Raves For the Work of JASON STARR!

"Starr has…a hard-edged style that is clean, cold and extremely chilling."
—*New York Times*

"A fearless, pitiless writer."
—*Laura Lippmann*

"I really don't know how Jason Starr does it: I start out thinking I'm only going to read a chapter and an hour later I'm on page eighty."
—*Bret Easton Ellis*

"Hypnotically good. Some of the best new writing there is."
—*Lee Child*

"Paranoid noir…playing its own one-of-a-kind game."
—*Joe Hill*

"Diabolically well-plotted."
—*The Literary Review*

"Deliciously addictive."
—*Megan Abbott*

"The New York sound, the energy, dialog that's on the beat… Read it and you'll go hunting for Jason Starr's other books, I promise."
—*Elmore Leonard*

"A throwback to the spare, snappy crime writing of Jim Thompson and James M. Cain."
—*Entertainment Weekly*

"Run!" I say to the girl. "Get help!"

Somehow the guy and I fall onto the pavement, scuffling in the snow. He pushes me down, but I manage to get back on to my knees and grab him again. There's no way I'm letting go this time, not until the cops get here.

Then I feel the pain in my gut. It doesn't feel like a punch, though. It feels much deeper.

"Stupid fuck," the guy says. "Look what you made me do, dumbass. Look what you made me do."

I fall to my knees and see a blur of the guy and the bright red in the snow all around me. I'm in shock I guess because it takes a few seconds before I realize it's blood, and a few more to realize it's my blood.

I'm lying on my side, part of my face in the snow. I'm weak and shivering and feel warm blood oozing over my freezing lips. I hear a male voice, not mine or the guy who stabbed me, but clear and distinctive: I saw you, Steven Blitz…

The NEXT Time I DIE

by Jason Starr

A HARD CASE CRIME NOVEL

A HARD CASE CRIME BOOK
(HCC-154)
First Hard Case Crime edition: June 2022

Published by

Titan Books
A division of Titan Publishing Group Ltd
144 Southwark Street
London SE1 0UP

in collaboration with Winterfall LLC

Print edition ISBN 978-1-78909-951-5
E-book ISBN 978-1-78909-952-2

Design direction by Max Phillips
www.maxphillips.net

Typeset by Swordsmith Productions

The name "Hard Case Crime" and the Hard Case Crime logo are trademarks of Winterfall LLC. Hard Case Crime books are selected and edited by Charles Ardai.

Printed in the United States of America

Visit us on the web at www.HardCaseCrime.com

For my father

"The most painful state of being is remembering the future, particularly the one you'll never have."
—SØREN KIERKEGAARD

"If something is going to happen to me, I want to be there."
—ALBERT CAMUS, THE STRANGER

THE NEXT TIME I DIE

ONE

Late Friday evening, I'm in my home office, honing my opening statement for the Jeffery Hammond murder trial:

If a person isn't responsible for the thoughts that lead to their actions, are they responsible for the results of those actions and, furthermore, do they deserve to be punished as a consequence of those actions?

While I love how this succinctly presents the premise of our case, I worry that it sounds "too philosophical," especially as three members of the jury didn't attend college and one dropped out of high school. On the other hand, juror number seven is a college professor and another juror is a small-business owner with a degree in sociology, so simplifying the language too much might not be the best move either.

I delete what I wrote and type, *How can you send a man to prison for the rest of his life who can't control his*, when I hear: "I want a divorce, Steven."

Well, I *think* that's what Laura said. I was so absorbed in my thoughts that I didn't hear her enter the room and it's hard to believe she actually said this.

"Sorry, what did you just say?"

She's wearing what she wore at dinner—a black-and-white low-cut dress and heels. I'm in the jeans I wore at dinner, but bare-chested.

She gazes at me for a few seconds with no affect, then says, "You heard me. I've made a decision. I want you to move out. Tonight."

Like all couples, we've gone through our rough patches, but lately things have been okay—no big arguments, a fun recent weekend away in the Berkshires.

"Come on, what's going on here?" I say. "What's wrong? Do you want to talk?"

"I've made my decision," she says. "There's nothing to talk about. Our marriage is over, Steven. We're through. Just go. Get the fuck out. Now!"

Laura is my height, five-ten, but when she's in heels she can look especially tall, even a little intimidating, and right now this effect is, well, heightened because I'm sitting, looking up at her. I'm still straining, trying to figure out what this is all about, then it clicks—the sudden mood swing, the cursing, the unguardedness. I feel silly for not realizing it right away.

"Okay, I get it now," I say. "I thought something was off during dinner, the way you were talking so fast, jumping from topic to topic, and Tom and Angie noticed it too. In the kitchen, Angie actually asked me if you're all right and I told her, 'I think so.' I meant to say something to you after they left, then I got caught up in work and didn't have a chance to. But, just so you know, I'm not angry about any of this. I totally understand why you're—"

"Shut up! Just shut the fuck up!"

I've been having persistent headaches lately—work stress, or maybe migraines—and this isn't helping.

"You have to calm down," I say. "*Please*, Laura. There's no reason to make this more difficult than it needs to be. If you just relax and take a pill you'll feel much better and then we can dis—"

"I don't need a pill."

"I really don't want to argue about this," I say, "but we both know that's not true."

"I am not fucking manic. That's always your go-to explanation about anything that goes wrong in our marriage—'There she goes, she must be manic again, she must be off her Lithium.' This isn't about me, Steven, it's about you. I'm fine with me!"

I get up from my desk. I know I have to be patient when she gets like this; that's what her psychiatrist told me.

"Look, it's okay, Lau. I'm not going anywhere—now or ever. Whatever's going on here, we can work this out, if you'll just—"

She swats at me with both hands like I'm a rabid bat.

"Okay, okay. Just relax."

"Go!" she screams. "Now! Go to your fucking brother's. We're through!"

She marches out of my office and slams the door. My brother Brian lives about twenty minutes away, near Katonah, with his wife Robin and their two kids, but there's no way I'm going there, especially now, at nearly midnight.

I leave my office and find her in the bedroom. She has her back to me as she's looking for something in her dresser. On TV, the news is on—Bernie Sanders campaigning for the Nevada Caucus, which he's expected to win in a landslide over Biden and Buttigieg.

"Look, Lau, this really is the wrong night to be doing this. I have a huge case coming up on Monday—you know how important this is for me, for my career. Maybe if you *weren't* off your meds right now you'd realize how unfair it is that you're—"

She slaps my face hard, jerking my head to the side. I wasn't expecting her to hit me, but I'm not surprised. She's hit me before during manic episodes. Once, she broke my nose.

"See?" she says. "This is exactly what's wrong with us. *This*— right here. You always think everything's about you and you never listen to me. You just tell yourself a story in your head and you believe it. *I* told you our marriage is over and I want you out of here right now. That's all that matters."

It's getting difficult to control myself, to stay calm and understanding, but I tell myself, *This isn't her, this is just her disease. Don't get sucked into a big argument now. Then it'll be about something else, then it'll be about* you.

I breathe deeply, then say, "If you could see this situation clearly and rationally, you'd see there's another side to this."

She cocks her arm, as if she's about to slap me again. Instead, she says, "If you had no idea this was coming then you're even more clueless than I thought."

"Look, I'm not an idiot," I say. "Obviously things haven't been perfect lately, but we had that nice weekend away in the Berkshires, didn't we? Hiking was fun and that picnic at Tanglewood was nice."

"The Berkshires!" she says. " 'Let's go to the Berkshires this weekend, Lau. It'll be good for us to get away, Lau.' What if I don't want to go to the fucking Berkshires? What if I don't want what's *good* for *us*? Did you ever think about that? No, of course you didn't think about that. 'It's too late, I already booked the Airbnb. We have to go.' You and your have-tos! Maybe *you're* the problem, Steven, not me. You ever consider that? Just because you're not diagnosed doesn't mean you're not sick. You know what I'm sick of? I'm sick of this shit, I'm sick of *you*! Maybe that's how I wound up with somebody else!"

She's flirted before when she's gone off her meds, but she hasn't actually *cheated*. I know our marriage is dysfunctional, but having an affair would be taking things to a whole other level.

"I hope you're not serious about this," I say. "Come on, you wouldn't really do that, Lau. You really wouldn't do that to us, would you?"

Her eyes are wide and venomous.

"What if I did? What difference does it make now?"

Don't overreact, Steven. You'll regret it if you do. Stay calm. Just stay calm.

"Okay, so then who is he?"

"I don't have to tell you anything."

"You said there's 'somebody else.' If that's true, and you're not just trying to get a rise out of me, then tell me who he is."

"Stop interrogating me. I'm not on fucking trial."

"What's his name?"

"*Her* name, you mean. *Her* name is Beth."

She's looking right at me, not blinking at all. She doesn't seem to be making this up.

"A woman? Seriously?"

"Does that surprise you?"

It does surprise me, but not as much as finding out she's cheating.

"Where did you meet her?"

"Why does it—?"

"I want to know."

"Okay. The post office."

"The post office? How do you meet somebody at the post office? Who even *goes* to the post office?"

"Well, that's where we met."

This doesn't sound like something she'd invent. My head is pounding like my brain is trying to escape from my skull. I feel gutted, nauseated, like I might throw up.

"You really did this, Laura? Please, tell me this isn't true."

She takes a step toward me, then stops, looking right at me.

"I know you want to think this is just my sickness," she says. "Maybe it'll make it easier for your ego or something, I don't know, but I'm in love with Beth. I don't love you anymore,

Steven—*at all*. Wait, I can do better than that—I've *never* loved you. How's that? Our marriage is a joke, it's *always* been a joke. I've been faking it for a long time. Everything we have is fake. *All* of it."

I stare at her for at least ten seconds, then I say, "I think you're right. I should go."

In the den downstairs, I call Brian on my cell.

"Hey," he says, "what's up?"

"I wake you?"

"No, what's—?"

"I'm coming over."

"To my place? Now?" He sounds concerned. "Why? What's going on?"

"I don't want to get into it."

"You okay?"

"Not really. I might have to stay a couple of nights, or longer."

"What happened, Steve?"

Now he sounds extremely concerned; could I blame him? I'd be concerned too if he wanted to mysteriously come over to my place late at night.

But I don't feel like explaining—not over the phone anyway.

"Don't worry, nothing life-threatening or anything like that."

"Then why—?"

"I'm leaving, okay?"

"Yeah…yeah, okay."

I put some clothes in a carry-on, including a suit to wear to court on Monday morning, and my laptop. I was planning to spend the rest of the weekend doing final preparations for the trial; now I'll have to work from Brian's.

This is, by far, the biggest, most high-profile trial of my career. Jeffery Hammond, a renowned abstract artist and a regular on Page Six and on the New York City social scene for years, was charged with multiple counts of first-degree murder for the brutal killings of three men. Although the body parts of one of his victims were found in a suitcase in his art studio in Nolita, and forensic evidence and witness accounts linked him to the other murders, Hammond pleaded innocent. We're planning an insanity defense, which is always extremely difficult to pull off, but in this case it might be impossible. Hammond is without a doubt a psychopath, exhibiting no empathy or remorse, but he has no history of schizophrenia, or dissociating from reality, and it's going to be a huge challenge to prove that he couldn't control his actions at the time of the murders and that the murders weren't at least partly premeditated. We plan to have a psychiatrist testify that Hammond experienced psychotic breaks prior to and during the murders, and another psychiatric expert will testify that late onset schizophrenia *is* possible, but the prosecution will have their own experts, who will try to discredit ours, and I'm sure the prosecution will play up the viciousness of the murders by showing graphic autopsy photos to the jury—which the judge has already declared permissible—and establishing Hammond as a calculated sociopath and master manipulator, which in fact he is. To have any chance of winning, especially with a less than optimal jury, I'm going to have to be at the absolute top of my game, but I don't know how I'm going to pull this off, now that I'm suddenly going through a divorce.

Speeding along Route 35, I'm trying to see through the frost and haze on the windshield. It's snowing, not heavily, but enough to slicken the road. It's still hard to accept that this actually *happened*, that my marriage is actually ending. Maybe I shouldn't have left. After all, dysfunctional crap happens in all marriages. I hear stories all the time at parties and on the train commuting into the city. Recently, Patti—a friend of Laura's, actually—found out that her husband Darren had been having an affair for years, even paying the other woman's rent, but they went to counselling and stayed together. If Patti and Darren could work things out, so could we.

The idea that things might not be as bad as they seem gives me hope. As I drive in the snow, I glance at my phone periodically, expecting to see "Laura" at the top of my texts list. She'll say she's sorry for everything and she wants me to come home to talk about what happened. I'm a reasonable person; I don't hold grudges. I could forgive her and we could work through this.

But she hasn't texted me.

There're only texts from Brian: *Sure everything's okay?? You sounded really weird*

And Terrence, a partner at my firm: *Look forward to the new draft. Reach out when you have a chance, I'm around all weekend.*

Terrence sent me some ideas for the opening statement earlier today and I told him I'd get back to him tonight.

I say to Siri: "Text to Terrence:…Working on it…period… Talk more in morning…period. Send text."

I'm surprised that there's still nothing from Laura, and now I feel like an idiot for rationalizing that this was an episode, a momentary lapse. If she went off her meds and had a fling that would be one thing, we could work through it. But telling me that she's in love with someone else implies that this has been going on for a long time. She was probably planning her exit strategy for weeks, maybe months, and I was too self-absorbed to see the signs. Or perhaps I did see the signs, but I was in denial. Maybe I'm still in denial if I can't accept my new reality.

"Goddamnit!" I shout. "Fuck! Fuck!"

It feels good to release stress—to rage. For a few moments, the pain in my head seems to wane, and I can see the situation more clearly, with less emotion. It hits me that the problem isn't that Laura is leaving me—the problem is that I left. I've been through so much tumult in my marriage, always staying and trying to work on things when a lot of men would've left years ago. But I made a decision—to stay in my marriage for better or for worse; I'm not a quitter, and I'm not throwing away a seventeen-year marriage just because she kicked me out during a manic episode. I'll fight to get her back, do whatever it takes.

I'm approaching a bend at the bottom of the hill. I usually slow here as this area is a known hotspot for accidents. Distracted by my thoughts, I don't slow as much as I should, though, and I have to pound the brakes. I skid a little, heading right toward a tree, and I experience the odd sensation of feeling the impact that hasn't happened yet, almost like it's *already* happened. Then I hear my first driving instructor, my dad, telling me, *Always turn in the opposite direction of the skid.* I do this, and thanks to my dead dad, I manage to stay on the road.

I have to catch my breath. The snow's coming down harder and my head's throbbing. I shouldn't be driving tonight. It's not just the weather; I'm too stressed and distracted to drive. But I'm not sure if I should go back now or wait till morning. If Laura doesn't take her meds, going back tonight could be pointless. Of course, if I do go back, Laura might not even be there—she might have gone to Beth's. Or, who knows, if the timing works out just right, I might arrive as Laura is leaving. I could follow her and meet this Beth, talk to both of them…

I need a cigarette. I officially quit about ten years ago, but I still smoke now and then, especially when under extreme stress.

I pull into a gas station just outside of Katonah. I park next to a few other cars, close to the road. When I get out, I feel the sleet, mixing with the snow, pelting against my face. The pain in my head is excruciating; I have to get this checked out.

Heading toward the minimart, I notice to my right, near another parked car, a guy and a girl arguing. The guy is older than the girl—he looks like he's around my age, forty-seven. She looks like she's about twenty, maybe a college student.

I try to ignore them. It's none of my business, after all, and I've been through enough tonight.

Then the girl screams, "Stop, you're hurting me!"

The guy's yanking on her arm, saying, "Just get in the car. Get in the fuckin' car."

This is the last thing I need tonight—to get in the middle of a domestic dispute—but he's hurting her; I have to do *something*.

I go over and say, "Hey, what's going on here?"

The guy pauses, still holding her arm, as he glances at me. The girl is looking at me too. She's pretty—shoulder-length blonde hair. They both look drunk, high, or both.

"How 'bout you mind your own fuckin' business?" the guy says to me.

I notice he's wearing an expensive watch—a shiny silver-and-gold Rolex. Somehow this detail makes the whole situation seem odder.

"He beat me up before," the girl says to me. She sounds desperate and looks legitimately terrified.

The guy yanks on her arm harder and says, "I told you to shut the fuck up."

With his other arm he opens the passenger-side door of the car and tries to get her to go inside.

"No," she says. "Stop it! Stop it!"

I can call the cops, but they won't get here for at least ten minutes, maybe longer during a snowstorm.

I rush up and grab the guy from behind. He's taller than me, and thicker.

"Let her go," I say.

"The fuck?"

He seems surprised I'm getting involved. I'm surprised too, but this son of a bitch caught me on the wrong night.

"You heard me," I say.

He lets go of her, then shifts around toward me, and shoves me hard. I fall back against the side of another parked car. Then he resumes trying to stuff the girl into his car.

"Stop it!" she screams. "I don't have to go! I don't have to go!"

I rebound off the car and grab the guy again and pull him away from the girl. He grabs me and rams us both back against the car I just bounced off.

"Run!" I say to the girl. "Get help!"

Somehow the guy and I fall onto the pavement, scuffling in the snow. He pushes me down, but I manage to get back on to my knees and grab him again. There's no way I'm letting go this time, not until the cops get here.

Then I feel the pain in my gut. It doesn't feel like a punch, though. It feels much deeper.

"Stupid fuck," the guy says. "Look what you made me do, dumbass. Look what you made me do."

I fall to my knees and see a blur of the guy and the bright red in the snow all around me. I'm in shock I guess because it takes a few seconds before I realize it's blood, and a few more to realize it's *my* blood.

The guy's grabbing the girl before she can get to the convenience store. They get in their car and peel away.

I'm lying on my side, part of my face in the snow. I'm weak and shivering and feel warm blood oozing over my freezing lips. I hear a male voice, not mine or the guy who stabbed me, but clear and distinctive: *I saw you, Steven Blitz.*

I have no idea what this means, why I'm hearing it, or where the voice is coming from. Then I'm in a large glass ball, and the ball begins to spin. I feel calm, at peace, removed, watching myself spin faster and faster, until the force of the spinning stretches and pulls me apart and what's left of me scatters and finally vanishes.

TWO

I'm on my back, staring at a ceiling, at a fluorescent light. My gaze shifts and I see blurry equipment—monitors, tubes. There's a tube in my mouth.

Hospital. Must be a hospital.

I recall the couple arguing, me intervening, the guy stabbing me. Good, at least my memory's fine. I know blood loss can lead to severe brain damage, so at least that's not an issue.

Then the pain hits.

I have a headache, but not much stomach pain. My head hurt before I got stabbed, so that's expected; but why don't I have pain in my midsection? Am I on opioids? Maybe my head is just distracting from my stomach. I once read that the brain can't register pain in more than one area of the body at once. It's why soldiers in battle might think they only have a broken arm when in actuality their legs have been blown off. I wiggle my toes and claw at the bed sheet with my fingers—at least I'm not paralyzed.

A dark-haired nurse enters.

"Hey, look who's up. How you feeling, honey?"

She's in her fifties, maybe Italian-American, has an accent—Brooklyn or Staten Island.

Leaning over me to look right at my eyes, she adds, "I'm Marie, it's nice to meet you. Don't worry, you're gonna be okay."

Nothing feels *less* reassuring than an overly sincere nurse telling you that you're "gonna be okay."

Because I'm aware that it would be difficult to talk, I don't even try, but I have a lot of questions. Like: What hospital is this? Has Laura or Brian been notified? I'm also concerned about the Hammond trial Monday morning. I have a lot more preparation to do. I haven't even nailed down my opening statement.

I reach for my cell in my pocket, forgetting for a second where I am and what happened.

"Hey, hey, take it easy," Marie says, maybe thinking I was trying to get up. "You're not going anywhere. Not for a while anyway."

She takes my temperature, then says, "A doctor will see you very soon, honey. You have some visitors waiting too."

I try to speak but I can't with the tube.

"Do you know where you are?"

I shake my head.

"Four Winds Hospital," she says. "You're going to be okay, so you don't gotta worry about that. Just worry about feeling better, okay, honey?"

Four Winds is in Katonah, not far from where I got stabbed.

There's a TV propped on the wall in front of my bed, but it's not on. My eyes shift toward the window. I squint as I adjust to the glaring sunshine and see what looks like fresh snow on the window ledge. Okay, it *is* morning, which means I've been unconscious for at least seven hours, which is bad, but not awful. The shorter you're unconscious the better off you are for the long term, but I can't have serious brain damage or I wouldn't be thinking as coherently as I am. Also, my memory seems fine. I know my name, date of birth, my parents' names, the name of my childhood best friend, my social security number. I'm not in a lot of pain; my main issue is the discomfort from the tube in my mouth.

Then I have a thought that has been lurking since I regained consciousness, but I haven't given it any attention until now:

Why am I alive?

There was so much blood—the knife must have severed a major artery. I once defended a client who was accused of stabbing someone, and I know from expert witness testimony how fast a person can bleed out with a major abdominal wound. I would have had a few minutes, five minutes tops, and the response time for an ambulance is at least ten minutes in the best-case scenario. During a snowstorm I shouldn't have had a chance and yet here I am, thinking clearly and, other than a mild headache, I'm basically fine.

I muster up the loudest moan I can. An aide, a guy in his thirties, hears me and comes over.

"Hey, how are you?"

I moan again.

"I know the tube's annoying," he says. "The doctor's on his way down."

I glance toward the TV.

"Oh, you want me to turn on the TV?"

I nod.

"You got it," he says.

He puts on CNN, then leaves.

In the corner of the screen I see the time: 9:23. So I've been unconscious for about nine hours.

There's an interview going on with some economist. I'm not paying much attention as I'm still absorbed by thoughts of blood, wounds and knives.

There are commercials, then the news returns. An earthquake in Chile killed "at least ninety-two people." Footage is shown of the devastation—bloodied victims, agony, horror. Next, from Chicago, there's a report about "a second day of mass protests" with protestors shown, bashing windows and some being dragged away by police in riot gear. I have no idea what these protests are about, but I've been so swamped at work lately that it's been hard to stay up on current events. Then there's a report of a small plane crashing in Maine, which killed the pilot and three passengers. After a story about the continuing search for a missing girl in Arkansas, the anchorwoman says, "Let's check in with Regina for the country's weather outlook." Then Regina says, "Looks like a chilly but sunny one up and down the Eastern seaboard to kick off your weekend..."

None of the news is familiar. It's Saturday, isn't it? How come there's nothing about the Nevada Caucus, or about that new coronavirus that's been spreading in Asia and Iran?

Regina is talking about the Nor'Easter, now centered off the coast of Massachusetts, when I hear, "Oh my God, Steven."

Laura has just entered. Although the nurse mentioned there was family waiting to see me, I assumed she meant my brother, his wife, and maybe their kids. After last night I wasn't sure that Laura would care, no less show up.

"You're awake, thank God. I was so scared."

She leans over and hugs me as well as she can with the tubes and whatnot. Then she kisses my forehead—a slow kiss, letting her lips linger. Finally, she pulls back and gazes at my eyes.

Something seems off about this—mainly the loving, gazing parts. Did she take her meds? Does she feel guilty about last night?

But something else seems odd.

She, looks, well, *better* than she has lately. She's in jeans and a plain black top, so it's not how she's dressed. Is her hair different? It looks a little longer, but maybe it's because she's been wearing it in a ponytail a lot lately and now it's loose and blown dry. Overall, she looks much happier and healthier than she did last night or, actually, the last several years. She also seems to care about me, even love me.

Is this what it takes to fix a marriage? Get stabbed in the gut and almost die?

I smile. If she's willing to forget about last night, I am too. I don't want my marriage to end.

"Can you understand everything I'm saying?" she asks.

It's frustrating to not be able to say, *Yes, I'm absolutely fine*. Instead, I nod.

"Do you know what happened?"

I nod again.

"It must've been so scary."

Teary eyed, she squeezes my hand. Am I imagining it or is she in better shape too, with leaner arms?

"Don't worry." Her sad face morphs into a smile. "I spoke to the doctors, including a neurologist. You mainly had a concussion. With your history, they just want to monitor you."

A *concussion*? How did I get a concussion from a knife wound? And what does she mean by my *history*?

"Don't try to talk," she says. "Just know how much I love you and how much Lilly loves you, and everyone else. Brian's here too, but he wanted me to come in first. I can't tell you how happy I am right now. When I got the call, from the cop, I thought that you…" She's about to cry. "I was so scared, Steve. I don't know what I'd do without you. But don't worry about Lilly, she's fine. Kaitlin came over and she's with her now. I already called Kaitlin and Lilly knows you're okay and you're going to be home soon."

I must have a very confused expression. Laura's had big mood swings before, but she's never gone from hating me to adoring me in such a short time. Oh, and I have no idea who Lilly and Kaitlin are.

"You're tired, I can tell," she says. "Why don't I let you rest and I'll go make some more calls. Do you want me to call work for you?"

I think about it, then shake my head. I'd rather make those calls myself.

"Okay, no worries." She kisses my forehead again. "I love you so, so much, baby."

Baby?

On her way out she says, "I'll come back in when the doctor comes to see you, I'm right outside."

What the hell was that all about?

What happened to her girlfriend from the post office? Why was she talking about people I don't know? Why didn't she mention anything about the stabbing? Do the police know what happened?

It's hard to think clearly. Maybe I'm delirious from the meds, but I have to make it into the city on Monday. Without me, we don't stand a chance.

"Steven."

I must've dozed. Marie is craning over me like I'm a baby in a crib.

"The attending, Dr. Chu, is here, then Dr. Assadi, the neurologist, wants to talk to you."

She sees my reaction.

"Don't worry, he doesn't think you suffered any serious brain trauma. He just wants to be certain."

I smile, not because I want to, but because I know she wants me to.

"Hello," Dr. Chu says to me, without making eye contact.

She checks the machines, whispers something to Marie.

"Goodbye," she says, exiting.

"Good news," Marie says to me. "I'm going to remove this tube from your mouth, so you'll be able to speak. It might be a little uncomfortable at first, okay?"

Removing it feels way more than a little uncomfortable, but I'm glad to have it out. She gives me a cup of water, which feels amazing too. I'm still confused, but confident everything will clear up soon.

Marie leaves, then a doctor in his mid-forties enters, with Laura trailing.

"Hi, Steven, Saleem Assadi."

"Hey," I say weakly.

He sees my hand move.

"It's okay, you don't have to shake. How are you feeling?"

"Could be worse. I'm alive."

He and Laura laugh politely, the way employees laugh at a boss's lame joke.

"Well, that's very true, very true indeed," Dr. Assadi says. "I'm just here for precautionary reasons, I'm not all that concerned, to be honest. You suffered minimal trauma to your brain. Can you recall what happened last night?"

"Yes…Yes I can."

"That's excellent," he says. "We want to monitor you just to make sure there are no complications. For that reason you'll be here for a couple of days."

"I have to go to work on Monday," I say.

"I'm afraid that will be impossible."

"I have to. I have a big case going to trial."

"You do?" Laura asks.

I have no idea why she sounds so surprised.

"Yes," I say. "You know I do."

"I understand," Dr. Assadi says to me, "but I'm afraid I can't discharge you."

"I *have to* be discharged," I say.

"It'll be okay," Laura says to me. "We'll figure it out." Then she says to Dr. Assadi, "When can he eat and drink?"

"You'll have to ask Marie and Dr. Chu about that," Dr. Assadi says. "I'm just the brain guy. Do you have any questions for me, Steven?"

"Yeah, about last night," I say. "Are there any details? I mean the condition I was found in, the exact time I was found?"

"I'm afraid I don't have all of that information, but there's a police report. I'm sure we could get that for you or put you in touch with the right person. If there isn't anything else, I have rounds—"

"The girl," I blurt out.

He stares at me. Then at Laura.

"The girl?" he asks. "What girl?"

"The guy she was with is definitely abusive and dangerous. Is she okay?"

"I don't know anything about a girl," Laura says. "Is that what you've been worried about? No, don't worry about that at all, sweetie. No one else got hurt."

First "baby" and now "sweetie?" The same woman who kicked me out of the house last night, who said she never loved me and is in love with somebody else?

"Wow," I say, relieved. "That's…that's great to hear. And what about the guy? I guess the cops caught him if you know the girl isn't hurt. What did they charge him with?"

Dr. Assadi and Laura exchange confused looks.

Then Dr. Assadi says to me, "Guy? What guy are you referring to, Mr. Blitz?"

"Was there another car there?" Laura asks. "The police said it was just you."

I must seem baffled too.

"No, the guy who *stabbed* me," I say.

Dr. Assadi and Laura still seem lost.

"What guy?" Laura asks.

"I thought you said you remember what happened last night," Dr. Assadi says.

"I do," I say, "every detail. I can describe him too—both of them. The police want to speak to me, I'm sure."

"Why would the police want to speak to you?" Laura asks with trepidation.

"Because I was stabbed," I say. "It's attempted murder. Manslaughter at best."

Laura holds my hand, like she's comforting a sad child, then says, "Nobody stabbed you, sweetie. You skidded off the road on Route 35 and hit a tree. Luckily, your airbag deployed or it would've been so much worse."

"No, that's not what happened," I say. "Why do you think that's what happened? Did somebody file a false report or was there some other mix-up with the police or something? I stopped to get a pack of cigarettes. Don't judge—I was upset and needed to smoke. Anyway, I was on my way to the gas station minimart on Thirty-Five, but in the parking lot there was a couple fighting. I tried to help the girl but the guy had a knife and he stabbed me in the gut. Then I heard a voice, I'm not sure whose voice, but it was definitely a male voice. He said, 'I saw you, Steven Blitz.' Then something really strange happened. I was…well, I was spinning in a glass ball, but simultaneously watching myself…What's wrong? Why're you looking at me like that?"

"A glass ball?" Laura asks.

"Yes," I say. "A glass ball."

She remains holding my hand as she glances at Dr. Assadi.

Then with absolute certainty that only makes everything more perplexing, he says, "No one stabbed you last night, Mr. Blitz."

THREE

They're gaslighting me—Marie, Laura, Chu, Assadi; they're all in on it. I don't know why they're doing it, or how they're doing it, or what the endgame is, but I know what's happening.

"Have you checked the security cameras at the gas station?" I say. "There must be one at the minimart, it could show the whole thing."

"The accident didn't take place at the gas station," Laura says.

"No, but the stabbing did," I say.

Laura smiles, like I'm a confused child.

"You weren't stabbed, sweetie," she says. "If you were stabbed you would have a wound, wouldn't you?"

I can't argue with this.

"Yes, there has to be a wound in my abdomen. A major one."

"So? Where is it?"

She lifts the gown I'm in a little to emphasize her point.

"See?" she says. "No injury. Your whole stomach's fine."

I feel with my hand. She's right, there's no wound, but something's not normal. I seem thinner weirdly—less fat and more ribs. What the hell?

"I don't know how that's possible," I say. "I know what happened." Then I notice a wound on my left forearm that's slightly older, has some scabbing. "And how did I get *that*?"

"You were moving some stuff in the garage and cut yourself. Don't you remember?"

The *garage*? What was I moving in the garage?

"It's okay, sweetie." Now Laura's looking at me the way a

psychiatrist looks at a mental patient, as if she's trying to act like she doesn't think I'm crazy, even though she knows I am. She adds, "You just need some more rest."

"I must concur with your wife," Dr. Assadi says. "Some rest would be a good idea right now. Sometimes a head injury of any magnitude can manifest with memory prob—"

"I'm totally fine cognitively," I say. "You said the concussion is mild, right? This is like a day at the office for Tom Brady. I know where I am, I know exactly what happened, I know everything."

"Sorry, Tom Brady?" Dr. Assadi asks.

"Yeah," I say.

Dr. Assadi and Laura seem confused.

"What's wrong?" I say. "Tom Brady. The football player."

They still look baffled.

"Okay, come on, this is ridiculous," I say. "*Tom Brady*. Six Super Bowls. Married to Gisele."

Dr. Assadi has a blank expression and Laura looks concerned.

"And how come there's nothing on the news about Bernie Sanders," I ask, "or the coronavirus?"

"Bernie who?" Laura says.

"Coronavirus?" Dr. Assadi asks. "What coronavirus is this?"

Maybe I *am* insane, or at the very least hallucinating.

"Maybe you're not actually here," I say. "Or maybe *I'm* not actually here."

After a deep breath, Dr. Assadi says, "Well, I have to do my rounds. Rest up, Mr. Blitz. I'll stop by later and check up on you."

He leaves.

"Don't worry," Laura says. "Everything'll—"

"Look, I can't explain why there isn't a wound on my stomach," I say. "But if I wasn't stabbed then something is seriously wrong with me, but I don't feel like anything's wrong with me. Actually, the only thing wrong is that I'm alive at all given how much blood I must've lost."

"Nothing's wrong," Laura says. "You're just a little confused right now and that's normal after an accident. You remember leaving the house, right?"

"Yes, and I remember everything you said to me before I left."

"What I said to you?"

This is a bad idea. If she doesn't want to get into it again, why should I?

"I remember leaving," I say. "And I remember driving in the snow."

"Do you remember skidding in the snow, right on the sharp turn at the bottom of that hill?"

"Wait, I did skid there, that's true. How do you know about that?"

Her expression brightens. "So then you *do* remember?"

"I remember skidding, yes, but I didn't *crash*. Actually, I got control of the car and continued on. Like I said, I went to buy cigarettes and got stabbed."

"No, that isn't what happened, Steven. But don't worry, I know the mind can play tricks. Like the doctor said, you were in a serious crash, you're on pain meds, so—"

"So you're saying I imagined getting stabbed. It was some kind of *fantasy*? Or, I know, maybe I'm *still* unconscious and you're a fantasy too."

"Look, let's just take a break from this right now," she says. "I think you're putting too much pressure on yourself. Just focus on resting and getting stronger, okay?"

It's frustrating that I can't convince her, but I don't see the point in arguing.

"Fine," I say. "I'll do that."

She kisses my forehead and is about to leave.

"Oh, meant to ask you," I add. "The people you mentioned before. Lilly and Kaitlin? Who are they? Some new friends of yours? Do they have something to do with the woman you met at the post office? Just so you know, I'm still willing to forgive you and work on things. I don't want to lose you."

"What woman from the post office? What're you talking about?"

"Come on, stop playing games. You don't have to do this. I told you, I'm not angry."

She's crying now.

"People make mistakes," I say. "It happens. And I know how hard it is for you to stay on your meds, how it takes your edge off…So? Who are Lilly and Kaitlin?"

Laura composes herself, then says, "Lilly is your daughter and Kaitlin is her babysitter."

"My daughter, huh?" I smirk. "So now you're going to tell me you have a secret family too?"

She stares at me like she's trying to win a no blinking contest. My attempt at ice-breaking levity obviously fell flat. I have no idea what's going on.

"After you get some rest, you and I are going to have to have a talk with Dr. Assadi," she says. "I'm sure, this…I'm sure this is all normal. I'm sure you'll be fine."

Laura glares at me for another long moment, then hurries out of the room.

Attempting to sleep is hopeless. My brain is churning.

Some time passes, then my brother arrives.

"Thank God," I say.

I'm thrilled to see Brian—I'm hoping he can clear everything up. He's a few years older than me and he's always been a great brother and my best friend. Stable, reliable—someone I can always count on. I've always looked up to him, especially when we were kids and he was the star of the family, excelling in sports and school, and I secretly wished I could be as confident as him. As adults, he's always been supportive, especially during times of crisis, like when our mother died while I was in college and when our dad died five months ago.

"I know you need your rest," he says. "I just wanted to check in on you."

"It's really great to see you," I say, then I notice that he looks tired, rundown. He needs a shave, but it's more than that. He has deep circles under his eyes and has a withdrawn, sullen vibe. "Are you feeling okay?"

"*Me?*" he says. "Shouldn't I be asking you that?"

"I'm serious," I say.

"Usual shit," he says. "You know how it is."

Actually, I don't know how it is. Things have been going well for him. He and his family just came back from a fun trip to Rome and he's been doing well at work. He runs a tech startup that's been growing rapidly, and he recently hired more staff and moved into a larger space.

"How's the family?" I ask.

"How do you think?" he says.

I don't know what he means by this, but he's acting like I should.

"What about you?" he says. "You must be feeling pretty out of it?"

"I think I got my second wind. Or maybe they just have me doped up on painkillers."

"As long as you don't get hooked on that shit."

Brian seems down, not like his usual self. I can't tell if something's wrong or if he's just concerned about me.

"Actually, I don't think I got hurt very badly," I say. "The worst part is what's happened since I got to this hospital. They're telling me I have memory issues, but I feel fine."

"Yeah, Laura seems a little…concerned."

"I know and I don't get it," I say. "Last night we had a really bad scene at the house. She went off her meds and told me she's cheating on me and wants a divorce."

"*What?*" Brian appears shocked.

"That was my reaction too," I say. "I mean, I know she can get irrational, but it was worse than usual. It was a big kick in the balls actually. I thought our marriage was over."

"Are you sure she said all that?"

"Of course I'm sure. Why wouldn't I be sure?"

"Sorry, I feel like I'm the one who's confused now," Brian says. "I've been out there in the waiting room with Laura for hours and…Are you sure she went off her meds?"

"Yes," I say. "We got into a whole thing about it. But she must've taken a pill today."

"Why didn't she mention anything about this to me?"

"Why would she? I mean, I don't think it's something she'd bring up."

"And she told you she's cheating on you?"

"Yes, with a woman named Beth she met at—get this—the post office. That's why I called you and said I was coming over, because she threw me out of the house."

Brian has a grave expression.

"What's wrong? What is it?"

"Nothing," he says. "I mean, Laura said you were having some memory issues, so I guess it's understandable that—"

"That what?"

He takes a moment, as if to find the right words, then says, "*I* was the one who asked you to come over last night, Steve."

"Come on," I say. "Don't do this to me too, Bri."

"I was having a rough night with Dillon," Brian says. "I think he's using again."

"Dillon?" I'm confused again.

"Yeah, Dillon."

"Who's Dillon?"

"Who's Dillon?"

"Yeah, who's Dillon?"

"Dillon's my son."

"Your kids are Lindsay and Emily. You don't have a son."

He shakes his head, looking down.

"Please, stop playing these games with me," I say. "I can't take it anymore. I have too much going on in my life right now."

"No, *you* stop playing games with all of us." Then, adjusting his tone, he says, "Sorry, I didn't mean it like that. I know you're going through something. I didn't mean to blame you for being confused."

"Come on, this is insane," I say. "Where's Robin? Is Robin here?"

"Robin?"

"Wait, so now you're gonna tell me your wife doesn't exist either?"

"Robin died years ago, Steve. I should talk to your doctor."

"Robin's *dead*? Come on, just stop the bullshit, all right?"

He stares at me, then says, "I'm not sure what's going on here, Steve. But if these are just symptoms, related to the accident, you have to report—"

"I wasn't in an accident, I got stabbed, goddamnit." I'm practically yelling. In a quieter yet just as frustrated tone, I say, "I don't have any memory issues, okay? I know what feeling confused feels like and it doesn't feel like this. I was on my way to your place because…wait, I know. My cell. Get me my cell and I'll show you the texts. I can't believe I have to do this, but if it's the only way. Aide! Aide!"

An aide enters. Not the one who came earlier—a young Asian guy.

"I need my phone," I say.

Seeming annoyed, maybe because it sounded like an order, he says, "I'll tell the nurse."

"There's no reason to do this," Brian says. "Everyone's just happy you're okay and Lilly's on her way over here with your sitter. She's going to be happy to see you too."

"Lilly, that's another thing," I say. "What's this insanity with Laura telling me I have a daughter?"

Brian stares, then says, "God willing, when you see her it'll all come back."

"Come on, not you too."

"Me too what?"

"Okay. So how old is this *daughter*?"

He seems baffled, then says, "She's six, Steve."

"So you're telling me I have a daughter, for *six years*, and just totally forgot about her? And yet I didn't forget about you and Laura and work colleagues and other people in my life. Just my daughter."

"It's okay," Brian says. "It's obviously just related to the accident. It's temporary."

Marie enters and says to me, "You're still awake and you're yelling. Well, energy's a good sign."

"Can I have my—"

"Here's your phone," she says, handing me a Samsung Galaxy.

"That's not my phone, I have an iPhone XR."

"This is the phone you had when you were admitted."

"No, it's someone else's phone because I have—"

"Chill," Brian says. Then he adds, "That *is* your phone, Steve. You do have a Galaxy. And what's an XR?"

"Can you just *stop*? Can everyone just fucking *stop*?"

"You're gonna have to calm down now," Marie says.

"Yeah," Brian says. "Maybe I should—"

"Okay, I'll prove it to you, watch."

I tap in my password—the one, I always use, HELLER, my mother's maiden name—and surprisingly the home screen activates.

"How is that possible?" I ask.

"Because it's your phone," Brian says. "Read our messages from last night, maybe it'll spark something."

The Galaxy screen is unfamiliar, but I find the message icon and tap it. The most recent text exchanges are with Brian.

> *On way!*

You sure you wanna drive in this?
It's a mess out there
can wait till tomorrow

> *Leaving in a few*

K

"See?" Brian says. "Now do you remember? You were on your way over to my house because I asked you to come by. And I'm sorry, I'm so sorry. The roads were bad last night. I should've told you to stay home."

He looks like he might cry.

Then I say, "I didn't send this, Brian."

"Then how do you think it got on your phone?"

"I remember what my last texts to you were. You asked me if everything was okay and you didn't mention anything about the snowstorm. And there was a message from Terrence about the trial tomorrow. That text isn't here either, which I guess makes sense since this isn't my fucking phone."

"You really have to chill, Steve."

"It's *not* my phone," I insist.

"You should rest now," Marie says.

"I don't need any rest. You can't force me to rest." I'm aware of how agitated I am, but I can't control myself.

Marie goes to the other end of the room, marks something on my chart, then exits.

"This is insanity," I say. "But I'm not insane. Everyone else is insane. You're insane if you think I'm insane."

"I don't think you're insane," Brian says. "You're just a little confus—"

"I'm not fucking confused either. Laura wanted a divorce and wanted me to leave so I texted you and told you I was coming over. This isn't my phone, that's why these weird texts are on it."

"Why would there be texts from me on another phone?"

"I don't know!"

"Look." Brian takes out his phone and shows me the screen. "See? The same conversation. How did the same conversation get on my phone?"

I ponder this, then can't believe I'm saying, "Maybe you're in on it."

"*It*? What's *it*?"

"The gaslighting, the game, whatever's going on here."

"Jesus Christ—"

"Well, there's nothing wrong with me. I only had a mild concussion, so how much brain damage can I possibly have? Besides, okay, let's say I *have* brain damage—more brain damage than they think, *bad* brain damage. Then I'd be forgetting things, right? Well, I'm not forgetting anything. I remember what happened last night, every detail, so I don't care what anyone says, there's nothing wrong with my memory."

Laura has entered.

"Hi," she says. "I have someone here who wants to see you, can she come in?"

"I don't know if that's a good idea," Brian says.

"Is it my daughter?" I say. "Yes, I want to see her. Definitely. Bring her in."

I feel like I'm calling a bluff that will hopefully end this whole charade.

Laura exits, then a few moments later re-enters holding hands with a cute little girl with long, wavy brown hair.

I'm surprised because I didn't think there would be an *actual* girl. More shockingly, she resembles me—same blue eyes, same thick eyebrows, same lips.

When she sees me her expression brightens and in a high-pitched voice she shouts, "Daddy!" and rushes over with her arms out wide, like she wants to hug me.

"Careful, Lilly," Laura says. "I told you, Daddy was in an accident."

"Can I hug his head?" Lilly asks.

"No, but you can hug his arm, if it's okay with him." Laura looks at me. "Is it okay with you?"

How am I supposed to respond? It's a scared-looking little kid.

I nod.

Lilly hugs my arm.

"So," Brian says. "How do you feel now?"

I know he's really asking me, *Do you remember who she is now?*

The answer to this is no—I have no idea who she is.

Maybe I *am* insane.

Squeezing my arm harder, the girl says, "I love you so, so much, Daddy."

FOUR

Although I'm ultra-aware that this is all some fantasy, or complex dream state, or odd effect of traumatic brain damage, it's hard to not get a little emotional. After all, Laura didn't want to have kids, but I've always wanted a child.

"It's okay," Laura says to me, holding my hand as the girl continues to squeeze my arm. "We know it's hard."

"You'll be fine," Brian says. "Just don't put too much pressure on yourself."

"Yeah, you don't have to worry, Daddy," the girl says sweetly. "We all love you so much."

"Okay, I think you're going to have to let go now," I say.

"Remember what I told you, be careful," Laura says.

"Oh-kayyy."

The girl backs away. Her eyes look so familiar, like, well, my eyes.

"So is this sparking something for you?" Brian asks. "Feeling a little better now?"

The girl's so adorable; I can't disappoint her.

"Yeah," I lie. "It's…it's so great to see you."

I can tell Brian and Laura know I'm full of shit.

"It's great to see you too, Daddy," the girl says.

Laura and Brian are teary and my eyes are welling up as well, but for different reasons. I'm not happy that I'm remembering, I'm upset that this insanity is continuing. And they're upset because I'm not going along with the insanity.

"I think it's time to let Daddy get some more rest so he can come home as soon as he can," Laura says.

"When are you coming home, Daddy?"

"He can't come home yet," Laura says, "but he will very soon."

On TV, on muted CNN, I see something that confuses me more than anything I've experienced since waking up in the hospital—which, of course, is saying a lot. It's so far out, so inexplicable, that I can only stare at the screen, mesmerized. It takes a while for it to even fully compute, and then longer for me to understand that it's not something I'm just seeing, that it's something I'm *experiencing*.

"Let's let Daddy watch TV and rest," Laura says.

"I have to go now, Daddy. See you later."

"See you soon," Brian says.

I don't know if I answer and I'm barely aware of them leaving. I'm still transfixed by what I'm seeing—the notification on the bottom of the screen:

PRESIDENT GORE TO ADDRESS NATION
ON INDIA–PAKISTAN CRISIS

What does that even mean? *President* Gore? President of what? Some environmental group? Also, what India–Pakistan crisis? What the hell is *happening*?

Okay, maybe it's a typo. Maybe the producer or whoever meant: Former Vice President Gore. But why would an ex-Vice President address the nation about *anything*?

It's getting weirder: there's footage of Al Gore in the Rose Garden of the White House, giving a press conference. He looks different than *actual* Al Gore—gray hair, but not as bloated. My heartrate accelerates. Over the years I've had occasional panic attacks and that's how this feels. The only difference is back then I didn't know where the anxiety was coming from, but now I know exactly why I'm panicking.

I'm not dreaming. I know what a dream feels like; it's not *this*. Dreams are erratic, they don't have this much logic, and the biggest difference—dreams end. How can I experience all this, in such detail, and still be asleep?

Now there's footage of Gore at what appears to be a summit, maybe at NATO headquarters. He's with Angela Merkel, who looks like the actual Angela Merkel, and a couple of men in suits I don't recognize.

My phone!

Even if my mind is inventing what I'm seeing on TV, it can't invent Google searches too, can it?

I go on Galaxy—not my real phone, of course, but the phone that somehow has my information programmed into it. The browser for some reason defaults to Excite as the search engine. *Excite?* Who still uses Excite? I type in "Google" but nothing comes up. I type "google.com" into the browser and go to the site of what seems to be a small interior design company in Amherst, Massachusetts. Am I spelling it wrong? I check three times—nope, no spelling errors.

Whatever. Using Excite I search for "Al Gore POTUS."

I'm expecting results to appear about Gore's failed Presidential run in 2000, or the times he contemplated running for President but opted not to.

What I'm not expecting to see amongst the first results is his Wikipedia page stating:

> *Albert Arnold Gore Jr. (born March 31, 1948) is the 45th and current President of the United States*

"What the fuck?"

I'm not aware of how loud I said this, but it must've been pretty loud because an aide pokes his head in.

"Sorry," I say, "everything's fine."

Yeah, right.

He leaves.

Back to Excite, I'm frantic, heading toward full-blown panic attack mode. Why does Wikipedia say this? Why not Trump?

Wait, and what's this right below?

Vice President Barack Obama

"Stop it, Steven," I say out loud to myself. "Just wake the fuck up already and stop it."

I search for more information about the Gore presidency. According to what I'm reading on sites like the *New York Times* and the *Washington Post*, he defeated Adam Stewart in the 2016 election in a landslide, with Obama as his running mate. I've never heard of Adam Stewart, nor do I recognize him in any photos. I do notice that Obama, in a photo from 2018, seems way younger than actual recent photos of him, with almost no gray hair. Guess the lack of gray makes sense, though, if he's never been President.

What about Hilary Clinton? I Google her—sorry, *Excite* her. She's still a Senator of New York with no mention of a presidential run.

Donald Trump? In 2014 he was convicted on three counts of sexual assault and is serving a twenty-year sentence at Sing Sing Correctional Facility.

I skim more articles on the Trump case, which not surprisingly got a ton of media coverage, as much as O.J. The prosecutor for the New York-based trial was Alissa DiStefano, whom I know well. How is it possible that I didn't know that she was the prosecutor on such a high-profile trial?

Well, because she wasn't, I actually have to remind myself. *Because none of this is actually fucking happening.*

I've read enough *Science Times* and clickbait articles over the years to know that there's a lot about the brain that can't be explained. If I didn't think my mental health was at stake, searching for information about all this nonsense would be a blast. There's so much more of this fantasy world I want to explore—politics, world events, sports, entertainment—but there's one search I need to do immediately: "Steven Blitz Attorney Manhattan."

Normally, my firm's website would come up. But in this bizarro world who knows what I might discover?

I brace myself, but surprisingly the results seem normal—well, almost. While I'm listed as an attorney, the actual firm's name is Richards & Harris, but now it's Richards, Davidson, Harris & Blitz. I'm *a partner*? And who is Davidson? My bio seems normal, though—undergrad at Rutgers, then NYU Law School—so I know I'm reading about *me*.

There are headshots of the attorneys. Terrence Richards' face looks puffier than it actually is, and the photo isn't the one on our actual site; it's one I've never seen before. My photo is unfamiliar as well; in it, I have a close-cropped haircut I've never had. To prove to myself that this isn't me, I feel the sides of my head, but I discover that—what the hell?—I have close-cropped hair. Using the camera app on the Galaxy I look at myself for the first time since waking up in the hospital and do a double take. It's like I'm looking at myself in an altered mirror. I'm aware it's me, but my face looks thinner, my cheek-bones more prominent. Admittedly I look better than actual me. Did they cut my hair when I was admitted? Oh yeah—who's *they*?

Lifting up the gown I'm wearing, I examine my body. I'm pleased that I look thinner than I actually am, but I'm a little *too* thin. I can see ribs that I've never seen before.

Reading all this fake information about myself is, on some

level, exciting. I still don't actually *believe* any of it, but I need to keep searching and discovering. Like an addictive video game, I can't get enough.

Back to Excite, I type: "Steven Blitz Facebook."

My Facebook page doesn't come up because Facebook itself doesn't come up. I search around, but Facebook doesn't seem to exist. Then I discover a Facebookesque site called MyWorld. The interface is different than Facebook—it looks like a cross between the old MySpace design and Google. I do a search for "Steven Blitz MyWorld" and, voila, my page appears.

I view a page that I apparently created but have no recollection of creating. The page has the same selfie of me with very short hair. There are other profile photos that I've never seen, wearing clothes I don't own. In a couple of photos, I have haircuts similar to my *actual* haircut, but in most of the photos I have very different hair. I also notice I have no gray in the photos, but my real hair is salt-and-peppery.

In a section called "family photos" that I never created, there are photos of Laura and me with our daughter, Lilly.

Again, I'm stunned by how much she resembles me. Is that why my brain is inventing all of this? Wish fulfillment? But, while a child qualifies as wish fulfillment, how does a possible nuclear war between India and Pakistan figure into this theory?

I scroll down and view photos of the three of us, taken three months ago at Disney World. In actuality, I've never been to Disney World, and yet I apparently took a recent trip there with my wife and daughter. Further down, there are more "family pics," taken mainly at birthday parties and playgrounds, and there are a lot of photos from a trip to Hawaii. About ten years ago, I attended a conference on Big Island, but Laura didn't come along. I certainly never went to Hawaii with Laura and a daughter.

I check out my timeline, which looks similar to a Facebook timeline, but is called "My News." There are posts that seem appropriate for me—politics and legal issues—but links to news articles are distorted. For example, a few days ago I linked to an article about the Nevada Caucus, but it was for the *Republican* Caucus, where Utah Senator Nick Wallace had "extended his lead" over Massachusetts Senator Michelle Brown. The only problem is I've never heard of Wallace or Brown. What about the Democratic Caucus? Why isn't there anything about Sanders, Warren, Buttigieg, or Biden? Just yesterday I apparently linked to an article with the headline, *Gore Threatens 'Massive Military Retaliation' in Pakistan*, and posted a comment: *Yeah Gore!* Not only don't I have any recollection of posting this—why the hell *would* I?—I don't even know what this crisis is about. I click on the article I linked to. Skimming it, I learn that Pakistan sent cruise missiles into India, killing hundreds, and India responded with an attack on Pakistan that caused major casualties. Ground forces have been clashing in both countries. According to Indian intelligence, Pakistan has been mobilizing its nuclear arsenal, and India has threatened a preemptive nuclear attack. Many of the articles compare the situation to the Cuban Missile Crisis and fear the worst international crisis since Dirty Monday. Because the term "Dirty Monday" means nothing to me, I do a search and discover that in 2015 jihadi terrorists in Italy detonated a dirty bomb in Rome that killed over a thousand people and a large portion of the city remains uninhabitable. The attack ignited an international "Never Again" movement, with protestors calling for total nuclear disarmament, but instead, in recent years, the United States, Russia, China and other superpowers have increased their arsenals.

The idea that there has been a dirty bomb attack in Italy

with tremendous suffering and loss of life is too shocking, disturbing and, well, weird to fully absorb.

Then I have a new thought: what about my parents? If I have a daughter now and Al Gore is President and nuclear war appears imminent in India, why can't my parents still be alive?

Wow, what if I could actually see and hug my parents again? I would even want to experience the fantasy version of this.

I find a site which has a public database for deaths in the United States and enter my father's name—Robert Blitz, New York. He's apparently still dead, although the date of death is incorrect. He actually died on April 11, 2019, but according to the site he died on March 4, 2016. It's possible it's a mistake, although I've never seen a mistake like this. The information about my mother is correct—Sarah Rachel Blitz, wife of Robert Blitz, and mother of Brian Blitz and Steven Blitz, did in fact die on February 11, 1993.

The accuracy of some information is the most baffling part of all of this. If I'm hallucinating, why isn't *everything* off? Also, why are the differences so closely related to reality; why aren't things *more* outrageous? Why do people I know in the real world even exist in this invented world? Why isn't there an entirely new cast? Why is Laura still my wife? Why don't I have a different wife, or no wife at all? Why am I still in Westchester, New York? Why am I not in Australia, China, or on another planet, or in another universe?

The Jeffery Hammond murder trial.

Scrolling through my contacts, I see some names I recognize and some that are completely unfamiliar. Then, going through the contacts, I find "T Richards." Odd, because I know I didn't enter Terrence's name that way; I entered it with his full name.

The unfamiliar email app opens, linked to an account from "Steven.Blitz@RDHB.com," which apparently is my work email address. I decide I'm just going to act like everything's normal, like the trial is happening. Maybe this is key to ending all this nuttiness—fake it to make it.

I tap out a message:

Hey Terrence

Crazy night! I was involved in an altercation up here. I'm okay, don't worry, but I don't think I can make opening statements. Can we delay? Let's strategize. I know you can handle if necessary, but I really want to be there. This is so fucked up, I know. I'm still hoping I can make it Monday. Talk later.

Steven

Trying to center myself, I shut my eyes. I've read a lot about Eastern philosophy, watched various gurus on YouTube, and try to meditate as often as I can. I like the basic philosophy of Buddhism, especially the concept that all human suffering comes from falsely identifying with the ego rather than the true self, but I've always found it hard to calm my mind fully. I try to focus now on my slow breathing, on the inhales and exhales, but thoughts keep intruding, mainly about the little girl, Lilly. Why does she look so much like me? Why does she seem to love me?

Stop it, just focus, damn it. Focus.

But the harder I try to quiet my thoughts the louder they become. At the peak of my frustration, the phone, still in my hand, vibrates and chimes. First off, I always have vibrate disabled for all notifications. Secondly, what's up with that melodic ring tone? I always use the default tone and usually keep my phone on silent.

The caller is displaying: "Terrence."

"Hey," I say.

"Hey, just got your message."

Something about Terrence's voice sounds odd. Is it deeper? Maybe he just woke up.

"Wow, that was fast."

"An altercation? What the hell's going on, man?"

I explain how I got stabbed, leaving out how I inexplicably don't have a stab wound, figuring, why get into it?

"Shit," he says. "That's awful. Can you talk? Well, obviously you can *talk*. But how are you, man? You okay?"

He still sounds off, but it's a relief to be talking to a work colleague, to experience a semblance of normalcy.

"I'm hanging in, maybe a little loopy from the meds, but other than that…"

"Oh, that explains it."

"Explains what?"

"I was just kind of, well, *very* confused. I don't know anything about this case you're talking about."

Here we go again.

"Come on, not you too," I say.

"What do you mean?"

"Come on, seriously?"

"I don't know what you're talking about, Steven. Opening arguments? Opening arguments for what? We have nothing going to trial this week."

"For fuck's sake, how is this happening?"

"How is what happening?"

"The Jeffery Hammond murder case. Come on, Terrence, don't mess with me like this. I've been through a lot already and—"

"Jeffery Hammond? Is he some new client? Did you say *murder* case?"

"Please, not you too," I say. "Why the fuck is this happening?"

"Does your doctor know you're having these issues?"

"There's nothing wrong with me," I say, realizing that I certainly must *sound* like there's something wrong with me. In a much calmer tone, I continue, "So you mean to tell me that you really have no idea who Jeffery Hammond is."

"No, I don't."

"He's our highest profile client. Jeffery Hammond the artist slash serial killer, emphasis on slash. That was your joke."

"I have to be honest with you, Steven. This is all super disturbing."

"Yeah, tell me about it."

"I'm worried about you."

"I'm worried about me too."

"I...I don't know what to say except you really need to report this to your doctor."

I breathe. "Okay, can I ask you a question?"

"Sure."

"I mean, maybe the answer to this is obvious, but if you have no idea who Jeffery Hammond is, then anything's possible... Have you met my daughter?"

"Lilly? Of course I have. Are you *serious* right now?"

"So you *are* in on it."

"In on what?"

What's the point?

"Never mind."

"Look, man, I guess you're just a little out of it, it's all cool. I'm just sorry you have to deal with this, I mean after everything you've been through."

"What else have I been through?"

Bring it on. I'm ready for anything now.

"Come on, you know what I'm talking about....Your cancer."

"My *cancer*." I'm too confused to panic.

"It's just not fair," he says. "I mean just when you got the all clear and were getting back into the swing of things."

"And what kind of cancer did I have?" I ask, like I'm totally removed from the situation, inquiring about somebody *else's* cancer.

After a pause, he says, "Brain cancer. But why are you *asking* me this?"

Ah, now it's starting to make sense. Well, at least this one point makes sense within the context of this nonsensical reality. That's why I have the close-cropped hair and I'm leaner, because I recently had chemo.

I touch my head, feeling my crew cut, and toward the back there's smoothness, *a lot* of smoothness. It feels like a scar— from surgery.

There's only one problem with this scenario, of course—I didn't have surgery because I didn't have cancer. I've never had cancer. I'm perfectly healthy.

"Brain cancer, huh? At least I apparently beat it. Well, that's good to hear. Are there any other deadly diseases or children I don't know about?"

"Look, let's—"

"No, I appreciate your concern…I appreciate everybody's concern, really I do. I mean, I have no idea how I survived a knife wound that deep. Sorry, I can't mention the knife, because apparently I wasn't stabbed. Oh, yeah, and I don't have a daughter named Lilly or *any* daughter, and Al Gore isn't the forty-fifth President, Donald Trump is. I'm still hoping it's the meds—some sort of crazy reaction I'm having. I don't know why I'm even bothering to explain this all to you, though, because you don't exist, you just exist in my mind—in my fantasy or dream or whatever the fuck this is."

When I'm through with my rant, Terrence says calmly,

"Donald Trump President? Maybe President of Sing Sing, but that's about it."

"Yes, I know he's in prison because I read about it online. Look, I can't explain any of this. Maybe it's just a fantasy, or you're in my dream, in which case I guess it doesn't matter whether I miss the court date or not."

"Again, there isn't any court date coming up," Terrence says. "I'm just glad to hear your voice and that you're okay. Rest up and see you soon, man."

"Yeah, see you back in reality," I say and click off.

Feeling sort of amused by all of this now, wondering what my brain can possibly think up next, I do an Excite search for "Jeffery Hammond murder trial." As I've been preparing for months to begin the trial tomorrow morning, of course I know his case inside out. Since he was arrested, his case has gotten nationwide media coverage, and as lead attorney on the case I've received more media coverage than I've ever gotten before. I've been on CNN several times, as well as *Good Morning America*, *The Today Show*, NPR and just about every other major news station.

I've experienced so many surprises already this morning, that I'm feeling jaded, like nothing can possibly shock me anymore.

Come on, let's see what you come up with next, I tell myself as I wait for the results to load. *Bring it on, brain.*

Among the top results, there's nothing about Jeffery Hammond, the Jeffery Hammond I know. Other Jeffery Hammonds appear, however. Jeffery Hammond a dentist in Brooklyn, Jeffery Hammond a minister in Elkhart, Indiana, Jeffery Hammond a violinist in Boston, Jeffery Hammond a film producer in Burbank. I'm already confused because I've done searches for *my* Jeffery Hammond many times and there are always many results.

I'm amazed by my mind's inventiveness and attention to detail, though. Normally I'm an ultrarational thinker. I don't believe in conspiracy theories, or extraterrestrials, or life after death, and I've always been left-brain all the way, with very little creative talent. Even my dreams are straightforward, not very inventive. I can write legalese, but I once tried to write fiction in college and got nowhere. Unless I'm writing about myself in some context, I get stuck, and I've always been amazed by creative people, how they can create something out of nothing.

Which begs the question: if I don't have a great imagination, how did I create all of *this*?

I go through several pages of results, scanning for other Jeffery Hammonds, and then I finally find a result for the Jeffery Hammond I know. I feel relief—well, a bit. The result is for a series of photos taken at a gallery opening in the Meatpacking District on July 14, 2019. This doesn't add up in the real world because Jeffery was arrested in March, 2019 and during September he was in prison on Rikers Island, awaiting trial.

The photos have other oddities. While it's definitely Hammond, he's lanky and his hair is longish, shoulder-length—in some photos he even has a man bun—while in reality he's stocky, bordering on overweight, and has short hair. It's not just his body—his whole style seems different. He's known for always wearing the trendiest designer clothing as, prior to his arrest, he hobnobbed with some of the world's best-known fashion designers. Now he looks ordinary, even drab, wearing mainly jeans and T-shirts.

More jarring than his appearance, Hammond's art seems different. Overall, it doesn't seem as complex or as accomplished as the art of his I'm familiar with. The style seems similar, but the raw energy isn't there. It's still dark and disturbing—there's one painting of a decapitated couple otherwise enjoying an upscale dinner that's very Hammondesque—but it's less abstract than the work I've seen, and it just doesn't stand out in the same way. It seems provocative for the sake of being provocative without any underlying artistic merit. I've read critiques of his work; an art critic at the *New York Times* described his work as "post-modern expressionism" and another compared it to some of Dali's masterpieces. But this stuff seems much more obvious than the Hammond paintings I know, without his trademark "emotional energy," and there's no sign of his best-known works, including the ones that are in MoMA's permanent collection— *Man Drowning* and *Manhattan Midnight*.

On other pages, I find more references to Jeffery Hammond, but I can't find anything about his arrest, or the murders. The day after his arrest the *New York Post's* headline was *THE ART OF MURDER*. I've seen that headline all over the internet in previous browsing sessions, but, when I search for it now, nothing comes up. There's only one possible explanation for this—there are no articles about Jeffery Hammond the murderer because he hasn't been caught.

The idea of a free Jeffery Hammond terrifies me. In preparing his defense, I spent hours interviewing him at Rikers Island, and even then, with guards close by, I didn't feel safe. Although he had a calm demeanor and spoke in a polite, engaging tone, I could sense the rage inside him. Maybe it was the vague deadness in his eyes, as if he were looking but not quite seeing. He projected a menacing vibe, as if he could lash out at any moment. Meeting with him for hours, getting a closer glimpse of the darkness inside him, only intensified these feelings. The way he spoke about grooming, stalking, murdering, and sawing off the limbs and heads of his victims—usually dismembering them while they were still alive—in a detailed, matter-of-fact tone, as if he were describing an average, mundane day, was truly horrifying. I went through a difficult moral quandary about whether I should take the case on at all. While I was going to argue that Hammond was insane and delusional when he committed the murders, I didn't really believe that he deserved any leniency. I finally decided to go ahead and defend him, with the excuse that all defense attorneys use—that I wasn't really defending him, I was defending his rights, and putting my belief in justice over my moral beliefs. I knew I was kidding myself, of course. I was working on the case for one reason and one reason only—because it would help take my career to another level. I was in it for me, not him.

I find a link to Hammond's MyWorld page. It's Jeffery Hammond—he's still recognizable—but it's also not Jeffery Hammond, or at least not the Jeffery Hammond I know. Beyond his physical appearance, this Jeffery Hammond appears to be living a normal, happy life. His posts are mainly about art—reviews, links to his exhibits. There are several photos of him working at a modest, bare-bones art studio in Astoria, Queens. In one photo, taken in what looks like upstate New York, he's holding hands with a handsome, muscular, tattooed guy I've never seen. I recall that Hammond once mentioned that he used to paint in Queens before he purchased the large space in Nolita, but in this world it seems like that move never happened.

As I search deeper, I recognize some of his paintings—all from early in his career. Hammond certainly doesn't seem to have achieved the same level of fame and success in this world. No major gallery openings, no after-party shots with celebrities or after-auction shots at Sotheby's. He seems like a mildly successful artist who hasn't broken out yet, and probably never will. Many of his posts are promotional about small gallery openings and other appearances, and he even has links to buy his works on eBay and on a site called "Artsy." I've never heard of Artsy, but I assume it's my fantasy world's Etsy.

In most of the photos of him at art galleries, he's with people I don't recognize. While I'm just Hammond's attorney and it's not like I know everyone in his life, I *have* seen many photos of him at galleries with other people—just not *these* people. Also, there's no sign of any of the men he's on trial for murdering—Mark Corsi, Danny Montoya, or Jeremiah Ferg. This is extremely odd because I've done many searches for information about Hammond's past, and the men have appeared with him in numerous photos.

I continue searching, hoping to somehow find something, a tidbit of information that gives me an "aha" moment that somehow confirms that I'm not losing my mind after all, that there's a logical, obvious explanation for what's going on that I just haven't figured out yet.

I'm into maybe my ninth or tenth page of search results, and most are less relevant. I'm about to give up when I see a result that catches my attention, from the *New York Post*, with the headline: *BODY FOUND INSIDE SUITCASE ON SIDE OF ROAD IS MISSING LONG ISLAND MAN*. It's dated Feb 11, 2016 and the snippet of the article reads: "...with artist Jeffery Hammond..." I click on the headline and read about how the dismembered body of twenty-seven-year-old Eduardo Ortiz was discovered on the side of a road in Kings Park, New York, on Long Island. Skipping ahead, I read how Ortiz was last seen with Hammond, leaving a party in West Hampton, but Hammond apparently wasn't considered a suspect in the case or even a person of interest. I've never heard of Eduardo Ortiz or about any involvement by Hammond in this case. The dismembered body in a suitcase certainly sounds like a very Hammondesque crime, though, as that is exactly how he disposed of Jeremiah Ferg's body.

I read the article a few times, but I'm not any less confused. I search for more articles about Eduardo Ortiz's murder. Apparently, the killer hasn't been found, but aside from the *Post* story about the discovery of the body, and a few earlier articles from the time he went missing in January 2016, there's no mention of Hammond.

I'm more confused than when I started searching for information. Is it just a coincidence that Hammond was questioned in this case, or is Eduardo Ortiz another one of his victims? And how come I can't find anything about the murders that I *know* Hammond committed?

I do a search for Jeremiah Ferg and several mentions of him come up on the first page of results. This isn't surprising because Ferg was a successful advertising executive. What's surprising is that Ferg apparently still is a successful advertising executive. According to what I'm reading he wasn't dismembered and placed in a suitcase by Hammond or anyone. He's very much alive. In an image search, I see a photo of Ferg taken on a red carpet, at some industry awards events, on, apparently, November 20, 2019, about nine months *after* he was killed. I flash back to images of the autopsy photos of Ferg that I viewed many times—bloody, barely human-looking body parts, including his severed head—and I even interviewed the medical examiner extensively about them, receiving more gruesome details, and yet here's a photo of Ferg, very much alive, grinning for photographers.

I search for information about the other victims, expecting to find that they're alive too. There is no mention of Mark Corsi's murder, and I find many pictures of him on MyWorld, taken this year, including a selfie he posted just two days ago.

When I search for Danny Montoya, a victim Jeffery Hammond murdered and left decapitated in a dumpster in West New York, New Jersey, I can't find any reference to this.

I wonder—is it only the Hammond murders that have vanished from the internet? What about the other cases I've worked on?

I search for information on some of my past clients and biggest cases over the years. I'm relieved that Alan Caldwell, who was acquitted for grand larceny in 2009, is alive and well, living in Clearwater, Florida, where he actually lives. For a few moments this gives me hope that the Jeffery Hammond situation is simply an anomaly, but then I can't find any reference to Caldwell's case or that I was his attorney. I can't find anything about the Roger Bellamy or Alexandra Newman cases either. I do find a reference to the Victor Brunetto case, but Brunetto was convicted—in actuality, he was acquitted—and his lawyer was "Leslie O'Donnell," not me. I do find references for mainly white-collar cases, where I've supposedly had defendants, but I don't recognize any of my clients' names. Who's Diane Winchester? Greg Horner? Carrie Anne Rizzo? Alexis Tatums?

Maybe it's this room's fault—claustrophobia and stale air are driving me insane. I have to get out of here, breathe in some real air, and then maybe my mind will clear.

Or am I deluding myself, missing the big picture?

What if, like in *The Truman Show*, everything that I'm experiencing has been created? What if this room, the news on CNN, the search results on my phone, my "daughter," are just plot points for someone else's pleasure? Right now, I'm relying on information I've found or been told, but information can be twisted, distorted.

I search for "Truman Show." Somehow, I'm not at all surprised that the search produces no relevant results. I go to

IMDB.com and look up Jim Carrey—nope, no *Truman Show*. *Dumb and Dumber* is there, but some movies of his I don't recognize. What's *The Last Sunrise* with Julia Roberts from 2003? Or *The Carpenter*, a drama in 2007 where he played Jesus? Either I forgot about two Jim Carrey films or someone planted this "information-loaded" phone in my room. Obviously, someone's fucking with me because this isn't even my phone— it's a freakin' Galaxy. Everything that has happened in this room has been fake. The doctors, CNN reporting about non-existent wars, the "family" visits. Laura isn't really Laura, and Brian isn't really Brian. Actors, lookalikes, were hired to impersonate my wife and brother. My "daughter" has to be an actress too.

The stabbing is more difficult to explain.

Maybe the stabbing is the only experience that I hallucinated and everything else has been staged. My mind has been fucked with, I've been brainwashed or programmed to believe that the stabbing happened, and actually I did skid off the road and hit a tree. I do remember skidding during my drive, so is it possible that the accident did actually happen, and the stabbing was uploaded into me? Listen to me—*uploaded into me*, like I'm artificial intelligence. That's how I feel, though—like someone's experiment.

But if any of this is true, who would go to these lengths to mess up my life? Had to be someone with a serious vendetta. I don't really have any enemies and, other than Laura asking for the divorce last night, I haven't had any recent falling-outs. At work, my main focus lately has been the Jeffery Hammond murder trial, but I don't see how that could be related to what's happening. I've been helping Hammond, I'm his main ally, actually his *only* ally, so he wouldn't have any reason to screw me over. Could it be someone from years ago? I was an angry kid and there were kids I bullied in elementary school and sleepaway camp. Is one of them a sociopath neurologist now who's acting out an elaborate revenge scheme?

I feel like I'm losing it, torturing myself, searching for answers that don't exist or matter. Whether I'm creating this or someone else is, I have to find a way out.

FIVE

The blade is halfway into my gut, but I don't have the strength to scream.

I open my eyes, confused, then realize I'm still in the hospital room.

It's dark out, so I must've slept for at least a couple of hours. Time feels distorted—and if this isn't an understatement, I don't know what is.

I check in with myself, do a personal inventory of my physical and emotional state. The pain in my head has subsided; I'm definitely calmer. Is the nightmare over?

For a moment I have hope, then I feel my head. Fuck, still a crew cut, still a scar. The CNN announcement bar displays *BREAKING NEWS: WAR IN INDIA* over images of missiles blowing up buildings in New Delhi and carnage and agony in the streets.

I look at my phone—well, the Galaxy—and see the time and date: February 22, 2020, 11:47. I'm assuming P.M. but I can't take anything for granted.

Watching images of the bloody war, I doze again.

Sunshine. It's a new day, Sunday, one day until the trial. I have to get out of here.

But I know they won't just let me leave—especially now that they've seen me acting so confused. I'm going to have to convince them that I'm better now, that my memory has been restored. If I keep telling the truth, that I don't recognize this world, they'll want to give me psych evals and I'll be here for days.

A nurse, one I haven't seen before, comes into the room and checks my vitals.

"I'm suddenly feeling much better," I lie.

"That's great," she says, taking my blood pressure.

"Can you tell the doctor on call? Or Dr. Assadi?"

"Are you feeling any dizziness or pain in your head?"

"No, none," I say, although I have a headache. "But it's more than that. My memory's back totally. I remember everything now."

"Oh, right," the nurse says, "I saw that on your chart. Pressure's looking good."

"Will you tell the doctors?"

"Of course."

Later, when a doctor comes by, on rounds I guess, I report my sudden improvement. I tell her that my memory is perfect now and that I feel great. She says that she'll contact Dr. Assadi as soon as possible to let him know.

"When do you think I can go home?"

"I'm afraid I can't answer that right now," she says. "But I will say that you're looking good physically, you're definitely heading in the right direction."

"Is it okay if I get out of bed and walk around the room?"

"I don't see why not," she says. "But you should probably have a nurse or physical therapist here to help you."

A young physical therapist comes to see me, and she makes sure I can walk without balance issues. Again, I report that my memory has been fully restored, although actually nothing has changed.

While I'm eating breakfast—cardboard pancakes, mealy scrambled eggs, murky coffee—Laura arrives. Like yesterday, I'm struck by how much more toned her body is and by her overall calm Zen vibe.

"I heard your memory's back." She's excited.

"Yeah," I say, "but unfortunately I didn't forget how good pancakes taste."

"And your sense of humor's back too," she says. "But seriously, you remember everything now? You remember Lilly?"

"Of course I remember Lilly."

"Oh, thank God," Laura says. "Lilly was very upset last night."

"Is she okay now?"

"Oh, she's fine. She didn't *say* anything, but you know how she gets."

"She doesn't express herself," I say, hoping I'm right.

"Exactly," Laura says. "I tried to explain to her that you're going to be okay, that it's just temporary, and I'm so happy that turned out to be true."

"Where is she now?" I ask.

"Home with the sitter."

"Kaitlin."

"Right." Laura smiles. "You really do remember. And what about the other things you said to me? About getting stabbed? The woman in the post office?"

"Yeah, I have no idea what that was all about," I say. "I guess I was just loopy from the meds."

She leans over and hugs me, then kisses me. Flashing back to the real Laura asking me for a divorce the other night, her attitude still seems absurd, but admittedly it feels nice too. Why wouldn't I rather have an adoring wife than one who despises me?

"So you remember everything about Lilly? I mean, specific things?"

"You mean like our trip to Disney World a few months ago?"

"Yes."

"Or Hawaii, to Big Island."

"Wow, you really are back." Her face glows. "Thank God. And what about work? You remember everything going on there too?"

"Yeah, yeah of course. Actually, I had a talk with Terrence earlier and, yeah, there are no issues there at all."

I manage to steer the conversation away from the areas where I have major gaps, and when Laura leaves to try to make a nearby yoga class, she seems convinced that I'm in fact normal now. The irony, of course, is that I actually *am* normal, just not normal in this fictional world that either everyone is pretending to be in or I've cast them in.

Later, Dr. Assadi arrives.

"I hear you've had sudden improvement," he says, maybe incredulously.

"Yep, feel great, doc."

I explain to him how when I woke up my memory was fully restored.

"This is great to hear," he says, "but not unusual. The brain can be fickle. I was hopeful that your symptoms would be temporary."

"So I can be discharged now?"

"Not yet, I'm afraid. I'd still like a neurosurgeon to examine you and weigh in, and I'd like to run a few tests."

"What sort of tests?"

"Cognitive function, memory—"

"I don't want any more tests."

"Well, I'm afraid the tests are necessary, Mr. Blitz. We have to ensure—"

"Look, I'm an attorney," I say. "Let's not go down this road, okay?"

I was hoping I wouldn't have to pull the lawyer card, but he isn't giving me a choice.

"I understand your frustration," he says, "but in my opinion it's not advisable—"

"It's also not advisable to give me treatment that I don't need."

"That isn't the case."

"You confirmed that I didn't suffer any brain damage."

"Yes, but you presented symptoms—"

"Symptoms that don't exist anymore."

"Still, we need to make sure there aren't any underlying—"

"Or maybe you just want to make sure you bill my insurance for as much as you can. Exactly how much is this consultation with the neurosurgeon and related tests going to cost?"

He fake smiles, and is clearly annoyed as he says, "I don't prescribe unnecessary treatment, Mr. Blitz."

Matching his expression, I say, "In that case, I don't think you'll mind if I request a full investigation from my insurance company, and get second and third opinions about every test you've prescribed for me since I've been under your care. Maybe we'll look for corroborating cases, see if any of your former patients share my concerns."

I'm getting through to him. I see the panic in his eyes.

"I have an idea," he says. "Just to reassure myself, I'll review your treatment plan with my entire team, okay?"

"I think that's a great idea," I say.

He leaves.

Lo and behold, about a half hour later, a nurse informs me that I'll be discharged today.

When Laura returns from yoga, she's thrilled.

"I was hoping for this during Savasana," she says. "I'm so happy right now."

Later, after I fill out paperwork, an aide wheels me to the hospital front doors with Laura walking alongside. The nurse has returned "my" leather jacket to me, a jacket I've never seen before. It's soft, high-quality leather; it looks too small, but it fits perfectly.

At the door, I'm allowed to get out of the chair and Laura and I head into the parking lot.

Breathing in the invigorating winter air makes me feel like I've spent years in prison, not a couple of days in a hospital. Hopefully, real clarity will return soon and everything will start to make sense again.

Despite the below-freezing temperature, it feels comfortable in the bright sunshine. Some of the snow has melted but there's still several inches on the ground and piles of snow where the plows have left it.

"Do you feel steady?" Laura asks.

The real answer: physically yes, mentally no. My anxiety is crazy high as I'm not sure what to expect next.

"Yeah, I feel great," I say.

"You don't sound it." She interlocks her arm with mine. "But it's okay, I have you, and I'm not letting go."

The woman who callously dumped me and kicked me out of my own house won't let go? Okey dokey.

Laura stops in front of an Explorer and opens the door.

I almost say, *Whose car is this?*

She has a Honda and I crashed a Toyota. I've never been an SUV fan, figuring they only make sense for families. But since I have a family now I guess this makes sense. Or "sense."

I get in on the passenger side. The car has distinct dog odor and there's dog hair all over the seat and the floor. Well, guess I have a daughter *and* a dog.

"So what kind of shape is my car in?"

"Oh, I forgot to tell you," Laura says. "It was towed, but I called the Porsche dealership and they said they'll repair it. I guess until then you can use the Mercedes."

This is confusing as well, since I don't have a Porsche *or* a Mercedes. I can't afford either. But I've always wanted a Porsche.

"You sure you mean Porsche?" I ask.

"Yes." I can tell she's concerned, fearing I'm having a relapse.

"I mean as opposed to our insurance company," I say, purposely not referencing Aflac in case we have another carrier.

"No, the dealership says they can handle it." Then with a knowing smirk she adds, "Don't worry, soon you'll be able to resume your midlife crisis."

Midlife crisis? What midlife crisis? I've handled my middle-age well. I have a stressful career, but I hike, meditate, try to eat healthy, limit my acting out.

As we head out of the hospital lot, I tilt the visor to block the glare from the sun on the melting snow. So far everything looks the same—the way things should look. Familiar landscape and landmarks—a church, an elementary school. Although I'm still in an unfamiliar car, breathing in dog odor, and there are countless other mysteries unresolved, I'm hopeful that getting out of the hospital will at least begin to solve my problems.

Then we approach the strip mall where I often stop for Starbucks.

"Can we pull over and get a coffee?" I ask.

"Sure," Laura says.

We're going too fast for the entrance to the lot, though, and I say, "Where're you going?"

Confused, Laura asks, "What do you mean?"

Then I see why she's confused. Why *I'm* confused.

At the location where the Starbucks is supposed to be there's the blue-and-yellow façade of a Blockbuster video store. Of course there haven't been any Blockbuster stores in years, except one in Oregon. Years ago, I was a shareholder of Blockbuster, loading up on the stock when they were competing against

Netflix, convinced that they would ultimately put Netflix out of business. Needless to say, I was wrong.

Well, so much for things clearing up when I get outdoors—apparently things are only going to get weirder.

"I mean, where…where do you want to stop?"

"Dunkin' Donuts," she says. "Unless you want to wait until we get home."

"Home's fine," I say, comforted to hear that Dunkin' Donuts exists, but suddenly jittery, eager to get home.

"Are you okay?"

That question, or variations of it, is getting annoying as hell, but I do a good job of hiding my frustration.

"Never felt better," I say. "Looking forward to getting back into the swing of things."

As we head along Old Post Road, toward South Salem, I'm still perplexed about Blockbuster. Are they still renting DVDs?

"I hope you're not thinking about going into the city tomorrow," Laura says.

"I don't see why not," I say.

"I think it's a bad idea. I think you need at least a day at home to rest and recuperate. I've already told Jackie I might not be coming in tomorrow."

I have no idea who Jackie is, but by Laura's tone I have a feeling I'm supposed to know. I also don't know what she means by "coming in" since she doesn't have a job.

"No worries," I say. "Let's just see how I feel later on and discuss it then."

"No worries?" she says. "Why did you say that?"

"What do you mean?"

"It just doesn't sound like you," she says. "It sounds, I don't know, British."

So saying *no worries* isn't "a thing"? Is saying *a thing* "a thing"? Am I going to have to censor the way I speak?

"Must've picked it up from TV," I say.

Staring straight ahead at the road, she doesn't say anything. I don't either, figuring, at least at this point, I'm better off keeping my mouth shut.

SIX

Our house used to belong to Laura's parents. Shortly after Laura and I got married, her parents relocated to Arizona and gifted the house to us. Financially, it was a great deal because the mortgage was fully paid off and our only major expense was property taxes. At times we discussed selling it, but the house was big—three bedrooms, an oversized living room, a large deck in the backyard—and we didn't think we could get similar space without moving further north, away from the city, which would've made my commute to work much more difficult.

The downside of living in the house that Laura grew up in, from my point of view, was that it never felt like it was truly *ours*. Over the years we did minor renovations, but couldn't afford to do any major work, and sometimes I felt like a permanent houseguest.

As we pull into the driveway, I'm confused. It's definitely, recognizably our house, but it looks much, much better.

The vinyl siding has been upgraded with stone-veneer, and the front lawn has been dramatically re-landscaped; now rows of bushes and mature pine trees line both sides of the lawn, leading to the street, which is odd because my actual front lawn doesn't have bushes *or* pine trees.

"Happy to be home?" Laura asks as she cuts the engine.

"Elated," I say, though I'm not sure whether I should feel happy or terrified.

Getting out of the car, it does feel good to take deep breaths and savor the familiar winter scent of distant burning wood.

"You okay?" Laura asks.

I stop near the front stoop, gazing back at the pine trees.

"Fine," I say. "I'm just, um, soaking it all in."

Inside, a dog begins barking.

"Somebody's excited to see you," Laura says.

She's reaching in her handbag for her keys. I notice the lock on the front door is unfamiliar. It shouldn't be. We just had it replaced last month.

"It's okay," I say.

I take out my keys and, sure enough, one of them fits.

Amazing.

When I open the door, a large gray-and-white dog—it looks like a Siberian Husky—is still barking like crazy, sounding more aggressive than excited.

"Wasabi, stop it," Laura says to the dog. "Calm down, just calm down."

Wasabi? I've always thought Wasabi would be a cool name for a dog...if we ever got one.

The dog has backed away a little, but is still barking at me ravenously, like I'm an intruder.

"That's so weird," Laura says. "I don't know why he's acting this way."

I do. At least I'm not the only one who knows that none of this is normal.

"It's okay," I say, holding out the palm of my hand so he can sniff it. "I'm friendly, I'm okay, I'm okay…"

Wasabi continues to bark, but not quite as aggressively, as he familiarizes himself with me.

"You haven't even been gone two days," Laura says, "and he's acting like you're a delivery guy."

I glance around, noticing that the inside of the house has changed. It's the same coffee table, but there's a new plush beige sectional, a different rug—what happened to the deep red Afghan one Laura's parents had gotten us as our wedding present? There's a larger TV—also on the wall, but it seems higher and farther to the left than my actual TV is. Also this one's a Toshiba and we have a Sony.

But the biggest difference is all the toys and children's books strewn on the couch and the floor.

"Lilly, we're home," Laura calls out.

Wasabi has finally calmed down and is licking my hand. He seems like a pretty great dog and, oddly, I already feel a bond. I hear the patter of footsteps upstairs, then, "Daddy's home! Daddy's home! Daddy's home!"

Lilly comes charging down the stairs and says "Daddy!" once more before she leaps up into my arms.

I catch her, almost stumbling, as she hugs me and I'm hesitant for a second or two, then I hug her back. It feels so nice to be appreciated and missed that, for a few moments, I forget that she isn't really my daughter. I feel absolutely no attachment toward this kid, no love, but it feels nice to pretend.

"I missed you so much, Daddy."

"Yeah. Me too…" I don't know what to call her so I go with, "…kiddo."

She pulls back a little to face me, appearing perplexed. "You never call me kiddo."

"So it's a new thing," I say. "Nothing's wrong with new things, right?"

"I love new things," she says and kisses my cheek.

"To celebrate Daddy coming home, I'm making his favorite meal," Laura says, "spaghetti and meatballs."

This is true—I've always loved spaghetti and meatballs.

I put Lilly down.

"Do you want to play with me, Daddy?"

"Um, sure, we can—"

"Daddy still needs rest," Laura says, "so maybe you can play a game, but no running around."

"Oh-kayyy," Lilly says.

Then I notice a young woman coming down the stairs. She's slender and tall—a few inches shorter than me and I'm six feet—with long, wavy, dirty blonde hair, and she's in skinny jeans and a tight top. She seems college age, around twenty.

"Hi, Mr. Blitz," she says. "Welcome home."

I realize she must be Kaitlin, the babysitter. I also realize that I've never seen her before.

Or have I?

She looks extremely familiar. We've met somewhere, I know we have, but not as my daughter's babysitter.

"Is something wrong?" she asks.

I'm thinking, *Where do I know you from? I know I've seen you before. Your face, especially your eyes—I know those eyes.*

"No," I say, trying to not sound confused. "Um, but thank you."

"You're welcome to stay for dinner, Kaitlin," Laura says.

"That's okay." Kaitlin sounds disappointed. "I already called an Uber."

So Uber exists. That's strangely comforting.

"Okay," Laura says. "Hopefully next time."

Laura heads into the kitchen. Am I imagining it, or is Kaitlin paying too much attention to me?

"I wish you could drive me instead," she says in a hushed tone, so only I can hear. "I need to talk to you."

Nope, not imagining it.

Lilly has dashed into the living room, calling out, "Come on, Daddy."

I'm on my way to join her, when Kaitlin finishes coming down the stairs and cuts me off. She's squishing up to me so close I can feel her cleavage against my chest.

"I was so scared when I heard you were at the hospital," she whispers. "I don't know what I'd do if something happened to you. Especially now."

I have no idea why she was so concerned about me to the point of feeling scared. And why *especially now*?

She's still too close to me, invading my space.

Then it clicks—how I know her. She's the girl from the parking lot, the one who was having the argument with that man on Friday night—the man who stabbed me. The girl's hair looked different then, though. It's much longer now, almost down to her waist.

"Wait," I say, "you were *there*."

"There?" She sounds confused.

"At the parking lot," I say. "On Friday night. You were with that guy—having a fight."

Now she's making eye contact, showing concern. "Um, what're you talking about?"

"The parking lot, in the snow. I'm the guy who tried to save you."

She still looks baffled.

"You really don't remember?"

"Remember what?"

I don't want to push it, as I know pushing it won't accomplish anything. I don't want her to think I'm insane, or realize that I'm insane, because there still is a very significant chance that I *am* insane.

Taking a step back, I say, "Never mind. I really think you should just go now."

"But we really need to talk," she says. "You sure you can't drive me? I'll cancel the Uber."

What could she want to talk about? Why the urgent tone?

"No, that's…that's impossible," I say. "I just got out of the hospital, remember? I can't drive tonight."

"Okay." She seems upset. "But I'll see you tomorrow at seven, at Pound Ridge Mall, right?"

"Um, I don't think I can," I say.

She moves in tighter to compensate for the step back I took.

"I know, you have to spend time with Lilly now. But tomorrow I have to see you, okay? We have *a lot* to talk about."

She kisses me on the lips.

At that moment, from the other room, Lilly calls out "Daddy! Where are you?"

I maneuver past Kaitlin, wiping my lips in case there's lipstick or gloss. My pulse is pounding as I try to process what just happened, but I'm aware that the longer this goes on, the harder it will be for me to dismiss it as some sort of fantasy, hallucination, or dream. After all, there's one thing that all dreams have in common—they end. And this isn't ending. It's getting weirder and weirder. But if this *is* a dream I'm angry at myself for inventing this perverse scenario. Having an affair with the young woman I tried to save, who's also my daughter's babysitter? What the hell's wrong with me?

Kaitlin follows me into the living room.

Lilly and I play a Mario Kart game that I haven't played before, on a Nintendo console called a TS that I assume is this world's version of a DS. Kaitlin sits on a chair to my left, intermittently watching us play and texting and maybe Snapchatting on her phone—if Snapchat exists.

My phone vibrates and I look at the display, a text from "Brian": *I NEED TO TALK*

I glance over at Kaitlin who's staring at me intensely. Very stealthy of me to have entered her in my phone as my brother, Brian, in case Laura saw an incoming text. God, this version of me is such a total prick. I'm just glad this isn't the real me.

Lilly says, "Daddy, why are you so bad?"

"Yeah, Mr. Blitz," Kaitlin says. "What's wrong with you today?"

"I'm not sure." My voice is unsteady. "Maybe I just need some more time to recover from my injury."

"It can't be *that* bad," Kaitlin says. "I mean they wouldn't have released you if anything was seriously wrong, right?"

Thinking, *Yeah, nothing seriously wrong except I have no idea who you two fucking are*, I say, "True enough."

"Can I kiss your boo-boo?" Lilly asks.

Call me crazy, but I don't feel comfortable with a strange child kissing the top of my head, even if she's supposedly my daughter.

"It's okay," I say. "I think after the spaghetti and meatballs I'll feel better."

"Bye, Lil," Kaitlin says, "see you soon."

As they hug, when Lilly has her back to me, Kaitlin takes the opportunity to glare at me again.

As Kaitlin is leaving, Laura comes out from the kitchen and says, "Bye, see you soon."

"Bye, Mrs. Blitz."

Well, at least Laura doesn't seem to have any idea that something's going on. God, listen to me—*something's going on*, as if something actually *is* going on that I need to keep a secret, which there isn't, at least not in *my* reality. Besides—I remind myself—it's actually *Laura* who's the cheater, not me.

"Daddy, come on, it's your turn."

I continue playing Mario Kart with Lilly, aware that, although I've never played this game before, I feel like I have. Sitting on the couch next to this little girl I never met until yesterday feels familiar too, like we've done this before.

"Daddy, watch out!"

I didn't see a bus coming right at me and it hits me head on, destroying my car. At that moment of impact, I flash back to the parking lot—the knife going into my gut. My pulse has accelerated and it's hard to catch my breath.

"I think…I think I should take a break."

"Okay, Daddy."

I watch her play for a couple of minutes, then Laura announces, "Dinnertime!"

The dining room table and chairs have changed too. We have a set from Crate & Barrel that we had for years and moved up here from our apartment in the city. But here we have a modern, sleek table—a stainless-steel base with a matte-wooden top—and matching chairs.

"You're sitting in my seat," Lilly says as I sit down in the seat closest to the windows.

"Whoops, sorry." I move to the seat at the head of the table.

Giggling, Lilly says, "Now you're in Mommy's."

As I sit in the seat opposite her, I say, "Your Daddy's a silly guy."

Laura serves the food—spaghetti with meatballs and a salad. It tastes like her usual cooking, but I've never seen the pale green plates or this silverware before.

"Is it okay?" Laura must've noticed my expression.

"Everything's great," I say. "Nothing like a home-cooked meal."

As we eat, I do my best to try to not seem too lost and confused, trying to talk as little as I can, and interjecting an occasional "cool" or "wow, that's awesome" to keep the conversation going. Of course, I'm totally lost most of the time, like when we're talking about the deadline for summer day camp applications and other stuff I'm supposed to know, like Lilly's playdate schedule and afterschool activities at "Rippowam." The Rippowam Cisqua School is a private school in Bedford that must cost twenty or thirty grand a year; how the hell are we affording that? Did we get some kind of scholarship?

But nothing confuses me more than when Laura starts telling me about her job again.

"This week is going to be crazy for me," she says. "I'm backed up with meetings, including another one with Melissa Cohen. I think I might have to consider firing Michael."

I have no idea who these people are, but I'm more surprised that Laura's working.

"That's cool," I say.

"Why is it cool?"

"What?"

"That I'm firing Michael. You know I've been struggling with this decision. He has two kids, in a second marriage."

"I mean, not cool you're *firing* him. I just mean it's cool you're, um, keeping busy."

"I wish I wasn't busy with *this*. Parents with their time accommodations are out of control. How is it possible that so many kids have ADD these days? I know what you're going to say, that it went undiagnosed back in the day, but I just don't buy it."

Thinking, *I wasn't going to say that*, I say, "It sounds like you're handling it as well as you can."

"It must be fast food, all those hormones, vaccines. There has to be *some* explanation."

"Are you going in to teach tomorrow?"

"Teach?"

So she's not a teacher; does she have an administrative position?

"I mean to the school," I say.

"Yes, it's a usual day for me, it's going to be crazy…Also, I'm having lunch with Beth. It'll be good to catch up with her."

Beth. Could this be the same Beth she's leaving me for? Or *was* leaving me for?

"Are you okay?" Laura asks me.

My face must show something.

"Fine." I swallow a bite, then ask, "So what's new with… Beth?"

"I don't know, that's why I want to catch up with her."

I want to ask where they met, but I know I can't be that direct.

"I just mean in general," I say.

"I really don't know," Laura says. "I mean I know she and her girlfriend have been having some trouble lately, but I'm not sure if that's all better now or not."

It's the same Beth. It must be.

"What's the trouble about?"

Laura squints. "Why so many questions about Beth?"

"Just making conversation," I say.

"I'm just surprised," Laura says. "I mean, you've never asked about Beth before and suddenly you seem so interested."

"Maybe I'm turning over a new leaf."

"A new leaf?" Lilly asks, smiling. "Where's your old leaf, Daddy?"

Laura and I look at each other and laugh. This fun family moment feels good and oddly familiar.

When we're finished eating I say to Laura, "You sit, I'll clear the table."

"Thank you," Laura says. "Oh, I meant to ask you. What ever happened with Benito?"

"Benito?" Again, I have no idea what she's talking about.

"Yeah, Benito," she says.

I want to avoid her reporting "new symptoms" to Dr. Assadi and having to deal with all that again. I'm still hopeful that after a good night's sleep this—whatever this is—will end, and my normal life will resume.

"Oh, *Benito*," I say. "That went well."

"How did it go well? You mean you're *paying* him?"

"No," I say.

"So you're not paying him?"

"Right."

"He just agreed to walk away?"

"Yeah, walked away. Can you believe it?"

I have no idea what the hell I'm talking about.

"No, actually I can't believe it," she says. "What did you say to him exactly?"

"I don't recall exactly. I mean I said just how I felt. You know, my…position."

"Wow, after all that drama."

"Yeah. Crazy, huh?"

"But it's wonderful news. But why didn't you tell me? I mean, before the accident."

"I guess I meant to, but I forgot."

"Well, I'm so glad you remember now."

After I finish clearing the table, I announce that I need to "catch up on a little work," and I head upstairs.

There are changes upstairs too—the walls were previously off-white, now they're very light blue, and there's nicer, much more expensive hardwood flooring; it looks like the hickory option that we once priced with a contractor but couldn't afford. The house smells different too. It has the odor of a house where a child lives, or maybe it's just Bounty fabric softener, which we never usually buy.

Another big change: my office isn't my office. Now it's Lilly's room, which makes sense—well, in the context of Lilly's existence making sense.

I go into the master bedroom, which doesn't seem to have any similarities to my actual bedroom, except that the objects in the room are occupying the same space as they do in my actual bedroom. We've always had a king-size bed; now we have a California king. The lush, high-thread-count duvet cover and bedding are unfamiliar, the walls have never been this color—subdued, pale yellow—and the dressers and other furniture are much classier and higher-end. I open a couple of the dresser drawers and don't recognize any of my clothes.

The master bathroom has been completely renovated with marble, including a new vanity, and an enclosed glass shower. When I catch a glimpse of myself in the mirror I'm jolted as it's hard to recognize myself with a slimmer face and close-cropped haircut and an overall trimmer physique. Also, since when have my teeth looked so white? I'm a grinder and there's no evidence of that anymore either. Are they even *my* teeth? It looks like I might've had at least several of them replaced with veneers.

When I open the vanity, parting the mirror, I'm able to glimpse part of the back of my head where I have the surgery scar. Then I look inside the vanity where there are several pill bottles. One, made out to Laura, is an empty bottle, labeled Amoxicillin. Another bottle is labeled Eskalith, or lithium. I wonder if Laura is taking medication regularly now, which would explain her stable, normal behavior. There are several bottles prescribed to me, but where's my Lipitor, which I've been taking to control my cholesterol? The only medication I recognize is one that Dr. Assadi mentioned they were giving me in the hospital as part of my post-cancer treatment. The date on the bottle is current and the instructions are to take "one pill daily." I consider blowing it off, but decide that even in a fake world I don't want to do anything that might jeopardize my health. So, with a gulp of water from the faucet, I gulp a pill then return to the bedroom.

I notice that the alcove in one of the far corners has been converted to an office space and there's a PC there—a Dell. I have no idea why I don't have a Mac, why all of my Apple products seem to have been replaced. How did I become a "PC guy"? I try to log on, but my password doesn't work, even though it's the same one I use for my phone and *that* worked. I try variations, then am able to reset it by entering the name of my childhood best friend, Richie—who is apparently *still* my childhood best friend—and having a message sent to my phone.

It still doesn't feel like my computer, but apparently it is—a bootup message appears: *WELCOME STEVEN*

I open the browser and check the news—increasing tensions between India and Pakistan and the likelihood that the U.S. is going to wage nuclear war dominate the headlines.

Then I check the stock market. The Dow is at 19,046, which doesn't make any sense because I'm positive that on Friday the Dow closed at about 28,000. The chart of the past ten years doesn't seem right either; neither does the twenty-year chart. Where is the crash in 2007? The bull market that started around 2014? Instead, there was a crash in 2015 and a mild recovery in 2017. I'm not a Wall Street expert, but the chart resembles the chart of the blasé stock market of the late seventies and early eighties.

Individual stock prices seem just as perplexing. Amazon at forty-eight? Netflix is trading at just above two dollars a share and hasn't split once since its IPO. Also, I notice a news item that Netflix is considering bankruptcy options. Meanwhile, Blockbuster is at fifty-two a share and has split nine times in the past twenty years. In addition to their steady DVD sales and rentals, Blockbuster has apparently become a dominant player in "the burgeoning streaming market," and in the overall entertainment industry, with a massive film and TV production wing. They've also morphed into a major consumer electronics retailer, competing against Best Buy online and at their physical stores.

I try to log on to my Ameritrade account, but my log-in doesn't work and the system doesn't recognize my email. I try some of my older email addresses that I rarely use, but I can't log on with these either. I'm sweating, fearing that all my money is gone, even though I know this thought is illogical, since how can you lose money in a world that doesn't exist?

I notice a filing cabinet that I've never seen before under my desk. I pull it open, surprised that it's so neat and well-organized. I've been meaning to get organized with my filing, but haven't gotten around to it. There's no doubt, though, that it's my handwriting on the file labels. On a file marked medical I find what appears to be my recent blood tests although the doctor referenced, Dr. Adam Feinstein, is not my actual doctor. Also, my cholesterol is normal, even on the low side, in all the reports. Then I notice material from Sloan Kettering in Manhattan, which I assume is related to my brain cancer.

Browsing through the files, I find one that's marked *Financial Accounts*. Inside, there's a folder at the front labeled *Charles Schwab*. I've never had a Schwab account but a recent statement, from last month, has Steven Blitz on it. There are several pages that I skim, then I stare at the account balance:

$2,842,654.43

In reality, I have barely two hundred thousand dollars in my investment accounts total—*including* retirement funds. We should've saved much more, but I had some off years, and Laura quit working and some bad investments in internet stocks and fledgling biotech startups didn't help either. But now, in this fantasy version of my life, we're doing great, which explains how we were able to renovate the house, get nicer cars, and pay for private school for Lilly.

Taking a closer look at a recent statement, I see that I made most of my money in—yep—Blockbuster. I currently own shares worth over $287,000. Recently, I sold shares worth a little over $798,000 and shifted the difference into bonds and fixed income, a move that I seem to have timed perfectly. During this period the Dow dropped 18 percent, perhaps in response to the unstable global situation.

Admittedly, I'm impressed with my savvy investing prowess, especially at a time when the overall stock market hasn't been booming. This fantasy version of Steven Blitz might be a lying adulterer, but he sure as hell knows how to invest.

Then I think: *Why can't I make more?*

With all the knowledge I have about the actual world, there have to be ways I could profit. Not only investing—I could invent products and drugs that haven't been invented yet, start my own business. Does *Shark Tank* exist? Does Mark Cuban exist? If so, Cuban will salivate when I tell him about my ideas. Or I could go to Hollywood and pitch *The Truman Show* and other movies and TV shows that I know well. Why not *Star Wars*? I do a search, disappointed that *Star Wars* exists—but only the original three, so I can tell George Lucas all about my great ideas for the sequels. *Friends* and *The Godfather* exist, but not *Breaking Bad, The Sopranos*, and *Game of Thrones*, although two of the novels in the *Games of Thrones* series exist—the first book and the sequel, *A Clash of Kings*. The other novels in the series haven't been published; maybe I can describe the plots to George R. R. Martin and somehow get paid for it.

What else can I create?

I already know there's no Facebook and Google, and I can't find Twitter either. YouTube exists, but it doesn't seem to be nearly as popular as it actually is, and the logo looks different. I can't find Snapchat or Instagram, but there's an app called

"Pictora" that seems to have similar functions as Instagram.

Searches for childhood and college friends also produce surprises. Some people look vastly different—heavier, thinner, older, younger. When did my friend Dave, my first college roommate, who had always been clean-shaven, grow that thick beard? Melissa, my high school girlfriend, is in amazing shape, and has posted lots of bikini shots while on a recent vacation with her fit, handsome husband. The last time I Facebooked Melissa, within the past year, she was very overweight and single. But the most jolting surprise comes when I visit my friend Rob's MyWorld page and see the most recent posts were on his birthday in July, from friends and family, with comments that include "I hope it's a beautiful day in heaven," "I miss you more every year," and "Gone, but never forgotten." Going back through his timeline I discover that Rob was killed in a plane crash while on vacation in Antigua in 2014. This is particularly shocking since, in the actual world, I just had drinks with Rob in the city last week.

Exploring what's different, or the same, about this world is interesting, but it also feels pointless. I don't really *believe* that Rob is dead, or that any of this is *real* information. Still, even if it's only for pure amusement, I have to know what's going on in sports.

Tiger Woods is a top golfer and the Williams sisters remain top tennis players. Michael Jordan exists, and Wilt Chamberlain, Babe Ruth, Mickey Mantle, Pelé, Secretariat, and Joe Namath exist or existed. I'm realizing that most, if not all, of the changes in the world seem to have occurred over the past twenty years. The most recent events and information seem the most screwed up, but I'm not sure what the significance of this is; if there is any.

For example, I remember Friday night, the night I was stabbed, the Knicks were playing the Indiana Pacers. I check the results and see that the Knicks in fact played on Friday night—but against the Miami Heat, not the Pacers. This alone confuses me, then I check the box score. Why are LeBron James and Stephen Curry playing for the Knicks? According to what I'm seeing, James scored 37 points and Curry scored 32 in Friday night's game. I click on an article about the game with the headline *Curry and James Power Knicks to Sixth Straight*. I go to the NBA standings—the Knicks are in first place in the Eastern Conference. This is ridiculous because they're actually near the bottom. Also, I see that they've won NBA championships four out of the past six years.

Checking current baseball, I recognize some names, but some don't make sense. Who's Danny Noll, who hit fifty-two homers for the Yankees last year? Where's Aaron Judge and Giancarlo Stanton? The Mets won the World Series in 2013 and 2016, which isn't true, of course. Older information seems more accurate, though—Derek Jeter and Bernie Williams both played on the Yankees on their 1997 and 1998 championship teams, and the Mets won the World Series in 1986.

Lastly, I check the recent history of the NFL. I've been a diehard Jets fan, but I've never seen the Jets win a Super Bowl. The last time they won it all was in 1969, well before I was born. Since this is *my fantasy*, the least my brain can do is let me experience the thrill of the Jets winning the big game.

Wrong.

The Jets haven't won another Super Bowl, or even played in one.

Some things never change.

As I tuck Lilly in, she asks me to read her *Madeline*, which is the same *Madeline* I know by Ludwig Bemelmans.

I have a feeling I'm supposed to have done this before, although I can't remember the last time I read a children's story out loud.

Sitting on the foot of the bed, I begin: "In an old house in Paris that was covered in vines, lived twelve little girls…"

Lilly interrupts and says, "Read it the way you *always* read it."

Of course I don't know which way that is, so I say, "Maybe mixing things up is good sometimes."

"No," she says. "I want things to stay the same."

I continue reading, trying different pacing, inflections, and character voices, but apparently, I can't get it right as Lilly keeps interrupting every time I get something wrong, telling me how I'm *supposed* to say it.

When I'm finished she says, "Again."

Although I don't know this kid at all, I do know when I'm being manipulated.

"Nope." I get up. "It's time for bed."

"Beddy-bye," she corrects me. "Say sweet dreams and kiss me on my head."

After I do this, I say, "Sweet dreams, kiddo."

"Not kiddo." She giggles, enjoying this game she thinks we're playing. "Do I have to tell you how to do *everything*?"

"Okay, just sweet dreams."

She smiles. "That's better."

I flick off the light, then shut the door. Is it possible that I'm already liking this kid, feeling attached?

Too bad this isn't my actual life because there are a lot of positives here. I'm a father, I have a happy wife, I'm wealthier, I have a nicer house and nicer cars. Okay, I'm apparently an adulterer, but I could fix that. I can become a better man, or revert to the man I actually am.

I get ready for bed, still trying to feel at home in this unfamiliar house.

After I brush my teeth, Laura says, "Did you arm the alarm?"

"Oh, not yet."

I go downstairs and discover that it's a new, unfamiliar, high-end video surveillance system. I can't arm it because I don't know the code.

When I return upstairs, I say, "This is a little embarrassing, but I don't remember the code."

"Oh, it's okay, sweetie," Laura says. "I mean, you're doing so well. You remember everything else, so what's the big deal if you forgot one thing?"

She tells me the code and I go back down. It takes a while, but I finally figure out how to set it.

A few minutes later, when I lie next to Laura on the spacious bed, she continues to stare at the thick hardcover novel she's reading: *Twisted City* by Maxwell Kennedy. I've never heard of the novel or the author, but I'm not a big reader so this doesn't necessarily mean anything.

"One sec," she says. "You're right, this book is great. Good suggestion."

I notice amongst the stack of books on my night table, four are by Maxwell Kennedy. Guess I'm a fan.

"I had, um, a feeling you'd like Kennedy. He's, um, right up your alley."

I get into bed next to her, liking her lavender scent; she must be into essential oils now.

"I think I have a great idea for a TV show," I say.

"Wait." She finishes reading a page then closes the book and places it on her night table. Then she says, "TV show? You don't even like TV."

I love TV, I'm always binging shows—at home and on my iPad on my commute to and from work.

"That's not true," I say. Then, not wanting her to think I'm having more memory issues, I add, "I mean, there are *some* shows I love."

"Okay. Like what?"

"Like, um, *Seinfeld*."

"Besides *Seinfeld*."

"Can I tell you my great idea?"

"Go 'head."

"Well, it's called *The Sopranos*."

"*The Sopranos*?" She sounds puzzled. "What's it about? Opera singers?"

"It really doesn't sound at all familiar to you?"

"Why should it? Have you told me about it before?"

"No, I, um, guess I haven't. It's just something that's been, well, percolating."

"Percolating, huh? So? What's it about?"

"Well, it's about a dysfunctional mob family in New Jersey. The mob boss, Tony, is living a double life, trying to run the crime family and manage his own family life. Oh, and he has psychological problems and sees a therapist."

Looking unimpressed, Laura says, "It doesn't sound like something *I* would ever watch."

Actually, Laura loves *The Sopranos*; we recently re-watched the entire series.

"Trust me, you'll love it," I say. "And nowadays it would be a huge hit with binge watching."

"What's that?"

"Um, nothing," I say. "Here's another idea. What do you think of this title?...*Game of Thrones*. It's based on a novel, but maybe I can get the rights."

"Okay, seriously what's going on with all this? Since when do you have ideas for TV shows?"

"Maybe it's because of what happened to me," I say. "I mean, there's nothing wrong with me. But, still, you know, a traumatic experience can change a person's perspective, spark creativity. There are things I want to do now that I've never done before."

She snickers. "Well, for the record, I think the mob boss idea and Game of Whatever are awful ideas, so don't give up your day job."

Using the remote, she flicks on the 60-or-so-inch wall-mounted TV that faces our bed, and CNN comes on. On the bottom of the screen there's an announcement:

GORE: ALL OPTIONS ARE ON THE TABLE, INCLUDING A PREEMPTIVE NUCLEAR STRIKE

"God, it's so scary," Laura says. "What if there really is a nuclear war?"

It's hard for me to actually feel *scared*, since I still don't believe what I'm experiencing is real. But the idea of Al Gore starting the third world war seems too absurd to take seriously.

"What's so funny?" Laura asks.

I'm aware I'm smiling.

"Nothing," I say. "I mean, you don't really think there's going to be a war, do you?"

"If Pakistan nukes India there will be," she says. "Unless we nuke Pakistan first and then Pakistan and maybe Russia nuke us."

"I have a feeling everything's going to be okay," I say.

I begin rubbing one of her legs, noticing how it feels much more toned than her actual leg.

"What are you doing?" She sounds surprised.

"Do you mind?"

"No," she says. "It feels good. It's just…surprising."

"What is?"

"It's been a long time. You haven't seemed very interested lately."

Continuing to caress her leg, I kiss her neck, under her chin, then say, "I'll never lose interest in you, I promise."

My hard-on is pressing against her thigh.

"Wow," she says. "Are you sure you really want to?"

Remembering her telling me that she never actually loved me, I say, "Are you sure *you* want to?"

"Of course I want to," she says. "I *always* want to. It's just that you just got out of the hospital."

"I feel fine...obviously."

"I can see that, but also, you've been so...distant...for such a long time, and now you suddenly seem so into me. It's just confusing, that's all."

"It's not sudden," I say.

"I've been worried a lot lately," she says. "I've been worried that you're unhappy, that you even want to...I don't know."

Holding her tighter, looking into her eyes, I say, "I'm sorry for whatever I did to make you feel that way, but it's not true, okay? That's the last thing I want and I promise I'll never make you feel that way again...Can you promise me something?"

"Okay, what?"

"If you ever have any doubts about anything, if you ever are attracted to someone else—maybe even your friend Beth—promise me that you'll come talk to me first before you—"

"*Beth*? Is that why you were acting so weird at dinner? You really think something's going on with me and Beth?"

I wish she knew how ironic it is that she's making my suggestion sound absurd, like an impossibility.

"Of course I don't think that," I say.

"That's crazy. I'd never—"

"Don't say that." I pause. "I mean, things can always change, and your intentions can change, but I just want you to know... *I'm* not changing. I know I can get, well, a little too self-absorbed at times, but I'm here for you, and I'll always be here."

I watch her smile.

"I don't know what's going on with you, Steven Blitz, but I like it."

With CNN and crisis-mode President Gore in the background, we begin having sex. Amazingly, it feels like it did when we first met, like we're discovering each other's bodies for the first time, which, in a way, we are. Thanks to my sleeker build, I feel sexier than I have in a long time, and it feels great to feel connected to Laura again. Not just physically connected; it feels great to feel close.

Afterwards, snuggling, she whispers, "I want to stay like this forever."

Hoping I never leave this fantasy state, I whisper, "Me too. Me too."

SEVEN

I wake up around 6 A.M., my naked wife hugging me from behind. I'm elated that I'm still here, that my new life hasn't faded.

"You're up already?" Laura squeezes me tighter, kissing the back of my neck.

"Guess I'm just excited."

"I can tell."

I smile. "You can go back to sleep if you want."

"No, I have to get up now anyway, but I don't want to let you go."

"Me neither."

"This feels so great. It feels like a dream."

"I know."

After I shower, I go online to do a quick "fact check."

The country is still on the brink of nuclear annihilation, the stock market is still a little above 19,000, LeBron James and Stephen Curry are still on the Knicks, and Excite is still the premiere search engine. If this *is* a dream, the details have remained remarkably consistent. The days are passing like normal days—with sleep cycles, sunrises and sunsets. What kind of dream or fantasy functions like this, with so much order? Nothing *feels* fake and don't the shrinks say that I should always trust my feelings? If anything, it feels like my old life is the fantasy and *this* is real.

After I shower in my luxurious bathroom, I enter a walk-in closet. I notice a stylish Hugo Boss suit that must have cost over a thousand dollars, easy.

"Sweet," I say.

Off to the side are what must be my work suits. I choose a stylish, slim-fitting Brooks Brothers suit and a Calvin Klein button-down. The outfit looks too small for me, but it fits perfectly.

After I put on a new-looking pair of light brown Mephistos, I head downstairs. Although the kitchen has been renovated with new maple cabinetry, a granite countertop, new appliances—when did we get a Sub-Zero fridge?—it seems like things are stored where I would expect them to be. The coffee is still in the cabinet above the sink, the mugs are in the cabinet adjacent to the stove.

I'm sitting on a breakfast stool, sipping a cup of hazelnut, when my phone vibrates as a text arrives from "Brian," but actually Kaitlin: *I HAVE TO see you later. A LOTTTT to discuss!!!*

I'm trying to decide if I should respond and, if so, how, when Laura enters in her yoga clothes.

"I missed my Ying class this morning, but I'll make the Vinyasa," she says, as she turns on the coffeemaker. Then she sees how I'm dressed and says with a surprised look, "You're going to work?"

"It's Monday morning," I say. "Why wouldn't I—"

"I don't think going in today's a good idea."

"Come here," I say.

I pull her in close and kiss her with passion, my hands massaging the back of her neck.

Then I shift back a little, but my lips are still practically touching hers, and say, "As you saw last night, there's nothing wrong with me."

"I know," she says, "but Dr. Assadi said—"

"Trust me, I'm fine. I promise if I feel off in any way, I won't go, or I'll come right home. I won't do anything stupid, okay?"

She seems reluctant, but says, "Okay, but be careful." She

kisses me again, then says, "Make sure to tell the driver to not let Madison sit next to Lilly because they haven't been getting along. I know you told him once already, but sometimes he forgets stuff."

Of course, I have no idea who the driver even is, but I assume Laura's talking about a school bus. There's going to be a lot to learn about my "daily routine" that I know nothing about, so I'm going to have to get used to learning on the fly.

"Will do," I say.

When Laura leaves, I sip some more coffee and peel a banana, but I'm too excited to eat. I'm eager to go into the city. Partly it's out of curiosity—I have to see what the world is like outside of Westchester—but I also want to find out what's going on at work, why Jeffery Hammond isn't on trial for murder.

I hear honking from outside. I glance out and see the school bus has pulled up in front.

"Fuck me," I say.

I rush up to Lilly's room and see she's still asleep.

"Come on, out of bed now. Your bus is here."

Stirring, she mumbles, "Bus?"

"Just get dressed!"

I hustle downstairs, open the door, and shout at the driver, "One sec! She's coming!"

I dash up, two steps at a time, and see that Lilly is still in bed.

"Shit, come on. What did I just tell you?"

"You used a bad word, I'm gonna tell Mommy."

"You have to get dressed, the bus will leave."

"I don't have a shirt to wear."

"Where are your shirts?"

I open a dresser drawer that's filled with socks.

"You know where they are."

"No, I don't. I hit my head, remember? It's hard to remember some things so you'll have to help me, okay? You have to go to school. You can't miss school."

"Bottom drawer," she says.

I grab a pink shirt and give it to her.

"I hate that one."

The bus horn honks.

"Put it on. *Now*."

I help her put the shirt on, and the jeans she wore yesterday, then socks and sneakers. Then I practically drag her downstairs.

When I open the front door the bus is starting to pull away.

"Wait!" I shout. "Wait!"

As we run, it stops.

"Where's my lunch?" Lilly asks.

Fuck, I'm supposed to make lunch too? How do parents do it? How the hell do I handle this every day *and* do everything I have to do for myself?

"Can't you get lunch at school?"

"But you *always* make lunch and I like your lunch better."

"I forgot today, but I won't forget again, I promise."

We jog toward the bus, navigating around the piles of snow near the curb.

"Thank you," I say to the driver, a young guy who has a hipster beard; well, if hipster beards, or even hipsters, exist.

"Have to stay on schedule, Mr. Blitz," he says, not making eye contact.

"Sorry, it won't happen again," I say.

He doesn't respond.

Lilly gets in, the doors close, and the bus pulls away.

"Don't let her sit next to Madison!" I shout at the driver, but I'm not sure he heard.

After attempting to center myself with a couple of steady, deep breaths, I return to the house and finish getting ready for work.

In my office space in my bedroom, I find a sleek, leather briefcase and inside find folders and papers that don't look at all familiar, but I remind myself not to be concerned about this, that it doesn't matter. Eventually I'll acclimate.

I find a Calvin Klein overcoat in the closet near the front door and head out.

My key chain has the remote lock and ignition key for my top-of-the-line silver Mercedes. The best Mercs were always way out of my price range. Not anymore, thanks to my savvy investing in Blockbuster.

I drive to the Katonah train station. On most mornings I park in the same spot, but today my spot is taken, so I park in one of the only available spots toward the back of the lot. As I head toward the station, I don't recognize any of the cars, and I notice that there's a new-looking Toyota I haven't seen before, which is odd because I was at a Toyota dealership a few weeks ago and am familiar with the recent models.

It's almost seven-thirty, perfect timing, as I usually take the 7:39 into the city. On my phone I have the MTA ticket app. The app looks different from the app I know—it's red with white font, instead of blue with orange and white; actually, the entire interface is unfamiliar. Also, I see that there isn't a 7:39 to Grand Central, but there is a 7:38. Although this slight difference won't impact my day, it reminds me that as familiar as some of this feels, this is not the world I know.

On the platform, I activate my ticket.

Usually I recognize most of my fellow commuters and have several friends I chat with every morning, and sometimes on the evening commute too, if we're on the same train—third car from the front. Today most people seem unfamiliar, though, and I don't see my friends. Do my friends even *exist*?

I do recognize a few people, though. There's a thin, older guy whom I've never spoken to, but he smiles at me, and says, "Hi, Steve," as I pass.

"Hey," I say, and keep going, toward the front of the platform.

As I arrive at the position where the third car always stops, I see a poster for a movie—*Life and Death*—with actors I don't recognize. Who's Aaron Hardy and Lana Wells? By the way they're presented on the ad as big movie stars, it seems like I *should* know them.

Then, on another billboard, I see an ad for a TV show on NBC called *Cosby's World*, which displays grinning, healthy-looking Bill Cosby, and his adoring TV children and grandchildren surrounding him.

"Are you fucking kidding me?" I say out loud.

A guy nearby glances at me, but I'm too mesmerized to care. Does this mean that Cosby isn't in prison? What about the #MeToo movement?

On my phone, I do a quick search—nope, no Cosby rape stories. But just because he hasn't been convicted, doesn't mean he's innocent. Like Jeffery Hammond, Cosby is who he is—nothing can change that. I can't find any #MeToo articles either. Maybe I can start the hashtag and go after Cosby and other abusers, pioneer a movement. With what I know, there are so many great things I can do for the world—I could even cure diseases. While I don't know exactly how to cure any disease, I've read articles and seen 60 *Minutes* reports on breakthroughs in Alzheimer's, cancer, and HIV. If this information isn't known yet, I can at least tell researchers what I do know and this might be enough to kickstart treatments and cures. I can help so many people.

"Morning, Steve."

I turn and see a familiar face—my friend, Angie Garcia. Angie and I have been commuting into the city together for several years, since she moved to Westchester from New Jersey. I just saw her Friday night, the night I got stabbed. She and her husband Tom came to our house for dinner. Like everyone else, Angie looks different, though. She has her usual slender build and is in a typical conservative work dress, but her hair is shorter with blonder highlights.

"Hey there, good morning, Angie. It's really great to see you."

She seems taken aback, like she's surprised by what I said, or by my attitude. She seems angry, but maybe she's just confused.

"How was your weekend?" she asks.

She definitely seems annoyed. Also, it's an odd question since I just saw her and Tom, though I suspect, as far as she's concerned, that dinner never took place.

"Eventful," I say.

"Really?" Now she appears concerned. "I hope nothing bad."

I don't want to go into all of it, so I say, "Just some very, um, let's just say *unexpected* things happened, but I'm hoping some normalcy returns soon."

"Oh, okay," she says. "You didn't reach out to me so I was getting a little paranoid. You know how I get."

I have no idea what she's talking about. Reach out to her? Reach out about what?

"Yeah, there's nothing to worry about that. Everything's just been moving steadily along."

"Well, that's a relief," she says.

After an awkward pause, I ask, "So how was *your* weekend?"

"Frustrating," she says. "I was at my in-laws in Montclair and I just wanted to be with you the whole time."

I'm praying this doesn't mean what I think it means.

"Be with me?" I ask. "Be with me where?"

"Come on, stop it, Steve," she says. "I'm sorry I was upset. I'm not trying to make you feel guilty, I know you had stuff with Laura and Lilly, but I can't help how I feel." Her expression brightens. "But I have some good news for you—I was going to text you last night, but I thought I'd just tell you when I saw you. Tom is going away with the kids for a whole week—winter break. You can come over Friday night. Saturday too if you can get free. Any weeknights too, except Wednesday when I have my book club."

"Come over?" I ask. "Come over for what?"

She bites down on her lower lip a little while staring at my lips, then says, "Whatever you want."

Still hoping I'm somehow getting this all wrong, I say, "Uh, I'm not sure I get it. I mean, why would you want me to come over if Tom and the kids are away?"

"Gee, I don't know," she says. "But I have a pretty good hunch we'd find a way to entertain ourselves."

I'm having an affair with Angie too? I'd be even more disgusted with myself if I didn't know this isn't actually *me*.

"Sorry, but that's not happening," I say.

"What?" She seems confused, hurt. "What do you mean?"

There are a few people nearby on the platform, but no one seems to be overhearing. Still, I lower my voice, practically whisper, "I don't know exactly what you think has happened with us in the past, but nothing's going to happen going forward."

She stares at me, like she's trying to solve a riddle, then says, "What I *think* happened? You're joking right?"

"No, I'm very serious, Angie. Trust me, this isn't what either of us want. We're good friends, we've been good friends for a long time. This is just going to mess up our lives, our families."

"Why're you acting this way?"

"I'm just being honest with you. And Tom's a great guy. I don't know what's happening with you two, but you should try to work things out."

"How do you know Tom? You've never even met him."

So I guess Laura and I aren't "couples friends" with the Garcias, and I haven't played golf with Tom, either.

"I just *know* things," I say. "Things no one else seems to know. I can't explain how I know them or you'd think I was insane, but you'll just have to take my word for it."

She's still staring at me. "What happened this weekend, Steve? Were you really in an accident or did Laura find out something? I knew it was only a matter of time until she caught on that—"

"No, that's not it, and let's just keep it that way, okay?"

She glares, then says, "What if I don't want to keep it that way?"

It's not like Angie to make threats. Well, not like the Angie I know. "You have to," I say. "You have no choice."

A train arrives. When I get on board ahead of Angie I recognize a guy who I know is a big tennis fan because we once had an argument about who's better, Federer or Nadal.

"Hey," I say, smiling. "Go, Federer."

He looks away like I'm a crazy stranger.

I don't see any other familiar faces. Where's Alex, Dave, Rob?

I sit by myself, adjacent to two empty seats. Is this how it's going to be for the rest of my life—wondering if my friends still like me or even exist? And now that I've experienced how quickly things can change, how I can lose everything in an instant, how am I supposed to trust anything?

My phone vibrates. Another text from "Brian": *YOU'RE SUCH A FUCKING ASSHOLE*

Glancing toward the far end of the car, I see that Angie is seated, glaring back at me, over her shoulder, and it's obvious she just sent me the text. So I'm using "Brian" as Angie's name in addition to Kaitlin's.

I look up again and Angie's gone. She probably moved to another car, but for all I know she was never there.

I can't rule anything out.

EIGHT

When I get off the train at Grand Central and head up the long ramp at the end of the platform I'm prepared for the worst. Maybe I won't recognize anything, maybe it won't look like New York at all. Maybe it'll look like another city, or maybe cities don't exist. Maybe New York will be a barren wasteland and I'll wander around all day, feeling alienated, terrified and confused.

I'm relieved that Grand Central is still the Grand Central I know. Same big four-faced gold clock at the information booth in the center, Cipriani and the Apple Store on the second level and, up above, the celestial ceiling, which looks the same as it has in recent years, post the Jackie Onassis restoration.

The familiar surroundings provide some comfort. With renewed optimism, I exit the terminal onto Forty-Second Street, looking forward to seeing the rushing, agitated faces, and breathing in the fumes from the smoky pretzel stands and buses, but right away I notice that things are off. Where's that new office building that was recently constructed to the west of Grand Central? Why is the old structure still intact and occupied? Across the street the Chase bank is there, but two storefronts away from where it was the last time I was here—last week. As I head downtown on Madison, I see that other stores and restaurants are gone, including Madison & Vine, a restaurant where I recently lunched with a client. None of this causes panic, though. Maybe I'm just getting used to inconsistencies; am I in "the acceptance stage"? Or maybe it's because I'm in Manhattan, where things are constantly changing anyway, so what's the big deal if some stores and buildings are out of place?

Bryant Park looks unchanged, but I don't recognize the stores across the street from it. Where's the Chipotle and the Starbucks? As I approach Times Square, I'm prepared for a jolt, but the surprise is that it looks very similar to the Times Square of recent years—cleaned up, glitzy, Disney-esque, mainly filled with flagship stores of large chains. Some of the stores and businesses are the same—American Eagle Outfitters, Levi's, MTV, the Nasdaq—but there are odd differences. For example, American Eagle is on the east side of Broadway, as opposed to the west. The oversized billboards for current TV shows and movies are all unfamiliar. Actually, the only one I recognize is for *Cosby's World*.

In the middle of Times Square, I look up and around, trying to absorb it all, like a tourist who's never been here before, which is actually an appropriate feeling, then I head back across town to my office on Thirty-Ninth near Madison.

The lobby has the same old-New York, art deco style and Lawrence, the usual security guard, is on duty. Unlike most of the other people in my life I've encountered recently, Lawrence looks the ways he usually looks—a middle-aged paunch, dark sport jacket. He's standing at the desk.

"Good morning, Steven, how you doing today?" He's grinning, warm, like normal.

"Pretty good," I say.

"Knicks lookin' good, huh? How many in a row is that?"

Lawrence often talks about the Knicks, but usually about losing streaks.

"A lot," I say. "Hard to stop Curry and LeBron, huh?"

"The dynasty continues," he says.

Passing his desk, I notice that something seems off. I'm not sure what it is—the marble floor looks normal, the elevator bank looks normal. Then I realize what's wrong—the security turnstile is missing. I check my wallet and discover that the work ID card that I normally scan every morning is gone too.

The interior of the elevator looks the same, though, and there's the same ping when I reach my floor—fourteen.

A slender woman, about thirty, whom I've never seen is at reception, but this isn't unusual—she could be a temp.

"Hey, good morning, Steven," she says, brightening like she knows me.

"Morning, how was your weekend?" At least I'm getting good at playing along with the craziness.

"Great, thanks," she says. "You have a few voicemails. Two over the weekend and one a few minutes ago."

"Thanks," I say, continuing inside.

The office looks nicer than it has ever looked; it's clearly undergone a renovation. The carpeting, desks, cubicles— everything looks upgraded. I already assumed my firm was doing well, going by my inflated financial accounts, but this provides more evidence.

"Morning, Steven," a stocky guy with a trimmed salt-and-pepper beard whom I've never seen before says to me.

I look behind me and watch him veer into one of the larger offices, so he's likely one of our partners.

I enter my office—but it's not *my* office. Nothing is familiar —not the desk, not the books or anything else on the shelves, and certainly not the photos of a teenaged boy and girl on the desk.

As I'm leaving, a totally unfamiliar woman—short dark hair, maybe forty—enters. She seems as confused as me.

"Hey, Steven," she says.

"Hey," I say.

"Looking for something?"

It must be her office.

"No, I was just uh…" I can't think of an excuse. "Don't know why I went in there actually. Monday mornings."

She smiles. "I don't think I'm awake yet myself, and I'm into my third cup of coffee."

"Only one for me, but I obviously need another."

"See you at the meeting."

"Um right," I say.

I don't know what meeting she means, but first I need to find my office.

I head in the opposite direction, peeking in every office I pass, looking for anything that might seem familiar, but nothing does. I'm about to give up when, for the hell of it, I decide to go around a glass wall into one of the large corner offices—I *am* a partner after all. Sure enough, I spot a photo of Lilly on the desk.

Not surprisingly, nothing in my office is recognizable—well, aside from the photo of Lilly, which isn't *actually* recognizable. The desk is much bigger than mine and my favorite Aeron chair isn't here; instead there's a larger, dark brown leather-cushioned one that I can't imagine choosing. There's a Compaq PC when I actually use a MacBook Air. I've never seen the books on the shelf—some law-related, but also a biography of Al Gore, and naturally a thriller, *Panic Attack*, by—who else?—Maxwell Kennedy.

Friday, I worked late, preparing for the Jeffery Hammond trial, and I remember leaving a couple of folders with non-confidential material on my desk, but the folders aren't here. Then I spot a tall, dark wooden, maybe mahogany, filing cabinet along the wall opposite the desk. Browsing the files, I recognize my handwriting on some of the documents, but otherwise they could be some random attorney's files. As I expect, there's nothing about Jeffery Hammond, and the idea that an evil-to-the-bone psychopath like Hammond is out there, free, still disturbs the hell out of me. What about the men I know he's killed—but are actually still alive—the ones whose horrific autopsy photos have been engraved into my subconscious? Is he plotting to kill them now? If so, should I warn them? Or what if there are new victims, like Eduardo Ortiz on Long Island. One thing is for sure—if Hammond hasn't killed, he will. Killing is his nature, he can't stop himself. He's told me this himself many times.

"Hey, man."

Terrence has entered my office; well, a *version* of Terrence. He's gained weight, especially in his midsection, and his face is pudgier. He used to have a clean-shaved head, now he has a close-cropped afro. And what's with the cologne? He's never worn so much of it before. It's like he's half Terrence/half smarmy used-car salesman. Still, it's nice to see another semi-familiar face.

"Hey," I say, still crouching by the file cabinet.

"Coming to the meeting with Elizabeth?" he asks.

Elizabeth?

"Yeah, of course."

"Everything cool?"

"Why wouldn't everything be cool?"

"Well, that phone call over the weekend was pretty, well, weird, man. I mean, you told me that you'd see me back in reality. I didn't know what that—"

"Oh, sorry about all that," I say. "Just some stuff going on at home and there was just a little misunderstanding."

I know this doesn't make much sense. Believing that I have a big murder case going to trial when that case doesn't even exist isn't a "misunderstanding." It's flat-out disturbing behavior.

"You sure?" he says. "Because I was convinced it was related to your health issues."

I'm lost for a moment, then remember that I had a brain tumor.

"Oh, don't worry about that," I say. "I just had a checkup with my neurologist and all is well in that department. Just one of those things."

I turn to face him as I get up.

"Good to hear," he says. "I want to go over the Livingston situation and catch you up on the litigation last week."

I have no clue what any of this means.

"Sounds great," I say.

"But first," he says, "I have to tell you what happened Friday night."

He closes the door to my office. Then when he turns back toward me and says, "So I did it...I finally hooked up with Ashley."

I have no clue who Ashley is, or why he's bragging to me about a sexual conquest. This is definitely not normal Terrence behavior.

"Ah." I'm not sure what else to say. He already thinks I'm having serious memory issues, so I don't want to give him another reason to be concerned.

He tells me about the "wild weekend" he spent with Ashley, our receptionist.

When he's through, I say, "You know this is really a bad idea, Terrence."

"What is?"

"Having an office affair, especially when you're a partner at the firm."

"It never stopped you before."

So I've had office affairs too? Great.

"Well, if I've made mistakes I won't make them again," I say. "But what you're doing isn't fair to Ashley, or to your wife."

"My *wife*?"

I see he's not wearing a wedding band.

"You sure you're okay, man?"

I know if I go on, he'll just think I've officially lost my mind. What will that accomplish?

"Sorry, it's just been a long weekend. I shouldn't have intruded."

"Seriously, I think you need some more rest. But I don't know why you're wasting your time moralizing on *today* of all days. Didn't you hear Gore last night? Nuclear war could break out anytime. This could be the last day of our lives. We might as well have some fun when we can, right?"

"There won't be a war."

"Gore sounded pretty damn serious last night."

"Think about it," I say. "If India does something like that the terrorists will just use it as an excuse for another Nine-Eleven. Gore obviously knows that so I'm sure he's pressuring both sides to work it out."

"Okay, what's this you're talking about now?"

"What do you mean?"

"Nine-Eleven. Is that some kind of code name or something?"

I smile, like he's making a joke, even if I don't understand what the joke is.

But then I can tell he's not joking.

"Wait," I say. "You're serious. You really don't know what Nine-Eleven is?"

"No, but I know what Seven-Eleven is."

My pulse quickens as I try to process all of the connotations at once. Last night it didn't occur to me to check if 9/11 or the Gulf War happened. Is it possible that none of it did?

"Please tell me this isn't a joke," I say.

"A joke? I don't even know what the hell you're talking about."

I think about checking on my phone or laptop, but I'm already rushing out of my office.

"Hey, where're you going? What about the meeting?"

I'm already exiting the office. It seems like an instant later I'm rushing along Fortieth Street, then crossing Seventh Avenue —the ten-minute walk feels like it's taken a minute.

Ironically when the 9/11 attacks happened I wasn't far from where I am right now—at my office in Midtown. I'd just arrived for work and Jen, another attorney, told me that a plane had hit one of the towers. I called Laura, who was working in the city then too, to make sure she was okay, and then my coworkers and I huddled around a TV in the office and watched people jumping to their death and the second plane hitting the South Tower. The memories of that day are so clear; but if it didn't happen the connotations would be mind-boggling. It means that all those people who died that day and in the Gulf War and maybe the war in Afghanistan are still alive. What about Osama Bin Laden and Saddam Hussein? What about Al-Qaeda and ISIS?

At the Times Square subway station, I enter through the turnstiles using a MetroCard that I already have in my wallet, and that has fares on it. My MetroCard has the exact same design—yellow with blue lettering—as the MetroCards I know. I board a 1 train, heading downtown. Already I get more evidence that 9/11 hasn't happened—on the subway map there's no mention of the 9/11 Memorial.

I'm over ten stops away, which in "subway time" is about two minutes per stop, or about twenty minutes. The subway is moving at a normal pace, but I'm so eager to get there it feels like time has stalled. Finally, we get to Chambers Street, and then the next stop is World Trade Center.

Amazingly we pull into the *old* World Trade Center station, the one that was partly destroyed and had to be rebuilt.

Only it's *here*.

As I step onto the platform I'm elated to see the crumbling, dirty walls, the leaking ceiling, and not the slick new train station it was replaced with. Best of all, there are no exit signs with direction to the 9/11 Memorial, just a directional sign to the World Trade Center.

"What the fuck?" I say way too loud, causing a few people nearby to glance at me as we head toward the exit.

Ascending the steps toward the street level, I flash back to the many times I went to the Twin Towers for business, or to have drinks or dine at Windows on the World. Watching the towers fall was the most surreal moment of my life…well, until the last few days.

I'm almost outside when I tell myself that this moment would be a fitting end to whatever's been happening to me these past couple of days. I'll look to my left and see the Freedom Tower, the Oculus, the 9/11 Memorial and my *actual* life will resume. I glance at my phone: 9:48. Actually the timing works out perfectly since the Jeffery Hammond murder trial begins at ten o'clock. I'm downtown already so I can head over to the courthouse, in time to make opening statements. Donald Trump will be President, I won't have a daughter, I won't be wealthy, my wife will be divorcing me, I won't be an adulterer, and a novel coronavirus will be spreading around the world. Everything will return to normal.

I'm staring at the Twin Towers.

It takes a while, maybe much longer than I realize, for this fact to set in, and even when it does, it doesn't fully compute.

I'm staring at the Twin Fucking Towers.

I'm still in too much awe to react. All I can do is stand there, staring, as if observing an alien ship that has just landed, like the ultimate deer in headlights.

I'm laughing uncontrollably, then I'm bawling, like I'm at a funeral. I'm semi-aware of people around me, giving me weird looks, but I'm too emotional to give a shit.

It's not enough to see the towers; I have to *feel* them.

I'm sprinting, weaving around people, but somehow not bumping into anyone. As I approach the South Tower, I glance up at the glistening steel that seems to go on and on forever. I flash back to more images from that day—the plume of smoke, people jumping from the shattered windows, shell-shocked Mayor Giuliani talking to the media, the famous photo of firefighters planting the American flag in the rubble. I also see flashes of the anniversaries since then—the grieving families, the names on the memorial, the beams of blue lights extending toward the heavens from the locations where the towers used to stand.

Only the towers are still standing.

I'm feeling the South Tower, caressing a corner of it with my fingertips. I wish I could wrap my arms around the whole building and hug it and never let go. Instead, I kiss the warm steel; feeling the seemingly impossible against my lips doesn't make this any less surreal.

It's here. It's actually here.

Not only the Twin Towers, the entire area seems intact—the promenade, the other buildings that were destroyed in *my* recollection of September 11, 2001, including Five World Trade Center and the Marriott Hotel.

An older Asian couple, maybe from Japan, is watching me.

"Come on, kiss it." I'm beaming at them. "You have to kiss it too! Don't take it for granted! Everything can vanish at any moment!"

They squint, as if confused, but seem to understand enough English to come to the conclusion that I might be insane, and they hurry away.

I have to experience what it's like inside.

I enter the lobby through one of the many revolving doors and gaze upward and all around, like I just discovered the Sistine Chapel. Every detail is exactly how I remember it—the long vertical windows, the promenade overhang above with flags from countries around the world hanging off. I'm getting more odd looks from people obviously perplexed by my expression of sheer bliss. They take all this for granted, just like everyone used to, including me. They're in the lobby of one of the Twin Towers on a Monday morning, what's the big deal?

I have to see what it's like at Windows on the World. How can it still be there?

I ride the elevator, still confused by my swirling emotions. I'm elated and amazed to be here, but should I feel happiness that 9/11 never happened or sadness that it did?

On the 107th floor, I exit and look around, stunned. The two-story restaurant looks pretty much the same as I remember it from the last time I was here in the spring of 2001. There are some minor changes in the décor, but it has the familiar plush red carpeting, curved booths with round tables, and of course the panoramic view of Manhattan, the Hudson, and the Statue of Liberty.

"Can I help you?" A red-haired woman, presumably the maître d', has approached me.

"I'm here," I say. "I'm really here."

"Yes." She seems a little confused. "Yes, you are. Can I—"

"Can I look around? Just for a few minutes. I just have to see…everything."

"Sure. I….I suppose that's okay."

I go to a window and stare down, again feeling the emotional impact of where I am and what I'm doing, especially when I recall the photo of "The Falling Man" who jumped from the tower. Now I'm here, in the same tower, *above* where the first plane hit.

"Hope you're not thinking about jumping."

In the reflection of the window, I see a gray-haired man behind me. I turn to face the man, who looks like he's in his sixties. He's in a waiter's uniform, smiling a little after his attempted joke.

"No, that's…that's not the way I want to go," I say.

"You and me both," he says. "Me? I want to go in my sleep. Just go to bed and never wake up. What's better than that?"

"True," I say, then a thought occurs to me. "Hey, I have a question for you."

"Shoot," he says. "Unless you got a gun. In New York, you never know, right?"

"How long have you been working here?"

"Twenty-eight years. God help me, right?"

I'm excited. "So you were *here*? On September eleventh two thousand and one?"

"I have a good memory. I mean, I once did a whole Sunday *Times* crossword puzzle and I barely cheated, but c'mon, how'm I supposed to remember where I was on some random date nineteen years ago?"

"Oh, that's just the last time I was here," I lie. "I was just wondering if you were here that day?"

He's getting impatient. "What day again?"

I tell him.

"What time?"

"Morning," I say. "After eight A.M., eight forty-five to be exact. It was a Tuesday."

He thinks about it, then says, "Must've been. I've always worked the early shift on weekdays and actually back then I was probably here even earlier. I used to help set up, not much anymore."

"Oh my God, this is unbelievable." I must be beaming.

"Why unbelievable?"

I reach out and hold his bony shoulders and stare at his eyes.

"Do you even realize how lucky you are? How lucky we *all* are?"

He backs away, wriggling free, and says, "Lucky? If I was centerfielder for the Yankees, I'd feel lucky. Spending my life here, I'm not so sure."

"Trust me, you're blessed." I shout, "Did you hear me? This man is blessed! *Everyone* here is blessed!"

People, maybe everyone in the restaurant, are looking over at me, like they think I'm out of my mind, but I don't care.

"Enjoy your day, everybody!" I shout.

I don't want to leave, but I have a feeling they'll ask me to if I don't.

I get on a down elevator with a group of people. I want to go to the observation deck and check out the other tower, but I need to get back to my office. I can come back here again soon —as many times as I want—well, as long as this doesn't end.

I shudder and feel light-headed; it's hard to stand.

"Hey, you okay?"

A guy in a business suit has to keep me from falling.

"Yeah, I'm fine."

"You sure? You almost fell."

"It's just the, uh, change in altitude," I say. "I'm fine. Thanks."

When we arrive at the lobby, I can stand, but I'm still shaky.

I go outside and gaze up at the towers, the steady breeze from the wind tunnel against my face. Nothing is permanent, but it's here now, I know what I'm seeing and feeling is real, and that's all that matters.

My phone vibrates—an incoming text. Still feeling blissful and fortunate, maybe even managing a dim smile, I check the display and see the message: *I SAW YOU STEVEN BLITZ!*

NINE

This is the entire text from an unknown number displayed as "anontxt." The message would be disturbing and confusing enough if it wasn't the same "final thought" I had after that guy stabbed me in that parking lot. Is this just some wild coincidence, or does this mean that after I got stabbed I had a premonition of this text? But how could I have a premonition about an event in another life, or another version of my life?

I read the text again, hoping to extract some hidden meaning, but *I SAW YOU STEVEN BLITZ!* is pretty straightforward. And I can't make anything out of "anontxt." I've had clients tell me how they've sent texts from online services to conceal the origin number of the text and I assume this functions the same way in this world. Some people use these sites for pranks, some for more nefarious reasons, but there is no way for the receiver to figure out who's contacted them. Well, maybe the FBI or a skilled hacker could figure it out if they really wanted to, but there's no way I can figure it out.

I tap on "anontxt" to try calling the sender, but only hear a generic voicemail message: *The party you have reached is unavailable...*

I have no more ideas. Someone is obviously trying to harass me, someone who knows something about me that I don't know. *Saw me? Saw me where?* Normally I'm not a paranoid person, but how can I not feel paranoid in this situation. Maybe this is all a set-up—maybe I'm here for a reason. What if someone is just setting me up to be here to witness the worst terrorist attack in the history of the United States?

I gaze up at the towers, expecting to see 747s crashing into them, but nothing appears to be amiss.

Could the planes be on their way?

I flash back to that morning. Sirens, chaos, people in agony, so many first responders rushing to their deaths.

Suddenly I feel the urge to shout, to tell everyone to run from the buildings, save themselves—but I don't. I can't. *"Everybody! Run! Get out of the way now!"* Imagine if I did shout that. *"Don't go in there! Not today!"* People would look at me like I was insane. The way *I* would have looked at me. If there's a way to warn people, this isn't it.

I look up again at the glistening towers framed by the deep blue sky and, thank God, spot no low-flying planes.

Not today. Not yet.

I descend to the subway.

The car of the 1 train isn't packed, but it's crowded—about twenty people. Thinking of the text—*I SAW YOU STEVEN BLITZ!*—I scan every face, looking for my threat. Like typical New Yorkers, no one seems to notice me; I could be invisible. Is this just an act, though? Is one of these people out to get me?

At Chambers Street, some people exit and new people board. I notice that one of the people left from before—a guy with short hair, a goatee, black-rimmed glasses, reading a weathered edition of *The Brothers Karamazov*—hasn't exited. He's about five feet away from me, leaning against a pole. Could he be the one? As the train lurches away, he glances up from the book for a moment and we make eye contact.

"Hey," I say accusingly.

He reacts as if surprised that I spoke to him.

"Yeah?"

"You know who I am." Purposely I say it as a statement, not a question.

He tries to ignore me, eyes shifting back toward the book.

"I don't know who you are," I say, "but I'm not afraid of you."

He looks at me again, angry now, and says, "What's your fucking problem?"

I realize I have no evidence that he sent me the text; it's just a wild hunch. I think of the adage—if you're wondering who the crazy person in the room is, then *you're* the crazy person.

"Sorry," I say, retreating to the middle of the car.

I have to give myself a break. It's easy to understand how a possible stalker, after everything that's happened, could rattle me. Maybe that's the motive of whoever sent me the text—to shift me off center. I have to stay focused—as focused as possible.

When I arrive at my office, Ashley says to me, "Hi, Steven. Matthew Goldstein called, he said it's urgent."

I have no idea who Matthew Goldstein is. Could he be my stalker?

"Can you call him for me when I get to my desk?" I say, mainly because I don't know how to contact him on my own.

As I enter my office, Terrence enters after me and says, "Where did you disappear to?"

"Oh, I, just had to, um, pick up some medicine." It's the best I can come up with.

"Do you want to know how the meeting went?"

"Oh, right, how did it go?"

"Sayers seems to want to take us on, but we really needed your input on the SEC stuff."

I have no idea what SEC stuff he's talking about, or why he thinks I could've provided any input. I've wanted to take on more white-collar cases, but financial crime is far from my specialty.

"Well, if he's taking us on I guess the meeting went well enough," I say.

"I said 'seems,' " Terrence says. "We're still in the mix, thank God, but we really need you to weigh in. He was especially interested in your work on that Bear Stearns case last year."

Bear Stearns hasn't gone under? Guess it makes sense since there wasn't a financial crisis in 2007 and 2008.

"I'd be happy to talk to him," I say, "but does it have to be today? I have, um, a lot on my plate."

"Are you sure everything's okay?" Terrence says. "Because if you need some time, I understand, but you have to let us know what's going on."

"I'm fine," I say. "Today's good. I'll reach out to Sayers asap, I promise."

Terrence seems skeptical but says, "Okay, thank you."

As I enter my office, my phone vibrates. I brace myself, ready to see another threatening text, but it's from Laura: *Hi baby :) How's your day going so far? Good commute in?*

New, caring Laura is still going to require some getting used to. I can't remember the last time the other Laura sent me a warm, friendly "just checking in" text. Not that she didn't have a kind side to her; it's just that as our marriage dragged on I saw a lot more of Mr. Hyde and a lot less of Dr. Jekyll.

We have a short text exchange where I tell her that my day is "going great so far," and she tells me that she's going to have a "fun surprise" for me when I get home, and we exchange "I love you"s.

I go online on my Galaxy and search for information about "9/11" and "terror attacks" and I'm not surprised I don't find anything. I'm also not surprised when I search for "Gulf War Bush Kuwait" and see that the Gulf War and all the events surrounding it, including the Iraqi invasion of Kuwait and the

U.S.'s Desert Storm response, transpired exactly how they did—or more accurately, I guess, how I remember they did.

Testing to see if the theory that I've been mulling holds up, I do a series of searches of events and facts prior to 1998, beginning from, well, the start of time.

The Big Bang happened, dinosaurs existed, Jesus existed, the Greek and Roman Empires happened, Shakespeare's plays exist, the Renaissance and Crusades happened, slavery happened in the United States, the Civil War happened, the World Wars and the Holocaust happened, Humphrey Bogart and Hitchcock existed and made their famous films, Marilyn Monroe existed and died from an OD in California, JFK was President and was assassinated in Dallas, Martin Luther King was assassinated in Memphis, all of the original *Planet of the Apes* movies were produced, AIDS was discovered in the early 1980s, the market crashed in 1987, Bill Clinton defeated George Bush and Ross Perot to win the 1992 Presidential election, the first World Trade Center bombing happened, and Clinton had an affair with Monica Lewinsky that led to his impeachment.

Obviously, I haven't exactly done thorough research of the earth and humankind's history, but as far as I can tell, it's sometime circa 1998 that events diverged from the world that I know.

A search of "Osama bin Laden" shows that he was killed in Saudi Arabia in 2003 in a car accident, so there's no mention of the Special Forces operation in Pakistan that actually killed him. Al-Qaeda exists, but the attacks mentioned in the early 2000s seem unfamiliar—San Francisco, Houston, Lyon, Barcelona. Of course the Dirty Monday attack in Rome is mentioned, although Al-Qaeda didn't take responsibility for that one. There was no U.S. invasion of Iraq in 2003. Saddam Hussein was killed by an Iranian assassin in Iraq, causing an Iran–Iraq war, and the current President of Iraq is Saddam Hussein's son, Uday, who I remember being killed after the 9/11 attacks. There was no long U.S. war in Afghanistan, but there was another war in Afghanistan that began in 2006, which involved Russia and the Taliban.

I can't find any mention of ISIS, however, or Brexit, or Mayor Bloomberg, or Colin Kaepernick kneeling, or Black Lives Matter. Consistently, it seems like this world diverged from my world at some point in 1997. This explains the Blockbuster-more-popular-than-Netflix phenomenon, as they were still competing in 1997, and why some movies and pop culture references remain and some don't. Excite existed before 1997, but Google didn't. Facebook wasn't created until 2003, and Etsy didn't exist in 1997 either. MetroCards haven't changed because the design was created pre-1997. *Dumb and Dumber* exists because the movie was released in 1994, but *The Truman Show* doesn't, possibly because that movie was released past the 1997 cutoff. *Eyes Wide Shut* doesn't exist, so it must've missed the cutoff too, but Nicole Kidman and Tom Cruise have acting careers, though I don't recognize any of their titles past the cutoff except for Cruise's *Mission: Impossible* sequels, which makes sense because the first "Mission" film was released in 1996. Also, Kidman and Cruise are still married, going on thirty years.

Some events after the cutoff occurred in both worlds. For example, the 1998 Yankees won the World Series that season—but against the Houston Astros, not the San Diego Padres, and George W. Bush won the 2000 Presidential election—although by a comfortable margin, without any ballot controversy in Florida—but I can't find any event *before* the cutoff that didn't actually happen in the world I know.

It will take more searching to pinpoint the exact date when

time as I know it changed. Maybe I'll even pinpoint the exact week, day, or even hour, minute, or second. While I'm not sure how any possible discoveries will change the situation I'm in, at least I'm gathering information. Maybe knowledge won't equal power, but it might make me feel less insane.

My phone rings.

"I have Matthew Goldstein for you," Ashley says.

How am I supposed to have a work call with a client regarding a case I know nothing about? It's going to take months of research just to catch up on everything I'm supposed to know.

Still, I have hope that a conversation with a client might spark something, maybe give me some insight into my current life.

"Put him through," I say, shaking my head. "Steven Blitz here."

"Hey, Steven, hope this is a good time."

"Time for what?"

"What do you mean?"

Great, already awkwardness. This was definitely a bad idea.

"For the strategy call before we get on the phone with HR."

I have no clue what he's referring to.

"Can I ask a question," I say. "You can just answer yes or no."

"Okay."

"Were you at the…" I can't believe I'm about to say this: "…Twin Towers earlier today? I mean, a half hour ago?"

"No, and what does that have to do with anything?"

He sounds believably clueless.

"Yeah, I'm sorry," I say, "I think we're going to have to delay that for a few days."

"What?" He's shocked and angry. "That's impossible, you know it is."

"Something's come up," I say. "Something…unexpected."

"This is ridiculous," he says. "My career's on the line here… more than my career. I can be arrested tonight."

"Why would you be arrested?"

After a pause, he says, "What the hell's going on here, Steven? Do you want to represent me or not?"

"I'm getting another call," I lie. "Sorry, I have to go."

How can I focus at work when there are so many more important things I could do with my time? I have knowledge that no one else seems to have. There's so much I want to do, but I can't do everything. I still want to get on the phone with Hollywood agents and start pitching *The Sopranos*, but preventing a 9/11-style terrorist attack has to be my top priority.

I see that Charles Schumer is still a Senator of New York. I get the number of his office.

"Senator Schumer's office, can I help you?" an upbeat-sounding guy says.

"Hi, I'm a constituent of the Senator's and I need to speak to him right away, or at least get an urgent message to him."

"I see," the man says. "Well, you can feel free to send him an email or a message via our website, but I'm afraid it's impossible to—"

"I'm not sure you understand," I say. "Thousands of lives might be at risk. There might a war, or multiple wars, if the terrorists aren't stopped."

I'm aware of how insane I must sound, but what am I supposed to do, stay silent?

"Sir, if you have any information about a terrorist attack, you need to contact the police or FBI immediately."

"I don't have any information per se," I say. "I just think your office and the Senator should look into flight schools in Florida and see if there's any unusual activity."

"Flight schools in Florida?"

"Yes, and…Is there a way I can speak to the Senator directly?"

"I'm afraid that's not possible, but I can give you the number of—"

"I know how to contact the fucking police, but they won't take me seriously—if your office can look into a man named Mohammad Atta. He might be taking flights classes there. Or just see if there's an unusual number of Middle Eastern men—"

"That name you mentioned, Atta…How do you spell that?"

"A T T A."

"A D D A?"

I pause. Do I really want to do this? He probably already thinks I'm batshit and if I keep this up he'll report me to the FBI and I'll wind up on a watchlist. Besides, how do I know any terrorist plan is actually in the works? It's been almost 19 years since the actual 9/11 happened, and it hasn't happened in this world yet, and maybe it never will.

"Never mind. Forget the whole thing."

When I end the call I see that Terrence and Elizabeth have entered my office. I don't know how long they've been there.

"You could knock," I say.

"The door was open," Terrence says. "Have a minute?"

"Not really, I'm super busy actually."

"What was that call about?" Elizabeth asks.

I'm surprised by the question. "Why does it matter?"

"You were talking about flight school," she says. "Why?"

"Why were you eavesdropping on my call?"

"We're concerned about you," Terrence says.

"Come on, not with that again," I say.

Elizabeth shuts the door.

"I just got off the phone with Matthew Goldstein," Terrence says. "He said he had what he characterized as a bizarre conversation with you. He said you couldn't recall any details of his case and you ended the call abruptly."

"That isn't true," I say. "I was very cordial with—"

"Consider this an intervention," Elizabeth says. "Goldstein is too important a client. We can't lose him."

"Fine," I say. "If you want me to call him back I'll—"

"We want you to go home," Terrence says. "Consult with your doctors, take as much time away as you need, but something is definitely off with you today, Steven."

"I'm perfectly fine."

"We don't see it that way," Elizabeth says.

"*You* might not think anything's wrong," Terrence says, "but *we* think something's wrong. It's called perspective. If this is related to your brain tumor, we'll be extremely sympathetic, but you have to be up front with us and let us know what's going on."

It's still difficult for me to believe that I'm a partner of this firm, especially with Elizabeth, whom I've never met before this morning.

After taking a few beats to gather my thoughts, I say, "I wish I could tell you both what's going on—believe me, I really do. But if I tell you, you'll never believe me."

Terrence and Elizabeth exchange bewildered looks.

Then Elizabeth says, "If you don't feel comfortable talking to us about it, you certainly don't have to." But she says it in a way that's clearly an invitation.

"Hell," I say. "I've been keeping it to myself since the weekend. Who knows? It might help to talk about it."

We go over to the conference area of my office; I sit in the chair and they sit on the couch across.

After an awkward silence, I say, "So where do I begin?" I turn to Terrence. "Okay, remember how I told you how I got stabbed Friday night? Well, that apparently didn't happen. According to the doctors, I was in a car accident, but I think I just skidded at that point and didn't actually crash. But I know I was stabbed because the girl who was there is actually my babysitter. Anyway, when I woke up in the hospital a lot of the world changed. For example, in the world I know, Donald Trump is President and you and I are working on a very high-profile murder case—we're defending the artist I mentioned, who's a serial killer and might still be." I look at Elizabeth, ignoring her perplexed expression. "And you—in the world as I know it, you're not here, you're not a part of this firm. Maybe you're working at another firm, or you're not even an attorney." To both of them, I say, "Oh, and do you have any idea how lucky you are to live in a world with the Twin Towers? In my world, there were horrific terrorist attacks on September eleventh 2001. We call it Nine-Eleven, which is why I reacted that way earlier. But anyway, my big advice is, don't take the Towers for granted—don't take anything for granted, because anything you think is permanent can be gone in an instant—poof."

I make a gesture with the fingers of my right hand, like I'm spraying fairy dust. They're looking at me blankly, like I'm a mental patient they're afraid to agitate.

"Look, I know how crazy this must all sound to you," I say. "I also know I'm not crazy or I wouldn't have any perspective on this, but I do have perspective. I believe that the other night I somehow latched on to another version of my life that, for some reason, twenty-two years ago, veered off from my other life, or my actual life, or whatever you want to call it. That's the theory I'm contemplating anyway and, again, I don't expect you to believe any of this. If I were you, *I* wouldn't believe it either. But I'm experiencing it so I have to believe it, I mean I have no choice. There are a lot of positives in this world, and not only the Twin Towers. I have a daughter now, a happy wife, and much more money than I had before. Some things are better in my world, though—like nuclear war isn't imminent and we have a better search engine called Google. Oh, and I'm actually much nicer than I am in this world. In the other world I was a devoted husband, I was honest and trustworthy. This version of me, seems to, well, be somewhat of a prick. I don't know, maybe I made bad decisions, went down a wrong path, but the good news is I have the power to change all that. I can be a better man now, a better husband." I look at Terrence. "You should make some changes too. I know that you can be better than you are now because I know the other Terrence Richards wouldn't callously screw a coworker."

Concerned, Elizabeth turns to Terrence. "What's he talking about?"

"I've heard enough of this bullshit." Terrence gets up and says to Elizabeth, "I think this situation has sucked up enough of our time for one day. Come on, let's go."

Elizabeth is getting up too, but very slowly.

"I want you out of here…now," Terrence says. "Come back when you work out whatever you need to work out."

"We need to talk," Elizabeth says to Terrence.

As they're leaving together, Terrence looks back over his shoulder and glares at me.

I made a mistake opening up to them about what I've been experiencing. I should've kept it a secret. I feel vulnerable now, exposed.

I leave my office and walk uptown along Madison. No one makes eye contact; I'm just another inconsequential, inter-changeable New Yorker. I'm aware of cars honking, drivers screaming for me to get out of the way. I realize I'm in the intersection of Madison and Forty-Second, holding up traffic.

A cabbie leaning his head out of a cab's window screams at me, "Come on, asshole, let's move it."

Feeling oddly invisible, like I might not even be here, I continue across the street and fade into the crowd.

TEN

At the Katonah train station, I get in my car and head home. The sun is bright and I'm squinting against the rays reflecting on the melting snow alongside the road. At a traffic light, I text Laura to tell her I'm on my way. She calls immediately.

"Everything okay?" she asks.

She sounds panicked, concerned. I flash back to how cold and distant she was when she told me she was ending our marriage.

"Fine," I say. "Just didn't want to push myself too hard on the first day back."

"Makes sense, and I'm glad too. I've been worried about you all day."

"That feels good."

"My worrying makes you feel good?"

"Yeah, actually it does."

"Remember, I have to pick up Lil later today from after school club, so I won't be home till six-thirty."

I don't remember this, of course, but it sounds like something I *should* know. "Oh yeah, that's right."

"Do me a favor and defrost the steaks? Unless you want something else."

"Steak sounds great. Hey, the light's about to turn, don't want to talk and drive."

"Smart. Can't wait to see you later. I love you, baby."

Recalling in my other life, Laura saying, *Our marriage is over, Steven. I don't love you anymore*, I say, "Love you too, baby."

✿

At home, Wasabi greets me. He's already getting to know me and I feel like I've known him much longer than a day. It's nice to have some time to myself. None of this seems to be going away so I might as well get used to it.

After I take the steaks out of the freezer, I change out of my work clothes and take a relaxing shower in my luxurious bathroom. In one of my dresser drawers, I find a pair of Dolce & Gabbana sweatpants and a comfy T-shirt; I put them on, then sit at my PC.

I log on to my brokerage accounts and see that I'm about twenty thousand dollars wealthier today. Maybe instead of figuring out how to get back into the swing of things at work, I should be thinking about how to wind down. At the very least, with the cushion of all this passive income, I don't have to grind the way I used to.

When I return downstairs, it occurs to me that I haven't checked our basement since I've been back from the hospital. Somehow, I'm not surprised to see that it's been fully renovated and, holy shit, there's a spectacular walnut pool table with yellow felt. I've always wanted a cool pool table so it makes sense that I splurged for this one. Hey, maybe I'm a great pool player now. I rack the balls and take several shots, missing all of them. Nope, still suck.

I'm about to leave the basement when I notice, off to the side, a door leading to a well-stocked wine cellar. There must be hundreds of bottles, mainly whites, which makes sense, as I've always preferred whites to reds. I choose a bottle of 2012 Pinot Grigio from Alto Adige. Back upstairs, I pour myself a glass and take it to the den, I put on some jazz.

A lot of this new life doesn't seem so bad; there are certainly lots of positives I could get used to.

On my phone, I do some more research to test my 1997 theory. On September 3, 1997, Princess Diana died with Dodi Fayed, so I make September 3, 1997 my new possible "cutoff date." Like most people, I remember where I was when I heard that Diana died—I was at a conference in Houston, having breakfast at the hotel restaurant, when Cara, an old law school friend, told me what had happened. It seemed surreal, back when surreal had a very different meaning for me than it does now.

I'm tempted to see what Cara is doing now, but I know if I go down that rabbit hole I'll start searching for information about everyone I know; right now I need to stay focused.

I search for "news events of 1997." Prior to Diana's death the Heaven's Gate mass suicides happened, Tony Blair was elected as Prime Minister of the United Kingdom, Hong Kong became independent from China, and the Pathfinder landed on Mars. After Diana died, Mother Teresa died a week later, but after Diana's funeral on September 6th, there weren't as many big events. The only major event I remember happening was the Florida Marlins winning the World Series on October 26, 1997 and the release of the movie, *Titanic*, on December 19th, and according to what I'm reading, both of these events actually happened.

I'm beginning to think that my theory about the timing might be wrong, as nothing seems out of the ordinary. Then I remember that the Super Bowl that season, played in January, was won by the Denver Broncos. I remember watching the game with my friends at a bar—John Elway defeating Brett Favre in a classic matchup. I go to a timeline of 1998 events, expecting to see that the Broncos won, but no, the site reports that in the 1998 Super Bowl, played on January 28th, the Green Bay Packers defeated the Denver Broncos, 31–13.

"Yes! Yes!" I shout.

Wasabi starts barking like crazy.

"It's okay," I say to him. "Calm down, it's all okay."

I pet him and scratch him under his chin until he stops barking.

"I think I'm starting to crack this, Wasabi."

Sometime between December 19, 1997 and January 28, 1998, the world changed. Now I just have to figure out what happened during that period that caused the world to diverge, and—oh, yeah—why and *how* I'm living that version of the world.

I finish the rest of the wine in one gulp and pour another glass, then continue searching. I can't find any major world events in that period that are different from my recollection, but I know there has to be *something* that can help me narrow this down.

During late 1997 and early 1998, I was in Manhattan, in my last year of law school at NYU, living in an apartment on Morton Street in the West Village with my friends Evan and Joe. I don't think I left town at all over that Christmas break. Wasn't that the New Year's Eve that we had a party at our apartment? No, that was in my *first* year of law school, because I was still dating Abby. On New Year's 1998, I was already dating Laura. We'd been dating since the summer of 1997, and on that New Year's at midnight we were with friends at the Telephone Bar in the East Village. Plowing through a bunch of MyWorld pages, friends and friends of friends, I find a photo from that night with the caption: *Remember this…?* And there we are, Laura and me in a packed crowd of New Year's Eve revelers. Apparently the world, or at least *my* world, changed in January 1998, sometime before the Super Bowl.

I strain to remember anything significant or memorable that

happened during that period, but nothing comes to me. I was doing an internship at a law firm downtown, but I can't even remember what cases I was working on. Otherwise, I probably went to the gym some days, bars with friends at night, but I can't recall any specific event during that period.

My phone vibrates. The display shows "Brian," but I cringe, knowing that it's one of the fake Brians in my contacts. When I see this one's from Kaitlin I mutter, "Fuck me," as I read the text: *Where are you???*

I was so absorbed, trying to unravel my past, that I forgot that I agreed to meet her this evening. I don't need any more stress right now, but I do need to speak to her, to make sure she understands that we can't see each other anymore.

I reply: *On my way!*

In the kitchen, I take two Tylenols for my headache. Upstairs, I dress quickly in Dolce & Gabbana black skinny jeans and a Givenchy black T-shirt—even my "casual" clothes are way nicer than anything I'm accustomed to wearing—and head out.

Before I drive off, I text Laura: *Running an errand. Be home soon!*

At a stop sign, I see her response: *What errand?*

Shit, now I have to lie: *CVS*

I'll have to stop at CVS later and buy something, to make my excuse seem believable. This is minor deceit, but it's still generating stress. How have I been living my life this way?

Kaitlin is waiting near the main entrance to Hunting Ridge Mall. She's in very tight jeans, a short black leather jacket, black boots with maybe two-inch heels. I've never had any interest whatsoever in younger women, so it's hard for me to understand, or believe, that I've had an actual affair with her.

"Hey," she says, as she gets in the car and shuts the door.

She tries to kiss me on the lips, like she did at the house yesterday, but this time I'm prepared and manage to turn my head a little at the last moment so she gets mostly cheek.

"Don't be so happy to see me." She sounds offended.

"We have to talk," I say.

"Yeah, we definitely do," she says. "What're you waiting for? Let's go."

"We're not going anywhere."

"What do you mean?" She seems distraught, like she's about to cry. "I don't get it. Why're you acting this way?"

Great, that's all I need—a big scene. I glance around, making sure no one's looking. There are a few teenagers near the mall entrance, but they're in their claustrophobic teenage world, talking and laughing, not noticing us.

"Look," I say to Kaitlin. "I know this situation, especially my shifts, must be confusing for you—trust me, it is for me too. The truth is I've been having some memory issues since I…" I almost said *since I died*. "I mean since the accident."

"You seriously can't remember *anything*?" She sounds beyond angry—livid. "And you expect me to believe that? I thought you were going to be okay after the accident. That's what you and your wife told me."

"I am okay," I say. "My memory's just a little gimpy, which is apparently normal after the trauma I've been through, so maybe you can just fill in some gaps for me."

"Fine." She crosses her arms in front of her chest. "What do you want to know? And do we have to do it here?"

I don't want to go anywhere. I just want her to get out of my car and go on with her life. Ideally, we'll never see each other again.

"What's the, um, nature of our relationship," I say. "I mean have we…?"

"Have we what?"

"Have we…had relations."

"*Relations*?" She sounds surprised or angry, it's hard to tell. "Yes, we've had fucking relations. A lot of fucking relations."

"Shit."

"What's *wrong* with you? Why're you acting this way, especially *now* of all times?"

I don't know what she means by this last part.

"Look, I came here to tell you that it's over, Kaitlin. I apologize for apparently starting something with you, which is totally inappropriate and out of character for me, and I really want you to be happy and find a guy—an age-appropriate guy—who you can have a normal relationship with. I'm not that guy. I'm really sorry, okay?"

I prepare for her reaction. Will she flip out? Start screaming and threatening to tell Laura?

She just stares.

"And it would probably be better if you stopped working for us," I say. "I don't know the best way to manage that, but maybe you can just say you're busy, taking classes, or you got another job. I don't care what the excuse is, but I think it would be best for everybody. Take some time to think about what excuse you want to give her. Whatever you come up with will be fine. Maybe you got another job for more money? That would make total sense."

"You'd really do this to me?" she says.

"We have no choice," I say. "Are you worried about the money? I know I can give you money. A lump sum to cover what you would've made from us for a year, okay? Or how about double? I'll pay you in cash, okay, but can we please just go our separate ways now and I'll figure out how to get you that money, okay?"

She doesn't move.

"What're you waiting for?" I put my hand on the ignition key, as if I'm about to twist it, hoping this encourages her to get going.

Instead she says, "Don't you even want to know what happened today?"

"No," I say, "actually I don't."

"Um, yeah, I think you do," she says. "The cops were at my house again."

I smile, hoping this is game playing, attempted manipulation. "Cops, huh? Nice one. What's this, something you're making up? You're trying to manipulate me, scare me? Whatever you say won't change my mind, Kaitlin. So please just get out of my car and go home. Or I can drive you home if you can't get a lift."

"So now you're going to tell me you forgot about that too? Well, that's convenient. Can I get into an accident and hit my head too? I'd love for this to go away, Steven. I didn't sleep last night. When I was around Lilly over the weekend I tried to pretend nothing happened, act normal—that *great* advice you gave me—but it's impossible. I keep seeing the blood—all that blood."

Panic is setting in. *Blood?* What the hell is she talking about? I've been through so much already, I'm not sure I can take another shock.

"Blood?" I try to stay calm, praying this isn't as bad as I fear it is. "What blood?"

"Oh my God, I can't believe this," she says. "This is a joke, right? I mean all of this, including your memory issues, right? Please tell me you're just fucking with me."

I want to repeat that back to her, but I say, "Tell me what's going on, Kaitlin. Why were the cops at your house...*again*? I need to know what's going on."

"Why do you think?" she says. "They found out."

"Found out? Found out what?"

"That my dad's missing."

I stare at her, trying to make sense of this. I can't.

She continues: "He didn't show up to work Thursday and Friday and so when he didn't show up today too, I guess people from his office got concerned."

"I…I don't understand," I say. "Where…where's your father, Kaitlin?"

She squints, suddenly suspicious. "Are you recording this?"

"Why would I rec—"

"Because you're a lawyer and I'm not a fucking idiot. If you think I'm taking the blame for this you're out of your mind, Steven. Besides, you did it, not me." She talks louder to the imaginary microphone, "You hear that, whoever's listening? He did it, Steven Blitz. It was him, not me! I'm innocent!"

Panicked, but with a fake smile, I grab one of Kaitlin's wrists, maybe harder than I intend to. "Keep your voice down. I'm not recording anything, I just want to know what happened."

"Ow, you're hurting me."

"Sorry." I let go, feeling desperate. "Please, I'm telling you the truth. I really can't remember anything that happened before Friday, so can you please tell me what happened with your father?"

"Wow," she says. "You're serious, aren't you? If your memory's this bad, shouldn't you be in the hospital or something?"

"Just tell me."

She lets out a frustrated breath, then says, "Okay, as you know, my father was an abusive prick, and the other night—last Wednesday—I texted you that he was threatening to stab me and you came over and…you seriously don't remember *any* of this?"

"What happened when I came over?"

"You two were fighting and you got the knife from him and you killed him."

Then I remember—*the healing wound on my arm*. Is that how I got injured, during a struggle with her father? Makes sense that I would lie to Laura and tell her that I injured myself in the garage. But why would I kill Kaitlin's father? It seems impossible, but is it? I know I'm not a killer, but without any memory of what this version of me did, how can I fully dismiss the possibility that I did it? After spending time at Windows on the World in the North Tower of the World Trade Center, how can I fully dismiss anything?

"During the fight, did your father cut me?" I roll up the sleeve of my shirt and show her the healing wound on my left forearm. "Right here."

"He might've. Wait, yeah, he did actually. You were worried about how you were gonna explain it to Laura."

"Jesus Christ."

"Why? How did you think you got the wound? You forgot that too?"

"What about…What about your mother?"

"What about her?"

"Well, where is she?"

"You know my mother died when I was a baby," she says. "You know I have no relatives, you know I'm alone."

"No, I don't know it. I don't know anything."

"This is crazy. I can't believe you're pulling this shit after everything you've already done to fuck up my life."

"I'm sorry," I say, "for everything I've done, but I can't help you solve all of your problems right now—God knows I have enough of my own to solve. I feel awful that your father's gone, and that you don't have a support system, I really do. I told you I'd give you money and your father must have money in his bank accounts too. Eventually you can get that money. Once he's missing for a certain amount of time you'll be able to claim those funds. But you're going to have to get someone else to help you because…" A thought hits me. Maybe this doesn't seem like a situation I'd get into, because I *didn't* get into it. "Unless…unless you're playing me."

"*What?*"

"Maybe you're lying about everything. I didn't get involved with you and I didn't kill your father, I didn't kill anyone. You're just trying to scam money out of me because you know I lost my memory and I'd be an easy mark. Is that what's going on here?"

"Did you really forget everything that happened?" she said. "Please, just tell me the truth, because this is scary and crazy enough *without* you freaking out on me."

She's right—I *am* freaking out, and if I *did* kill her father, I know that it's not a good idea to meet with her in public, especially since there are security cameras near the entrance to the mall and one of them probably captured her getting into my car.

I start the engine and drive away.

"Where are we going?"

I'm too absorbed to answer.

"I don't get it," she says. "First you want me to get out of the car, now you suddenly want to go somewhere?"

"Did you tell anyone you were meeting me here?"

"No," she says. "Of course not. Why would I tell somebody?"

"You didn't tell a friend, or even Lilly? You didn't text anyone about it, post about it, post anything ambiguous about it?"

"Look at you, suddenly getting all lawyerly on me."

"Are you sure or not?"

"I'm sure, I'm sure."

I drive for a while, toward the center of Katonah, and we're silent.

Then she says, "You know, if this were a movie I would probably be worried right now. I mean if we were in a movie and you started driving somewhere, it would be because you're planning to kill me too. You'd think that I could rat you out so I'm better off dead. Just so you know, if you try anything you definitely won't get away with it. That's why I wanted to meet at the entrance to the mall, where all those cameras are. They probably got a clear shot of your license plate too. See? You might be a fancy lawyer, but I'm just as smart as you are."

"Of course I wouldn't kill you," I say. "I'm not a killer. I wouldn't kill anybody."

"Yeah," she says, "except my father."

Staring at the road ahead, I don't say anything.

I park on a side street in a residential area, around the corner from Katonah Memorial Park. It's a quiet street, lined with mature oak and pine trees.

"Assuming you're telling me the truth about all this," I say, "where's the body?"

"*Assuming*?" she says. "So now you're going to tell me you don't remember that either?"

"Look, I need you to help me out," I say. "You're obviously scared right now, I'm guessing that's why you called me. If you want my help…if you want to get away with this and not go to jail, you have to tell me the facts."

"We buried him, of course."

I have to take a deep breath. "Where?"

"I can't believe you don't remember this part since it was your idea. At Ward Pound Ridge."

Frighteningly, if I had to pick a spot to bury a body, it makes sense that I might choose the Ward Pound Ridge Reservation since I've gone hiking there many times and know that area well.

"So we buried him together?"

"Yes," she says.

"Who dug the hole?"

"We both did."

I wish she sounded like she's lying, but she doesn't.

"Did we use shovels?"

"Yes."

"Where'd we get them?"

"*You* brought them," she says as if this is obvious.

"Where did I get them?"

"I have no idea."

Shit, as if I didn't have enough to worry about, now I have to worry about shovels, and trust that this version of me covered up a crime well enough. As a defense attorney, I know how difficult it is to cover up crimes. Every criminal makes mistakes.

"Do you remember what we did with the shovels? Did we get rid of them?"

"You said you would."

"What about clothes? What were we wearing?"

"Normal clothes."

"What're normal clothes?"

"I was in jeans and a sweatshirt."

"Shoes or sneakers?"

"Sneakers."

"Did you throw out everything?"

"No, but I washed my clothes, like you told me to."

I'm glad I told her that. It sounds like I was pragmatic, thorough.

"What about the sneakers?"

"I cleaned them too."

"Throw them out, I'll buy you another pair."

"But you said—"

"Just do it. There can't be any dirt in your house, or anything to connect you or me to burying a body, do you understand that?"

"Of course I understand. If you want me to throw out the sneakers I'll do it, but it'll cost you like a hundred and forty dollars."

"I don't care about the money—money is meaningless. What about when we buried the body?"

"What about it?"

"Did we do a good job? Did we bury it well?"

"You said we did. But it took forever. I still have a blister."

She shows me a hand, a roundish piece of skin hanging from her thumb.

"Shit," I say. "Did the police see that?"

"No."

"You sure?"

"It wasn't hanging off like this when the police spoke to me."

"Then you got lucky."

I look at my hands, which seem fine.

"You were wearing gloves," she says. "You had gloves and I didn't. You said you didn't think of it."

Why didn't I think of it? Does this mean I wasn't careful? What else did I forget to do?

I have no choice—I have to trust myself. After all, this version of me isn't an idiot. We have the same brain—well, sort of. At least we share similar experiences, and apparently had the same education and upbringing, so my ability to think logically shouldn't have changed, even if my morality has. I'm a defense attorney— I'm good at what I do. I know what evidence the prosecution would need to make its case and I must've been careful and hidden that evidence well. Or better yet, destroyed it.

"What about the police?" I ask.

"What about them?" Kaitlin seems annoyed.

"What did you say to them? What were their names?"

"I forget. I mean I wasn't paying attention when they told me. There were two of them. Men. Both said they were detectives. I think one of them was, like, hitting on me. It was really creepy actually."

"What did they ask you?"

"Normal stuff. Like if I knew where my father was, if he told me about any trip he was going on, stuff like that."

"What did you tell them?"

"What you told me to tell them. That I don't know anything. That I haven't seen him since Wednesday."

"Is that believable?"

"*You* thought it would be. He travels all the time on business, sometimes he's gone for like two weeks, so it's not crazy, but…"

"But what?"

"But I think they're suspicious."

"What makes you think that?"

"They know stuff. I mean, what was going on. I mean, how many times have I called nine-one-one on my father since I was a kid? A dozen? More?"

"So you're saying you think they think you did it?"

"Yes. I mean no. I mean, I don't know."

"What does that even mean?"

"They were asking so many questions," she says, "but I think I was good. I started crying, which makes sense, right? I mean, I *should* be upset that my father's missing, right? So I don't think *that* makes me look suspicious, I mean the crying part."

A car passes—an SUV, looks like a mom driving with her kids in the back.

"It sounds like you said the right things," I say. "I'm a lawyer, I'm sure I coached you well and if the police were actually suspicious of you they probably would've taken you in for more questioning today. But it's a big mistake for us to be seen together. We can't take this risk again. You just purposely met me where there's security cameras. Did you think about what would happen if the police got hold of that footage?"

She's crying. "Sorry. I was scared. The police came and I...I didn't know what to say."

As she continues crying, a thought hits me. I reach over and pat down her arms, then her legs.

"What're you doing?" I ask.

I feel around her stomach and back, but I can't find any device.

"Making sure the police didn't send you to me," I say.

I finish checking her.

"You really think I would do that to you?" she asks.

"To avoid going to jail, if that's what they promised you, sure, why not?"

"I'm the one who should be scared of you," she says. "You're the one acting weird, saying you can't remember anything."

"What about witnesses?"

"To what?"

"What do you think?"

"Just you and me were there."

"Are you sure?"

"Positive."

"Did you tell anybody?"

I think I see her hesitate.

Again I ask, "Did you tell—"

"No," she says, "of course I didn't tell anyone."

"You didn't text or post or blog about it?"

"Who *blogs*?"

"Did you tell any—"

"No, I swear."

I take out my phone.

"Are you sure," I ask, "because I've been getting some strange texts lately and maybe it's related."

"What?" She's concerned. "Why didn't you tell me?"

"I didn't know if they were related to this. I still don't know."

"Oh my God, show me."

I show her the text from the anonymous texter.

"It's from an unknown number," I say, "someone obviously hiding their identity. Do you have any idea who can be doing this?"

"No, but it's easy to hide your number. I have no idea, it could be anybody."

It seems like she's as confused as I am about the text, but it's hard to tell for sure.

"Well, let's hope it's not related." I maneuver to put my phone in my pocket. "I don't think it's a good idea to drive to the mall."

"I'll take an Uber," she says.

"Okay," I say, "but remember, we can't be in contact any-more. Not just because of what happened to your father but because it's over with us. It shouldn't've started to begin with. You seem like a great person and Lilly obviously adores you, and Laura too, but it's never going to work out with us, so you're going to have to just forget about me, okay?"

She's smiling.

"Wait, you're not joking. This is really, seriously, what you think this is about? You think I want to *be* with you? Like I actually *like* you?"

"Don't you?"

"No." She's laughing. "I just thought you were a sort of hot older dude and you were into me so why not?" She laughs again, amusing herself. "You really think I believed all that bullshit you told me about how we're soulmates? Oh my God, you *did* believe it. You're even more far gone than I thought. You really think I'd want to be with some creepy, unhappily married old guy who hooks up with his babysitter and cheats on his wife? I could never have any respect for you…ever."

Her words sting, even though I still don't feel like it's really me she's talking about.

She opens the car door, then says, "Funny, I wanted to meet up with you because I was scared and I thought you'd calm me down, give me some good advice. You used to seem so rational, so calm. But I guess that was all fake too, huh?"

She gets out, then cranes her head back, and adds, "Thanks for killing my father—you did me a big favor there, I hope he's in hell now where he belongs. But I have no interest in your money—you can keep it. I don't need you or any man to save me. I just don't want to go to fucking jail."

She slams the door and marches away.

Thanks for killing my father. While of course I still don't know all the circumstances, it sounds like she was in distress and I came over to help her. It also sounds like if I killed her father it was in self-defense and I might've saved her life, or at least saved her from further abuse, and the only mistake I made was covering up the killing and not just telling the cops the truth.

Driving slowly, I look over as I pass, hoping she'll be looking at me so I can smile or maybe wave goodbye. But she continues straight ahead, acting like she doesn't notice me.

Heading home, along Route 35, I'm so distracted, worrying about the body, and what I'll say if the police come to talk to me.

I have a feeling telling them the truth, that another version of me committed the murder but not me, won't go over well. Then I realize I'm approaching the gas station, the one where I got stabbed the other night.

Although there are cars behind me, I slow down to take a look. The area near the gas pumps looks pretty much the same, but the minimart has been remodeled and perhaps it's in a different location, as it seems like there's more space between the pumps and the storefront. I zero in on the spot where I got stabbed, flashing back to the intense pain I felt when the blade pierced my gut, and then the bizarre experience of being trapped in the ball of glass.

A car behind me honks as I slow to about five miles per hour.

"Okay, okay," I say, and I speed up.

Seeing the spot where I got stabbed felt surreal, like I was reexperiencing a dream I'd almost forgotten, but as I approach the bend in the road where I skidded that night in the snow, I slow again, flashing back to how I could feel the impact in anticipation of a crash, and then hearing my father's voice, telling me, *Always turn in the opposite direction of the skid,* and how I narrowly avoided hitting the tree. I forgot about hearing my father's voice and the feeling of déjà vu I had before I made that decision, and I'm elated, suddenly certain that this detail explains everything that's happened to me since Friday, *and* what happened to me in 1998.

ELEVEN

The car behind me honks again—this time a steadier, more agitated honk. When I reach the straightway at the top of the hill I stick my arm out the window and motion at the driver to pass. As the car goes by, the driver turns toward me for a moment and I can read his lips—*Fuck you, asshole*—and I wonder what would happen if I *didn't* let him pass, or if I reacted to his insult, perhaps by insulting him back? How would those seemingly fleeting decisions alter our lives? What if he arrived home several minutes late, maybe too late to save a dying relative? Then, what if he had to quit his job, which would affect the lives of his co-workers and, like a spreading virus, eventually the rest of the world would be affected? Meanwhile, my life would be altered too, which would affect the rest of my day, and ultimately the rest of my life. What if every decision we make creates new strands of our lives?

At the hospital, Laura and the doctors insisted that I was in a car accident on that bend, but I knew that I had actually avoided the accident and continued on to the gas station. What if at that moment, at the bend in the road, two strands of my life overlapped? What if one of these strands, one that veered off in 1998, reached the same spot at that bend at the same time, but either I didn't remember my father's advice or I didn't follow it, and I crashed into the tree? That's why I felt the impact that didn't happen, right before I made the decision to turn into the skid, because I was in a crash—in the other strand. Maybe, in my strand, I was killed that night in the parking lot, but instead of dying like I should have, I somehow joined this other version of my life that happened to intersect at that moment. Maybe all of our strands coexist, and maybe sometimes, if the strands overlap—maybe only if they overlap when you die—it's possible for your consciousness to move on to the concurrent strand and, in effect, your life continues.

As for how the 1998 strand of my life started, it could've been any random decision that I made that January, as innocuous as letting a driver pass me on a road. It didn't even have to be a decision. Maybe I jostled the arm of a guy at a bar, spilling his drink. Maybe that was enough to spin off another version of my life, causing ripple effects that altered world events.

Okay, yes, I'm aware of how insane this sounds—to seriously believe that a single decision I made in 1998, never mind a spilled drink, could change the entire fate of mankind—but I know what I've been experiencing, and if I can't trust my experiences, what can I trust?

As I watch the car I let pass make a left up ahead, I wonder if in another version of the driver's life, he's still back there, heading toward another destiny.

"Daddy!"

Lilly dashes toward me as I enter and leaps into my arms, almost causing me to drop the CVS bag I'm holding, which contains deodorant and aftershave.

"Hey, kiddo, it's so great to see you."

It *is* great to see her. It's amazing actually how I feel so attached to her, the way a father should feel when seeing his daughter. I'm not sure where the feeling is coming from, but I know I feel it, and that it's real.

I kiss her on top of the head, as if I've done it hundreds, maybe thousands of times before.

"I missed you," she says.

"I missed you too," I say. "Mmm, something smells good."

"Mom's grilling steaks."

"I meant the top of your head, but the steaks smell good too."

She laughs. "You're so funny. Hey, want to play with me?"

"How about after dinner, before bed?"

"Okay." She runs off.

I go into the kitchen, and see Laura with her back to me, tending to steaks on the grill. Music is playing, a love ballad by some soulful female singer I don't recognize.

I approach Laura from behind and grip her hips. She flinches a little, as if startled.

"Hey." She looks back at me smiling.

I kiss her neck, smelling lavender oil.

"Mm, you smell so good," I say.

"Somebody's happy to see me."

"If Lilly wasn't home I'd attack you right here."

"Ha, I bet you would," she says. "What's in the bag?"

"Oh, just some deodorant and aftershave."

"Since when do you need aftershave?" She sounds a little suspicious.

"I wanted to try one," I say. "My skin's felt a little rough lately. Is there anything I can do to help?"

"You can start to mash the potatoes," she says.

I help finish cooking, asking her all about her day. Although we've been together for about twenty years, there's so much to discover; it's like I'm in a new, exciting relationship.

At the dinner table, it's great to be with my family, with Wasabi under the table, patiently waiting for any scraps to fall. As Laura goes to the kitchen and returns with a bone for Lilly to give to Wasabi, I'm admiring how beautiful my wife is and how lucky I am. Why would I want to be with other women and make the selfish, idiotic decisions that led me to the point where I can lose all of this at any moment? Why wasn't a great family enough for me? Why did I need more?

"What're you thinking?" she asks.

It used to annoy me when she randomly asked me what I was thinking; it seemed so intrusive. But now I like it. I want her to *want* to know everything, and I want to get to a point where I can tell her everything.

"I'm thinking about how lucky I am to have you and Lilly in my life," I say. "I don't feel like I deserve it."

"Aw, that's so sweet." She looks happily teary. "I'm feeling pretty fortunate right now too."

The phone rings—the landline—jolting me like the first shock of an electric chair. Laura goes into the living room area, to the coffee table, and answers it. I watch her concerned expression as she says, "Oh, okay," and takes the phone into the kitchen to talk in privacy.

Naturally I fear the worst—it's the police telling her a body was found and that I'm a murder suspect. I thought that waking up in the hospital and not recognizing the world was a nightmare, but maybe the real nightmare is about to begin. I imagine Laura coming out of the kitchen with a venomous expression, furiously pounding my chest, screaming, "How could you, Steven? How could you? How could you do this to me? To our *family*?"

This scenario seems very real, like it's already happening. Then Laura pokes her head out from the kitchen and motions with her hand for me come join her, out of earshot from Lilly.

"What is it?" I ask, concerned, but relieved that she's not going berserk.

"That was Kaitlin," she says. "She's quitting."

I took an acting class in college. I was awful, but I do my best to act surprised and confused as I say, "She is?"

I'm not sure I'm pulling it off, but Laura is too distracted by her own thoughts to notice.

"Yeah, she says it's personal reasons, but she wouldn't give me any details. I feel so bad for her. She has that awful relationship with her father. I hope something didn't happen."

"Happen?" There's the bad acting again; I'm aware of how my face is heating up. "Why would something *happen*?"

"I don't know all the details, but obviously she has a bad relationship with him so it isn't so far-fetched that it's somehow related. I just wish there was something I could do to help."

"There's nothing—"

"I mean what if there's real abuse going on there? Obviously, she wouldn't tell us, the parents of the kids she babysits for. Maybe we should, I don't know, call the police."

"Absolutely not," I raise my voice.

"It was just a thought," she says, taken aback. "You don't have to snap."

"Sorry, I didn't mean that," I say. "It's just none of our business, that's all. It's totally inappropriate for us to get involved."

"Yeah, I guess you're right." She sighs. "I feel awful for Lilly too. She'll be devastated."

"It's probably for the best," I say.

"Why the best? Lilly adores Kaitlin."

"I know, and there are a lot of positives about Kaitlin…obviously…but with the issues she's having at home, is it really a good idea to have her alone around Lilly? I'm not saying I suspect anything, but in these situations, as you just said, we'll never really know what's going on there."

"Now you're scaring me," Laura says. "Do you really think that—"

"I don't think anything, I'm just being cautious, that's all, and why shouldn't we be? Besides, it's not like we're *firing* her.

It's her choice and if someone wants to leave, you have to let them go. What choice do we have?"

"Yeah, I guess you're—"

Lilly enters smiling and says, "What's up?"

"Nothing, sweetie," Laura says. "Mommy's just talking to Daddy."

"About what?"

"About nothing," Laura says.

"You can't talk about nothing," Lilly says.

"She has a point," I say.

"Go back and finish your dinner," Laura says.

"I'm not hungry anymore," Lilly says.

"Then go watch some TV."

"Okay."

Lilly dashes to the living room.

"Who's going to tell her?"

"I will," I say. "Don't worry about it."

After I help Lilly get ready for bed, she wants to play doctor. I agree and she opens her kit.

"What seems to be the problem?" she asks.

Although as far as I'm concerned we've never played this game before, I get the feeling it's maybe the hundredth time we've played.

"Um, broken ankle," I say.

"Okay," she says. "Let's take your temperature."

She sticks the thermometer in my armpit for about two seconds, then says, "Looks normal. How about your blood pressure?"

"Do you think high blood pressure might've caused my broken ankle, doctor?" I ask, enjoying this now, like I've probably enjoyed it many times before.

"Could be," she says, putting the cuff around my arm. Then she says, "Looks normal too. Time for a Band-Aid."

Band-Aid makes me think I might as well rip another one off and I say, "I have some bad news for you—Kaitlin's not going to come here anymore."

"She isn't?" Lilly asks, focused on adjusting the blood pressure cuff.

"I know you'll be upset, but there are some things in life we can't control."

"It's okay, Daddy. I'm not sad."

"You're not?"

"Nah, I didn't like her too much anyway."

"Really? We thought you did."

"She was always texting too much or looking at her Pictora. She didn't play with me enough."

When I tell Laura the news later, in our bedroom, she's elated and hugs me.

"What would I do without you?" Laura says.

Imagining her screaming at me, *Get out!*, I say, "Try not to forget this feeling."

"Why would I forget it?"

"Feelings are ephemeral. I think it's always important to remember that, you know, if things ever get rough."

"Why are you saying this?"

"Just promise me that we'll always give each other the benefit of the doubt, no matter what."

"I promise," she says, smiling and shaking her head, as if she just agreed to something frivolous.

Later, I'm in the bathroom, brushing my teeth.

"Steve, come quick!"

Fearing something awful happened, I rush into the bedroom where Laura is sitting up in bed naked, looking frantic and excited, pointing at the TV.

"Look, look!" she says.

It's CNN. Over a shot of the empty desk at the Oval Office is an announcement:

BREAKING NEWS
NUCLEAR CRISIS AVERTED, PRESIDENT GORE
TO ADDRESS NATION

"Sounds like Gore convinced Pakistan to back down," she says. "Thank God, I really thought this was going to escalate."

"I knew Gore wouldn't push the button," I say.

"That's true, you've been confident all along, haven't you?"

Recalling my *Yeah Gore!* post on social media, I say, "Yeah, I guess I was prescient."

"God, I can't imagine," Laura says. "I mean being in that position. The future of the world is at stake and you have to make a decision, and if you make the wrong decision millions of people might die."

"I don't know," I say. "I mean, is there really any such thing as a wrong decision?"

"What do you mean?"

"I'm just saying, I think every decision someone makes, whether it's good or bad, can lead to something positive or negative. The consequences aren't obvious from the decision itself."

"It's too late for this," Laura says. "You're hurting my head."

"Lemme give you a hypothetical situation," I say. "What if, let's say nineteen years ago, America was attacked by terrorists? What if a group of Islamic terrorists executed a horrific attack on our country? Imagine if, crazy as this may sound, the World Trade Center was destroyed."

"What do you mean destroyed?"

"I mean *totally* destroyed. Knocked to the ground. Both Towers."

"That's impossible, they're made of steel."

"What if hijackers flew airplanes into them, commercial jetliners filled with innocent passengers and crewmembers? Seven-forty-sevens headed from the East Coast to California so they're packed with jet fuel. So the planes hit the top of the towers and explode on impact and then the fire causes the steel to melt and the entire buildings buckle and collapse and buildings in the surrounding area are destroyed too. A few thousand people die, including hundreds of firefighters and other first responders."

Laura's staring at me. "That's a really sick thing to imagine, Steven."

"I know it is, but—"

"Maybe instead of thinking about writing a dumb TV show about mobsters, you should write science fiction instead. How do you even come up with this crap?"

"I said it's hypothetical."

"Still, you had to *think* of it. Hijacked airplanes crashing into the Twin Towers? You sure you're feeling okay? Maybe I should be worried about you."

She *should* be worried about me.

"You're missing the point," I say.

"There's a point?"

"Let's just, for the sake of argument, say it happened, okay? Oh and not just the Twin Towers. Let's say the Pentagon was attacked and passengers forced another plane headed toward the White House to crash in rural Pennsylvania so it was an enormous tragedy that led to us getting involved in multiple wars in the Middle East where there was even more horror and tragedy. My point is—"

"Yes, what exactly *is* your point, Steven?"

"My point is that in this scenario it's possible that a couple of decisions would've changed everything. For example, if somebody at the CIA had decided to investigate why so many Middle Eastern men were suddenly attending flight schools in Florida maybe the attacks would've been prevented, and that would've prevented the whole chain of events that followed from happening."

"Chain of events?"

"Wars around the world with massive casualties, new terror groups forming, right-wing factions taking control of governments. Brexit."

"What's that?"

"It's just an, um…a term I made up—you know, if Great Britain ever decided to leave the European Union it might be called Brexit."

She still looks perplexed, or maybe concerned.

"Never mind," I say. "What I mean is it's all about decisions we make that cause chains of events to unfold and it can create a new reality that coexists with other realities and these realities continue on simultaneously coexisting. So even if Pakistan and Gore made a good decision here, it doesn't necessarily mean world peace is on the horizon. Bad things can always happen. Just different bad things."

"You know what I think?" Laura says.

On TV, President Gore has entered the Oval Office and is sitting at the desk, about to address the nation.

"I think *this* is the idea for your movie or TV show," she says. "I don't know why you're wasting your time with law."

We watch Gore's speech about how "a potential tragedy unlike anything the world has ever seen" was averted today. It's a very stern and powerful speech and afterwards analysts compare Gore's performance to JFK's handling of the Cuban Missile Crisis. No wonder I've been posting all that praise on MyWorld.

"It sucks he didn't win in two thousand," I say.

"Why? If he did, he wouldn't be President now."

I guess this is true since 9/11 never happened, and Bush didn't lead the country into wars in Iraq and Afghanistan, and maybe a million people are alive who wouldn't be alive otherwise. How have all those people altered the world?

A little while later, when Laura dozes, on my phone, I go to Jeffery Hammond's MyWorld page. It disgusts me how clean-cut, how *normal* Hammond appears—confident, smiling, standing at the end of a pier, with his thumbs inside the front pockets of his jeans. He looks much fitter and healthier than I've ever seen him. I remind myself how this version of Hammond may seem healthier than the Hammond who was my client, but I know he hasn't changed. Maybe in a different version of the world there can be different Presidents, different wars, and different diseases, but one thing that never changes is psychopathy. If someone is a psychopath, they'll always be a psychopath, no matter what their circumstances. If Hitler or Dahmer grew up in different circumstances would they be better people? It's the same for Hammond. He's a remorseless psychopath, incapable of empathy, and nothing can change that. I know what's going on *inside* him—the shame, hatred, perverted dark fantasies. As his attorney, I had to play along, pretend that I wasn't on to him, even sympathized with him, but he couldn't fool me then and he can't fool me now. I'm not surprised he *looks* happy—this makes total sense. His personality has always been a mask, a façade, a con. People who didn't know him well loved him and he was always the most charming person in the room at his gallery openings. During our interviews, he was extremely engaging, always stroking my ego, as he tried to manipulate me, the same way he manipulated his victims. I recall how I struggled with my decision to take him as a client. Every defense attorney has to table morality, at least to some extent, in order to take on *any* case, but the decision to take on the Hammond case was different. While I'd defended many ruthless, hardened criminals, I'd never represented a serial killer—a guy like Hammond who had zero remorse or empathy, who I was certain was guilty. He wanted me on the case, though, because he believed I could get him off. He offered almost double my usual rate and I knew it would be a high-profile case, with nationwide media coverage, which would bring me more high-profile clients. In the end, I took him on, but I continued to struggle with the decision. During our many meetings, I always told Hammond that I believed he was innocent, and that I would try as hard as I could to get him off, but I was lying, of course. I didn't want him to get off. I wanted him to go to jail, ideally for the rest of his life.

I don't know if this version of Hammond has killed anyone yet, but I know he's fantasized about killing, or is planning to kill, because killing is his nature, and nothing can change that.

The other Jeffery Hammond lived with his boyfriend, Jeremiah Ferg, before murdering him. I search for more information about Ferg and Hammond's other victims, but, like the last time I searched, I can't find anything connecting Hammond to the murders, since the murders haven't been committed.

Am I looking at this all wrong? Maybe there's no information about his victims because his victims have changed. Maybe there are *other* victims.

Instead of searching for information about the victims I know, I search for information about unsolved murders that match Hammond's M.O. Maybe there are active missing persons cases for young attractive men in the New York City metropolitan area, or maybe a body or bodies have been discovered

with wounds similar to the ones that I know Hammond in-
flicted.

The first series of searches don't provide any promising
results. Two weeks ago, an unidentified male was discovered
near Schenectady, New York, but there's nothing about this
case that screams Jeffery Hammond. A couple of months ago,
on Staten Island, the body of a man was discovered, but the
victim had been asphyxiated and Hammond didn't asphyxiate
any of the men I knew about. He preferred to use a chainsaw.

Then, on the fifth or sixth page of search results, when I'm
about to give up, I see a link to a *Daily News* article that in-
trigues me.

Last year, in January 2019, the dismembered body of twenty-
nine-year-old Mark Miranda, a part-time model and a bar-
tender at a Manhattan nightclub, was found in the East River.
Hammond's art studio in Astoria, Queens is maybe five blocks
from where Miranda's body was discovered. Is this just a coincidence or did I just discover a Jeffery Hammond murder
victim that the police don't know about?

Reading more about the murder of Mark Miranda, I again
have an odd, intense feeling of, yes, déjà vu, as if I'm reading
about one of the Jeffery Hammond's victims from my other
reality. All of Hammond victims were in their twenties or
early thirties. Like the other victims, Miranda was handsome
and muscular—definitely Hammond's type—and he actually
has a strong resemblance to Danny Montoya, one of the men
I know Hammond killed, but who's still alive in this strand.
There's no mention of Hammond in the story or of the police
trying to connect the murder to the 2016 murder of Eduardo
Ortiz on Long Island. Then I find an article on a site called
LiveFeed—it seems a lot like BuzzFeed—that describes, in
more graphic detail, how parts of the body were found in dif-

ferent garbage bags, and I flash back to the autopsy images I know so well of his other victims. I feel like I'm definitely on to something.

My phone pings as a text arrives from "anontxt."

Laura stirs a little as I glance at the display:

I SAW YOU MOTHERFUCKER

Saw me? Saw me when? Does this mean earlier today, last week, or a minute ago? Is someone still here, watching me?

I get out of bed quietly and go to the window. Parting a small space in the blinds with my fingers, I peer out at the darkness. I can't see or hear anything, but that doesn't mean that someone isn't out there.

Then I have a crazy thought—could it be Jeffery Hammond?

I don't have any evidence to support this theory. It's probably pure paranoia—I was just searching for information about Hammond so it's natural that my brain would make the connection. Still, I can't shake the feeling that he's the texter, and rejecting this possibility seems as crazy as acknowledging it.

"What is it?" Laura asks, spacy, disoriented, the way she always is when she's just falling asleep.

I must've jostled her when I got out of bed, or maybe she heard the text arrive.

"Nothing, just work," I say.

"O…kay."

She settles down. I wait until she hasn't moved for about a minute, then pull the curtain aside again and look out toward the front lawn.

I can't see anything, just darkness.

I go downstairs, with Wasabi trailing.

At the bottom of the stairs, I whisper to the dog, "It's okay, you wait right here."

I check the security cameras. Front of the house, sides of the house, backyard, garage area all look clear.

I go outside, shutting the door behind me. I listen, but hear nothing except the light breeze crackling the branches.

"Hello," I say, but not too loud because I don't want Laura or Lilly to hear.

No response.

"Hello, is anyone here? I'm not afraid of you."

This isn't really true. I am a little afraid, but not for my own safety—I'm more concerned about Laura and Lilly.

"Hammond, is it you? Are you out there?"

No answer.

"Hammond if you're there, I know what you are. I know you didn't change."

Still no answer. I'm feeling crazy, like I'm losing control. I remind myself that I have no evidence that Hammond's here or that he even knows I exist. I have to get a grip.

Back inside, I take a series of slow deep breaths to center myself, then I go upstairs and check on Lilly, making sure she's safe and sound asleep.

Climbing back into bed with Laura, I'm still feeling para-noid. Somehow I get my heart to stop racing and I manage to fall asleep. I dream that I'm driving along a twisty road. At first, I'm someplace exotic, on an island, maybe Bermuda, but then I'm in Westchester. I'm approaching the bend in the road where I skidded the other night. Noticing that my hands are covered in blood, I panic, brake too hard, and the car spins out of control. Headlights come toward me, getting brighter and brighter, then, right as I make contact with an oncoming car, I wake up.

I don't know if I scream, but my pulse is pounding like I just ran a sprint. Next to me, Laura stirs, then settles again. I'm not sure what to make of the dream, if it's a premonition, more déjà vu, or random anxiety.

I want to close my eyes and have some peace, just for a few hours, but I know I'm kidding myself.

If death couldn't quiet my mind, sleep won't either.

TWELVE

Although I have no intention of actually going to work today, I put on one of my Brooks Brothers suits and go down to the kitchen. Laura is already in work clothes—a conservative, over-the-knees dress—finishing her coffee. What is it about this version of her? She looks gorgeous and sexy even when she's not trying.

"Good morning."

I try to kiss her on the cheek, but she turns her head, maybe not wanting to ruin her lipstick.

"How'd you sleep?" she asks. "You were stirring a lot."

"I was? Guess I was dreaming."

"You were talking in your sleep too."

Oh no, what did I say? My life is so mysterious, even I don't know who I am, or what I've done. But it's hard enough worrying about what will happen when I'm awake, now I have to worry about being unconscious too?

Trying not to show concern, I ask, "Hope it was something profound."

She smiles. "No, it was hard to make out what you were saying exactly. But you were breathing heavily, you sounded agitated."

"I was probably just having an adventure." I'm eager to change the subject. "When did you get up?"

"Made my six A.M. yoga."

"It's really great that you're doing yoga."

Confused, she says, "I've been practicing for years."

"I know you have been. I just mean in general. So many people don't take care of themselves, let depression take over."

She gives me another befuddled look, then asks, "So what's on your agenda today?"

I can't tell her the truth—that I'm not actually going to work, that I'm planning to have a talk with Jeffery Hammond, the serial killer I was defending in another version of my life, to find out if he's been stalking me in my current life.

"Um, it's a pretty full schedule," I say.

"Oh yeah, what's going on?"

Here we go with the lying again.

"Oh, I'm just, um, working on a new case."

"Oh really? Which one?"

"Not really *new*. Someone I worked with in the past who might have another case for me."

"So mysterious. Come on, tell me, what case?"

I might as well mention his name. If Hammond entered my life recently, or sometime in the past, I might've mentioned him to Laura.

"His name's Hammond," I say. "Jeffery Hammond."

"Who's he?" The name clearly means nothing to her.

"I haven't mentioned him before?"

"No, I don't think you have. I mean, unless I forgot. What does he do?"

"He's an artist."

"Really? I think I would've remembered *that*. Sounds interesting. What's the case about?"

"Oh, just a personal liability thing. Nothing very sexy." I reach out and grab her hips. "Speaking of sexy. How's *your* day looking?"

I try to kiss her, but again she avoids me, this time wiggling free and opening a cabinet above the counter, as if she's looking for something, but it was probably just an excuse to get away from me.

"What's wrong?" I ask, thinking she must be upset that I didn't give her enough information about Hammond. "I thought I brushed my teeth."

She doesn't smile.

"I shouldn't say anything," she says, avoiding eye contact.

"Now you *have to* say something," I say. "Come on, we can't say goodbye like this, I'll be thinking about it all day, and you will too."

She stares right at me, holding my gaze for a few seconds, then says, "Okay, fine, I guess it's better to get this out in the open, instead of letting it simmer…Have you been cheating on me?"

The question shouldn't surprise me, given my apparent history, but since I know that I—the real me—hasn't deceived her in any way, it feels like this is coming out of nowhere.

"What?" I say. "You're seriously asking me that question?"

It's easy to sound innocent when I genuinely don't believe I've done anything wrong.

"I can't believe it," she says, "but yes…yes I am…Are you?"

"No," I say, "of course not."

As far as I know, she has no evidence, and the less I say, the better off I am. Utilizing my defense attorney skills, I'm trying to be careful with my language.

"I love you," I say, "and I wouldn't do that…I mean that's not something *I* would ever do."

"I want to believe you, but lately you've been so…distant."

"Really? I thought we've been closer than ever."

"Since you've been home you've been great, like a different person actually. You've been nice and attentive and more passionate than you've been for months. Years, actually."

"So what's the problem, then?" I try to hold her again, but she won't let me.

"I don't know, the change is just a little…dramatic, that's all. I mean before the accident you were so removed, so mysterious, always staying late at work, and then there was the phone call incident."

Phone call incident? I have no idea what she's referring to, but I assume she means a woman called the house, or there was a suspicious call on my cell.

"Oh come on, you know that was nothing," I say.

"I know, I know, it's all just my imagination, that's what you always say. I'm just crazy and paranoid and jealous."

Did I really *say* all that?

"You're not any of those things," I say.

"That's not what you told me."

"Look, whatever I said, it's in the past and the past doesn't exist, and it doesn't even reflect who I truly am anyway."

"What're you talking about?"

"I'm saying I didn't mean any of that. Trust me, I didn't."

She gazes at my eyes like a human lie detector, then says, "Then why the sudden change? Is it the old cliché of the man who's cheating suddenly bringing home flowers and buying his wife gifts?"

"I haven't bought you any—"

"I mean metaphorically. Are you being nice to distract, or overcompensate for something? If something's going on, please, just tell me, Steve."

Should I confess about Kaitlin and Angie and whatever other women I might've been involved with? Old me wouldn't keep secrets like this. But if I confess to one thing, where do the confessions end? Should I also confess to murdering Kaitlin's father? What about other mistakes I might've made or crimes I might've committed? How do I confess to what I don't know I did, or to what I don't know is true?

After a long hesitation I say, "There isn't anything going on. I would never *willingly* do anything to hurt you, Laura. I hope you know that."

Of course "willingly" is as loaded as a word can possibly be loaded, but at least it helps me feel like I'm being somewhat honest. Also, my eyes are teary and the show of emotion has an effect on Laura. She grabs my shoulders, pulling me close, and kisses me, like she loves me as much as I love her. I'm relieved, but it's hard to totally trust this impression, especially as I flash back to her kicking me out of the house, screaming that she doesn't love me anymore.

"Yuck."

Lilly has entered; I don't know how long she's been there. Laura and I stop kissing, but we're still holding each other.

"Mommy and Daddy are allowed to kiss," I say.

"People only kiss when they get married," Lilly says.

"People kiss *during* marriages too," I say.

"*You* don't," she says.

"Oh yeah?" I kiss Laura again. "Well, we do now."

Laura laughs a little, then pushes me away gently, "Okay, that's enough." She grabs her handbag as she says to Lilly, "Mommy and Daddy have to go to work, and *you* have to go to school."

"I'm afraid Madison is going to sit next to me on the bus again."

"I'll make sure she doesn't, I promise," I say.

When Laura leaves, I get Lilly dressed and ready for school, and we're outside waiting for the school bus with time to spare.

I get on the bus first and tell the bus driver to please make sure Lilly and Madison don't sit together and he suggests that Lilly sit in the seat directly behind him.

"Thank you, Daddy!"

Lilly gives me a big hug, then gets on the bus happily. As the bus pulls away, I feel a parental pang of anxiety, and I already miss her. How can I have these feelings for a little girl I met a few days ago? It feels like I've always known her and I guess, who knows? Maybe I have.

I park my car at the Katonah station in time to make the 7:38. On the platform, I see Angie Garcia. When she sees me, she walks away in the opposite direction, toward the front of the platform. I'm going to let her go, then it occurs to me, Maybe I'm wrong about Hammond. Maybe, in this world, he has no idea who I am. But Angie definitely knows me and could have a motive to harass me.

I rush up alongside her. She continues walking.

"Can we talk for a second?" I ask.

She doesn't answer.

"Come on," I say. "There's no reason to have this animosity between us."

Finally, she stops, near where the front car will arrive.

"Fine, what do you want to talk about? Us? Is it about how you led me on? How you ruined my marriage without even stopping to think about me or my feelings?"

I'm not sure exactly what she's talking about, but I take her word for it.

"I'm sorry," I say. "I didn't mean to hurt you, honestly I didn't. I'm just trying to be logical."

"Logical," she says, like the word disgusts her. "Is this really the same man who told me that we're soulmates, and he wants to marry me when our kids get older?"

For fuck's sake, how many women did I use that lame soulmates line with?

I want to tell her, *Actually, this isn't the same man*, but I say,

"I get it. You're pissed off at me, and you have a total right to be. But can you just be honest with me about one thing—have you been sending me texts?"

"Texts?" She seems believably confused. "What texts?"

"Maybe to scare me, or intimidate me, or get some kind of revenge over me. If you are, I won't be angry with you. I've just been through a lot recently and I'm trying to heal now with my family, and I'd really appreciate it if you told me the truth."

She stares at me with a serious, non-blinking expression that makes me wonder if a confession is coming.

Then she says, "Tom and I are getting divorced. He said he suspected that I've been cheating on him so he met someone and he's moving in with her."

"Do you think it's possible that Tom's sending the texts? Maybe he's angry with me and wants to scare me or something?"

She glares incredulously, then says, "My life is in a shambles right now and you really think I give a shit about your stupid texts? You're a son of a bitch lying bastard, Steven Blitz, but I'm so happy to hear that you and your family are healing. That's just fucking wonderful."

Like we're in a scene in a melodrama, she marches away, back toward the middle of the platform.

It sucks that things with Angie and me got so messed up in this reality. In my old life, we had such a great connection and she always helped make my daily commute feel less like a grind and more like something I looked forward to. She truly was one of my best friends, one of the few people I knew I could always trust and rely on. For these reasons, I never considered crossing a line with her and starting an affair, because I knew I would risk losing her as a friend. Apparently in this reality, judgment, wisdom, and the ability to anticipate future consequences and act accordingly are qualities I've lacked.

The train arrives and she boards without even glancing in my direction. Let her stay angry at me. I want her to be happy and I know she has a much better chance of being happy without me around. Maybe someday she'll even thank me for not fucking up her life more than I already did.

From Grand Central, I take the subway—the 6 to 59th and then I switch to the N to Astoria. Although these are trains I've taken many times before and they look and smell like they should look and smell, I still don't feel like I'm in my world.

I exit at the Astoria Boulevard Station and head under the el toward the East River. Over the years, I've been to Astoria several times, usually to go to the Museum of the Moving Image or out for Greek food. As far as I can tell, the subway station looks the same as the last time I was here, and it's nice to see that a diner and a bodega look semi-familiar; I assume because they have been in business since pre early 1998.

I don't want to arrive too early, so I kill some time at the diner, sitting at the counter, drinking coffee. The caffeine's a bad idea. I have a lot on my mind and it's only making me more anxious.

At around ten-thirty, I leave the diner and head in the general direction of Manhattan, toward the East River. Using the Excite Map app, I walk for ten minutes or so, following directions to Hammond's studio. The Astoria I know is very gentrified—this version, not so much. I veer into an industrial area with old brick factory buildings and warehouses; several seem abandoned. His studio is in one of the more rundown-looking brick buildings, which is startling in comparison to the hip, upscale studio space in Nolita where the Hammond in my other reality works.

There are four buzzers, and #4 is labeled in pen: J. HAMMOND. Before I buzz, I hesitate, asking myself: *Do I really want to do this?* Hammond may very well not be involved in my current life at all. Do I really want to open this huge can of worms if I don't have to? I can try to forget about him, hope that our paths never cross. He's not my client anymore and, besides, whether he's killed people or he's planning to kill people or he's not a killer at all, it has nothing to do with me. Even if I'm the only one who knows his true nature, and I can help solve murders he may have already committed or prevent future murders he might commit, is it really my responsibility to get involved? After all, no one knows that I know. If I walk away right now no one will ever know.

Before I can weigh all the cons, I press the buzzer. I took the leap—now at least I'll know, I'll have more information, which can never be bad.

Or can it?

I have no idea if Hammond is here now or not, but I didn't want to give him any sort of heads up. If it turns out he knows me, and he's been harassing me with the texts, I want to catch him as off-guard as possible. I press record on my phone's voice memo app and then return the phone to my pocket. If Hammond says something incriminating, I want to make sure I have evidence to use against him—either to coerce him to leave me alone or by sharing it with the police. My goal is to stay in control, to have options.

"Can I help you?"

The voice comes from above. I retreat a few steps, then gaze up and see Hammond leaning out of one of the large windows on the third floor. While I know Hammond is a free man in this reality, it's still jarring to actually *see* him outside of a prison. After all, the last time I saw Hammond, just last week, was at Rikers, when we were reviewing our final preparations for his trial. At that meeting he was in shackles.

"Oh, I…good morning," I say. "How are you?"

This feels way beyond awkward. I'm totally unprepared for this and am regretting coming here at all.

"Sorry, do I know you?"

His tone sounds like he legitimately doesn't recognize me. He's about forty feet away and isn't Hammond myopic? In prison he was wearing glasses and he isn't wearing any now.

"Um, sort of," I say, because I don't know what else to say. "I was wondering if we could, um, talk."

"Are you delivering something?" Now he sounds confused and a little irritated.

"No, I'm here to, uh, inquire about purchasing some of your work."

I'm proud of myself for thinking fast, making this up on the fly.

"Oh. I usually only meet people by appointment."

"I figured that was probably the case, but I was in the area, so I thought I'd just drop by. Is it possible to see some of your work now? I won't take long, I promise."

He doesn't answer, as if he's mulling it over.

Then he says, "Okay, I'm coming down."

I'm not surprised he opted to meet with me. Given the current state of his career, I don't think he'd delay a meeting with a potential buyer.

About thirty seconds later, the door opens and I'm facing Hammond. He certainly looks much better than he did in prison—which isn't tough to pull off. Last week he was pasty, worn out, like he'd been through hell, which, in a way, he had been. Now he looks younger, healthier. His hair is back in a man bun and he's wearing a smock over old, ripped, paint-spattered jeans and a black T-shirt. His muscles are cut, like he's been working out. Still no glasses, but maybe he has contacts.

"Hey." My mouth is dry.

"Hey," he says, extending his hand to shake. "And you are?"

He seems to legitimately have no idea who I am. If it's an act—and it would certainly fit his personality to be fucking with me—it's a convincing one. During our interviews, he played mind games all the time, getting off on feeling a step ahead of me, like he always thought he was the smartest one in the room, and he probably was. I'm smart, was near the top of my class in law school, but Hammond is smarter.

"My name's Steven...Steven Blitz."

We shake. His grip is firm, too firm, and it lingers, like he's trying to make a point, or gain my respect, or...could he be *hitting* on me? It didn't occur to me that he might assume that's why I came by his studio—to hook up. I know he has promiscuous tendencies and he's called himself a sex addict. I'm reasonably sure, though, that I'm not his type. He usually goes for younger men.

"Nice to meet you, Steven."

He finally releases his grip. My hand is clammy.

"Come on, come in, I'll show you around."

While he seems normal and friendly, it's hard for me not to remember who he is and what he's done.

He leads me into a foyer area, created by two large, semi-detached half walls.

"How did you find out about me?" he asks.

He genuinely doesn't seem to know me. If this is acting, it's Oscar-worthy.

"Oh, actually," I say, "we know each other."

"We do?"

"Well, not *know*, but we met—briefly, at a gallery in Bushwick last year. You gave me your card."

I'm thinking fast, recalling that one of the photos of Hammond that I saw online was taken at a gallery in Bushwick last year.

He squints, as if trying to remember, then says, "The Terese Jenkins exhibit?"

This sounds somewhat familiar. "Yeah, that was the one."

"I don't give out cards," he says, like he thinks he caught me in a lie which, of course, he did.

"Oh, I don't know if it was a *card*. I mean you mentioned I should contact you if I wanted to see your work and I looked you up online."

"Oh, okay." This seems to appease him. "So what're you interested in exactly?"

"Well, I'm an attorney and big art collector and am interested in purchasing a painting or two. Hope it's okay I dropped by. Like I said, I just happened to be in the area. I mean, I can come back later or some other—"

"No, not at all. I was about to take a break actually. Great to meet you, Mr. Blitz."

"Call me, Steven."

In my expensive suit I look like a guy who has money to spend, so I'm not surprised he sounds intrigued, especially since this version of Hammond hasn't hit the big time yet.

"Well, it's nice to meet you…again," he says.

"Likewise." I'm smiling at the irony.

"Come on," he says. "I'll show you some of my newest work."

He leads me further into the space, which I now see is really a combination art studio and apartment. There's a big open space with several plastic drop cloths on the floor. The cloths make me shudder as I recall how he described to me, at length, with almost no emotion, how he dismembered victims in his art studio in SoHo. *I put down layers of drop cloths. I have nice floors and I didn't want to ruin them, of course.* These floors don't look so nice—just normal wooden flooring—but, I wonder, did he dismember Mark Miranda's body here before dumping his remains in the river? Were others killed here?

"Something wrong?" he asks, as if reading my mind.

"No, not at all." I swallow.

I continue looking around, at a large canvas—a work-in-progress—and other paintings, some propped up against walls, some hanging on the walls. All the art has Hammond's trademark stark bleakness with dull grays and blues contrasting with occasional bursts of bright red, but nothing in particular looks familiar. I'm no art expert, but the works don't seem to have the same quality as *Manhattan Midnight* and his other well-known works.

To the right, there's another half wall, and beyond it a bed.

"Sorry it's such a mess," he says. "Part of my process, I suppose. I have to work in chaos."

Wondering if there's hidden meaning in this statement, I say, "I wouldn't expect anything less...I didn't realize you live here too."

"Yes, it's my home studio. Not ideal, but what can you do? New York, right? I've gotten used to the paint fumes—hope they're non-toxic. If my skin starts peeling off, I'll know why."

The dark, dark, slightly inappropriate humor is very Hammond-esque and familiar. In our prison interviews he would smirk while describing gruesome murders.

"Can I get you something to drink?" he asks. "Water? Coffee? Orange juice?"

"Water's great."

As he goes to kitchen area, behind another half wall, I look out the back windows at a sliver of the East River. The area where Miranda's body was discovered isn't far from here, maybe a quarter mile away. There are mainly old warehouses between here and the river and, at night especially, the streets would be empty. Hammond could have easily killed Miranda in this apartment, dismembered him, wrapped the remains in a drop cloth and stuffed them in a suitcase. But would Hammond dispose of a body so close to where he lived? The Hammond I was defending always planned out his "disposals," which was one of the reasons I felt an insanity defense had little hope of working. Hammond was always methodical; in this respect, he murdered the way he painted. His work is chaotic and violent, but there is also great precision in his technique.

"Here you go."

I'm jolted. Hammond is standing right behind me with the water and I didn't hear him approach.

"Oh, thank you," I say, taking the glass from him. "Um, it's a nice view."

"Yeah, it is, I guess," he says. "I've been here so long I don't notice it anymore. That's the thing about views—no matter how beautiful they are, they never last. We always ultimately become complacent, indifferent. Familiarity is like amnesia."

I take a sip of water—I need it as my mouth feels like sand-paper.

"So you're an attorney, huh?"

"That's right," I say.

"What type of law do you practice?"

"Criminal defense, actually."

"Really?" His surprise seems genuine. "So now I'm connecting the dots here. Defense attorney—that's why you like the dark stuff, huh?"

"Excuse me?"

"My paintings aren't for everyone, *Something* about them must attract you."

"That's true, I guess I do like the dark stuff."

"So what type of criminal cases do you handle?"

"Everything from tax fraud to murder."

"Cool," he says with a smirk. "So if I ever get in trouble with the law, I know who to call."

I know he's joking, but I'm recalling the adage that there's truth in every joke. Although he's acting engaging and normal, I feel the same way about him in person as I did when I saw the happy photos on his MyWorld. It feels wrong that he's a free man, working on his art all day, rather than on trial for multiple murders.

"I'm here if you need me." I smile, playing along.

I turn to check out another painting, one of the ones leaning against the wall. "So how long have you been here?"

"Oh, a long time. It's not ideal, but I like the area. I used to paint in Manhattan at the Art Students' League. I used to find it inspiring to paint where Pollock and O'Keeffe worked—I was young and more romantic, I suppose—but in general I hate being around people."

This last comment comes off as extremely chilling. Maybe it's the subtext, or the way his eyes appear lifeless, the way they did in our prison interviews.

"Interesting," I say. "Have you ever thought about finding studio space in Manhattan?"

He gives me a strange, squinting look, then says, "Actually I once looked at a space there that I loved, but it didn't work out. Why did you ask me that?"

I wonder if he's referring to the studio on Mott Street, where the other version of Hammond works.

"Just curious," I say. "I like to have as much background as possible on the artists whose work I acquire."

"I see," he says. "So what kind of painting are you looking for?"

"No particular kind," I say, glancing around. "I'm a new

collector. I'm doing some redecorating and your art really stood out to me and then I did some research about you online."

"I hope you read some good things about me."

He's smiling. He really does have charm—which explains how he's been able to successfully lure in his victims.

"Yeah, you had a lot of, um, glowing reviews," I say, thinking instead about the articles I read about the murders of Mark Miranda and Eduardo Ortiz. "I think I, um, saw a comparison to Bacon. I can definitely see that influence."

"Ah, yes, I love Bacon. Thank you, that's very flattering."

"I see some Dali in your work too," I say, pouring it on. Glancing at a work in progress, I add, "This one's very compelling. I love the colors, the deepness and intensity of the colors and the textures. So, um, what inspires you?"

"Violence," he says.

"What sort of violence?"

"Oh, everything—murder, rape, torture, war. I don't feel any emotional connection to my art. I'm more interested in my reaction to the subject matter, exploring the interplay between reality and fantasy."

I get the sense that this is his sales pitch, how he's described his work for years to prospective buyers. I'm also aware how, on another level, he's revealing his genuine psychopathy. I know I'm right about him—there's no way he's changed, that sometime after early 1998 he miraculously became sane.

"Actually I heard about a murder right around here recently," I say. "A body was discovered in the river."

Although I'm dying to observe his reaction to this, I'm playing it nonchalant, looking away, casually checking out the other paintings in the room.

"Oh, right, I heard about that too," he says. "Heard about it on the news."

"Is that the sort of thing that…inspires you?"

Now I glance at him and see that his expression has changed drastically from just several seconds ago. He seems taken aback, offended, as if I touched on a sensitive issue. For the first time since I arrived here, I feel concerned for my safety. I'm taking an enormous risk. I know how easily he can snap—go from calm to extreme violence. No one knows I'm here, so if he decides that I know too much or am a threat to him in any way, I have no doubt that he'll kill me, dump my body in the river, and he won't feel any guilt or remorse over it.

"My paintings are always non-specific," he says. "I thought I made that clear."

"You did," I say. "I wasn't trying to—"

"I'm not a ripped-from-the-headlines sort of artist. I need to experience my art myself. It has to always come from me. It has to be personal."

"Good to know," I say. "I mean, I mean it's good to get a sense of your general aesthetic and work habits."

I don't know much about art and I fear it's coming through, and I worry that I sound full of shit, that it's raising a red flag for him.

"Of course," he says. "I want you to know as much about my work as you possibly can. Informed decisions are the best decisions."

I move closer to one of the largest paintings in the room, one of the ones propped up against the wall. It's a bleak, abstract riverfront landscape, with blood-red water. I wonder if the color of the water and the location alludes to the murder of Mark Miranda.

"How much?" I ask.

"I haven't priced it yet, but I can do five thousand."

The Hammond I knew routinely sold paintings for millions.

"That's definitely in my range," I say.

"It's negotiable," he says. "If you want to buy more than one I can give you a good deal."

"This one's interesting too." I'm gazing at a larger canvas of a maze of city streets, also with dominant blood-red coloring.

"Yeah, that's a personal favorite. It's seven thousand but you can have them both for ten."

"I think I'm probably only in the market for one right now."

I notice he's eying me differently now, as if he's trying to figure something out.

"You know, you do seem familiar now," he says. "I still don't remember meeting in Bushwick, though."

"It was very brief."

I feel like he's playing a game with me now, that he knows exactly who I am and he wants to see how I respond. I hope I'm just being paranoid, but I'm regretting my decision to come here.

"Where'd you grow up?" he asks.

"Long Island," I say. "How about you?"

"I was born near Philly," he says. "But I lived all over."

Of course I know his whole history. I know he grew up in Cherry Hill, New Jersey, then lived overseas in Africa and Asia—his father was in the military—before returning to New Jersey. I'm assuming his past, up until a divergence in early 1998, is exactly the same as the other Hammond's past.

"What about college?" he asks.

"Binghamton," I say.

"No college for me," he says.

"Actually, I knew that."

He seems surprised. "You did?"

"I told you, I did a little research."

"Right. Research before you invest. Makes sense."

Again, I wonder if he's playing an elaborate mind game with me. He seems benign, but is this all an act? Hammond has told me how he studied his victims, searching for any vulnerabilities that he could exploit.

"You have an interesting background," I say. "A lot of travelling."

"The perks of having a military dad."

"Do you think this had an effect on your creativity?"

In interviews he's mentioned how his unstable childhood had a profound influence on his art, but I want to see how he responds.

"Yes, in fact it has," he says. "I think the moving around made me feel like I had to constantly make new friends, and I think that's why I'm often open and experimental in my work. Also, the imagery of my childhood, especially violence I unfortunately witnessed, has had a profound effect on me to this very day."

I can't help wondering if that violence was before or after 1998. Or both.

"I'm sorry to hear that," I say. "About the violence you've witnessed."

He shrugs, holds my gaze a little longer than necessary. I want to get the hell out of here.

"Well, thank you, this has been amazing," I say. "I'll have to check with my wife, but I'm sure one of these will work out."

"You didn't take any pictures," he says.

"Oh, I wasn't sure you wanted me to."

"Most serious buyers take pictures."

He sounds irritated.

"I can take a few now," I say.

"Forget it," he says curtly. "I have to get back to work."

He backs up a couple of feet to create a clear path for me to get to the door, a not-so-subtle way of telling me, *It's time to go now*.

As I walk to the door with him trailing me, I'm aware of the vulnerable position I'm in. A serial killer, a pissed-off and maybe suspicious serial killer, is right behind me. He could grab something and smash it over my head and I'd have no way to defend myself. It's a ten second or less walk to the door, but it feels like minutes. When I open the door and step out into the hallway, I look back at him.

"Well, thanks again," I say, trying my best to act natural, despite the tremendous awkwardness. "Look forward to talking again soon."

"Yeah, okay, sure," he says, and slams the door.

Wanting to get out of this building as fast as I can, I hurry downstairs. When I get outside, I want to run or at least jog, but I maintain a steady, normal pace in case he's watching me leave. Only when I turn the corner do I begin to relax.

I know I might be exaggerating, letting my paranoia get to me, but I still feel like I was lucky to get out of there alive.

I jog a couple of blocks to put more distance between us, then I return to walking. I take out my phone and stop recording. I'm not sure what, if any, value the recording has. Hammond didn't admit to anything. While I believe there is a serious possibility that Hammond killed Mark Miranda, Eduardo Ortiz, and possibly others, there is nothing on the recording that would qualify as evidence that Hammond committed any murders. I can call in an anonymous tip, but I'm not sure how I can even get the police to investigate. I can tell them that I know he's a killer, but why would they believe me?

I ride the subways back to Grand Central and get on the first

Metro North to Katonah, the 12:20. I text Laura from my seat, *Hey, how's your day going?*

She replies: *Busy! Will pick up Lilly from playdate on way home.*

I send: *Awesome, love you!*

She replies: *Love you too!!*

I'm lucky to have a loving wife and a wonderful daughter. I have to embrace all of the many positives in my new life, and forget, or at least not worry, about what I can't control.

Looking forward to getting back to Westchester and having a nice, relaxing rest-of-the-day at home, I close my eyes, starting to doze, when my phone vibrates.

I half-smile, expecting to see a flirty, warm text from Laura— but it's from "anontxt."

With dread, I open the message:

YOU THINK YOU'RE SMART DON'T YOU, FUCK FACE?
YOU THINK YOU HAVE IT ALL FIGURED OUT HUH?
WELL GUESS WHAT? YOU DON'T!!!

So much for relaxation. My face is burning.

I read the message several times, as if searching for hidden meaning and clues. Could Hammond have sent it? Is he fucking with me after all? Did we meet sometime earlier in this version of my life? Is there something I don't know, some big piece of information that I'm missing? One thing's certain—it sounds like whoever sent the message is getting angrier, more belligerent, and maybe more impatient.

My phone vibrates again. It's another text from the same number, except this one is an image—Kaitlin and I in the woods with a dead body, presumably her father. My face is clearly visible as I'm dragging the body toward a dug-up hole. The picture must've been taken late last Wednesday afternoon.

In my other life, I was in the city last Wednesday afternoon, in my office, preparing for a murder trial, but apparently I was in two places at the same time, or at least different versions of me were in different places.

I know this is true, because *I'm* here, staring at the evidence.

THIRTEEN

It's the fifth time I've called Kaitlin and she still isn't picking up and my head's throbbing like my brain tumor's back.

"Come on, answer," I mutter to myself. "Just answer, for fuck's sake."

I'm expecting to get her voicemail again and I'm about to hang up again and call back, when I hear, "What?"

"Where are you?" I must sound as panicked as I feel.

"What do you want?" she asks.

"Where *are* you?"

"Home, but why do you even—"

I realize I'm probably talking too loud and cup my hand over the phone and say quieter, "What's the address?"

"You don't know my address?"

"You know I don't remember things."

After exhaling an agitated breath, she gives me her address.

"Don't leave, I'll be there soon."

"Why? I don't under—"

I end the call.

From the Katonah train station, the drive to Kaitlin's house takes about ten minutes. She lives just outside of town, in a modest two-level house with a four-step stoop and a very small front yard. As far as I know, I've never been to this area, and yet it looks vaguely familiar. Is this how people with Alzheimer's feel? I try to stay calm, focused, but it's hard not to feel anxious.

Before I get out of my car, I glance around the area for any sign of the police or a stakeout. I don't know exactly what I'm looking for—I doubt this is like a movie and that there's a van parked nearby with high-tech surveillance equipment.

Deciding that the coast is clear, I get out and approach her front door, still looking around for anyone suspicious. There are no people on the streets, much less any cops, and the several cars parked nearby seem to have no one in them.

I ring the bell once and knock a few times.

She opens the door. She's in jeans and a white hoodie and glares at me angrily.

"I don't get what's going on," she says. "Why're you here?"

I enter, having to push by her a little. She doesn't close the door so I reach around her and close it. I hear a TV on in another room.

"Are you alone here?" I ask.

"You didn't ans—"

"Are you alone?"

"Yes."

"Good, we have to talk."

"I thought you didn't want to talk to me again. What happened to it's too dangerous? You even made me quit my job."

She's right about the dangerous part, but what choice do I have? This is urgent, somebody has a photo that could put us in jail for the rest of our lives, and I just have to hope and pray that her phone isn't tapped and the cops don't know I'm here.

"I know," I say, "but I doubt the cops have you on full surveillance. It sounds like you're at most a person of interest, not an actual suspect, so it's doubtful that cops got a go-ahead for a legal tap."

"Why are you even here?" she says. "I told you, it's over with us—forever."

"I have to show you something," I say. "Something bad."

"If you caught something it's not from me."

"It's not *that*."

We're still near the front door, and there are windows close by.

"Let's move further into the house," I say. "I don't feel comfortable."

We go into the kitchen. There's a table with four chairs, but we remain standing.

"This is so weird," she says. "I mean, that we're here again in the kitchen."

"What's weird about the kitchen?" I ask.

"What do you think? This is where it happened."

"Where what happened?"

"Seriously?"

"You mean, where I—?"

"Where you killed my father. Yes."

I try to imagine the scene—the struggle, the screaming, the blood. But of course I can't remember an event in a house where, to my knowledge, I've never been. But, unlike when I was in the car, approaching the house, I can't deny that *something* about being here feels familiar. It feels like déjà vu, but maybe it's just my mind, teasing me. I'm having this feeling because I feel like I *should* have it; it isn't real.

"Seriously," she says. "How can you forget where I live? You've been here so many times."

"I have?"

"If you're not fucking with me, I really think you should go to a doctor, a *brain* doctor," she says. "Maybe this has to do with that tumor you had, not the accident. Or maybe—"

"Look, we have a problem—a *big* problem."

On my phone, I show her the photo I received.

"What is it?"

"Look closer."

She squints.

"Oh my God." Her eyes have widened. "Who took that?"

"I have no fucking idea. I thought you might know."

"How would I—?"

"You tell me."

Now her eyes narrow. "Whoa, what's going on here? Are you, like, *accusing* me of something?"

"No, I just want to know the truth about everything you know."

"I don't know any more than you do!"

"Well, I hope *that's* not true."

She shakes her head, "Sorry, but if you don't trust me, there's nothing I can do about that."

As she tries to turn away, I grab both of her shoulders, shifting her back toward me.

"You're fucking lying to me," I say, spraying saliva. "I know it."

"Are you going to kill me too?" she snaps back. "Is that your plan? You wanna get rid of me? Am I just like baggage now?"

I'm holding her shoulders much harder than I intended, hard enough to hurt her.

What the hell am I doing?

I release my grip immediately.

"I'm so sorry," I say. "I don't know why I did that. I…I'm not myself lately. That's what I'm trying to explain to you. I…I need your help, Kaitlin."

"I don't know what you want from me."

"I just want you to be honest with me," I say. "We're in this together obviously. I've been honest with you about my memory issues. If you're holding back on me about anything, it can get both of us killed. So I need you to just be smart and think about that."

She's giving me a different look now. I seem to be reaching her.

She sits at the kitchen table. I sit across from her.

Then she says, "There's only one person I can think of. But I thought…I mean I *know* I can trust him, so maybe I'm just being crazy."

"Who is he?"

I want to shake the information out of her, but I keep my cool.

"I don't know if I should really be saying anything about…I mean, I really thought I could trust him." She looks away for a moment, then looks back. "I've known him forever, he's basically my best friend. I've always been able to talk to him about everything and he knows all about what was going on with my father. You know…the abuse and all that."

"What's his name, Kaitlin?"

"Justin," she says like it's obvious. "You know, the older guy from Goldens Bridge? I've mentioned him to you so many times before…Oh, I guess you forgot that too." She shakes her head in frustration.

"How old is he?" I ask.

"Like twenty-eight—not *old* old like you, but still old. But I don't believe he'd actually *do* something like this. I mean, I guess he can be obsessive sometimes, like showing up at my house or texting me nonstop, but I don't think he'd—"

"Does he know about me and you?"

"Yes, and that's something I *didn't* tell you, so I can't blame you for forgetting, or not remembering, or whatever you want to call it. I told him once just because I thought, I don't know, it would convince him that I'm not into him? He's my friend, that's all, but sometimes he's wanted more. Actually, I feel sorry for him, you know? He lives by himself, I don't know where he gets money. The only reason he popped into my head now is when you showed me that picture I thought, maybe he resents you? I don't know if he sent it or not, I swear to God I don't. But if somebody followed us when we buried my father's body it could've been him. I mean, he's followed me before."

I'm angry at her for lying to me initially, and for all I know she's still lying. But getting emotional and accusing her seems like the wrong way to go. I'm still in the dark about most of my life and if I push away the few people who know my situation, who's left?

"Let's take a drive," I say.

Goldens Bridge is about a half hour from Katonah. In another lifetime, Laura and I used to drive this way when visiting our friends Mary and Roger at their lake house in Mahopac in the same area. I wonder what Mary and Roger are doing in *this* life, if they're still together, or even alive. There are so many friends and acquaintances I haven't even checked up on, maybe because I haven't had a chance to, or maybe because on some level, I'm afraid to. I'm learning that when you're thrust into living another version of your life there are some things you're better off not knowing.

During the whole ride, Kaitlin and I barely speak. Actually, the only words exchanged other than directions are when Kaitlin says, mainly to herself, "I can't believe we're actually doing this. This is so crazy."

I ignore her, watching the road.

When we approach the area where this Justin lives, I say, "Okay, you guide me from here."

"Keep going straight," she says.

We go through the main part of town, then, a few minutes later, we're in a rural area.

"Okay," she says, "make the next left right here."

We pass an occasional house and then it's mostly woods.

After maybe another mile, she says, "Slow down, it's that road right over there."

It's not really a road, it's more like a long, unpaved driveway. I drive along it into the woods and it seems to be going nowhere.

"Are you sure this is—"

"There it is," she says. "I told you he's weird."

What she'd told me was that he was her best friend. Basically. Then that he was "obsessive." Now he's "weird." What's next?

Up ahead to the right is a small, dilapidated gray house. Many shingles are hanging off or missing. There's a rickety-looking front porch with a broken railing. A red pickup is parked on a stretch of gravel.

I pull up in front of the house and cut the engine. I think I see a curtain move inside the house, on the second floor.

Then I say to Kaitlin, "Did he ever say anything to you about owning a gun or any other weapons?"

"Why're you even *asking* that?"

"Gee, well, the guy's been threatening me, and he has a photo, or pho*tos*, that could send us to jail for the rest of our lives."

"*Us*? Why us? I didn't do anything. You killed my father, not me."

"You're an accessory. You helped me bury the body."

"That's because you forced me to."

"Can you prove that?"

She has her phone out.

"Put that away."

"I'm calling the cops. I'm not getting into *more* trouble because of you."

"I said put it the fuck away."

Recognizing the seriousness in my tone, she pockets the phone again.

"Look, I'm not trying to scare you or intimidate you," I say.

"Yeah, sure you're not," she says.

"I'm just trying to be rational and logical. The fact is—whether we like or not—both of us are involved in this now, and, yes, from a legal standpoint that includes you."

"I didn't do anything!"

"Actually you did, and if I go down, you go down with me. That's the bad news. The good news is I'm not going down. This is what I do for a living—I get criminals off. If you listen to me, do everything I tell you to do, trust me, we'll get through this."

She seems to be absorbing all of this. A long time goes by. Maybe just thirty seconds, but it feels much longer.

"Fine," she finally says. "I'll do what you say, but after this, I never want to see you or talk to you ever again."

"Deal." I open the door a crack and say, "Stay behind me."

"You crazy?" she says. "I'm not going in there. The guy's been practically stalking me."

Her best friend.

"You have to come with me. You know him and I don't."

"We're probably just wasting our time coming here. I shouldn't have even told you about him."

"Well, you did. And even if you hadn't, we'd have to deal with him sometime."

I get out of the car. Reluctantly, she gets out too, breathing heavily.

As we approach the house, our shoes crunching the gravel, I know we're taking a risk, possibly an unnecessary risk. I have no idea what we're getting into, how unstable this guy might be. But what's the alternative? Wait for another anonymous message to arrive? Watch my life unravel even more than it already has and do nothing to stop it from unraveling further?

I press the doorbell, but it doesn't seem to work, so I knock a few times. I don't hear any movement inside.

"Maybe he's not here," Kaitlin says.

"He's here." I continue to bang on the door. "Come on, open up, Justin, we know you're here. We need to talk. Right now."

Finally I hear footsteps, heavy ones, then the door opens and I see Justin, I guess. He's taller than me, maybe six one, and stocky, like he could've played football or wrestled in high school. His longish, wavy hair is messy and it looks like he hasn't shaved in several days. He's in jeans, work boots and a dark hoodie with paint splattered on it. His eyes are glassy, like he's high.

"Yeah?"

I'm not sure where I've heard his voice before, but I know I've heard it somewhere. It sounds so familiar, but I don't think I've seen him before.

"I guess you know who I am," I say, hoping for a quick confession.

He studies me for a few seconds, then says, "Yeah, you're the old guy Kaitlin's been—" He notices that Kaitlin is next to me. "Wow, you're here too."

He pats down the sides of his hair, as if trying to look handsomer.

"Have you been texting me or not?" I ask.

"I dunno what you're talkin' about," he says. Then he says to Kaitlin, "Are you seriously *with* this old dude?"

"I'm not with anybody," Kaitlin says.

"Look it's up to you if you want to admit it or not," I say to Justin, "but it doesn't really matter. I'm an attorney, you might already know that. If I tell the police what you're doing they can use reverse encryption software to confirm your identity, and harassment and possible attempted extortion are serious crimes. You can go to jail for at least ten years, maybe longer."

Most of what I'm saying is total crap, but I'm hoping it frightens him.

Unfortunately, he seems unfazed.

With a devious half-smile, he says, "You really expect me to believe you're going to the cops? After what you two did? After what I *saw* you two do? And so what if you're a big-time lawyer? That just means you have way more to lose than me."

"So you admit it," I say. "It's been you all along."

"I'm not admitting anything." Then he says to Kaitlin, "I still can't believe you're with him instead of me. You don't know what you're missing, baby."

"I'm not your *baby*," Kaitlin says, "and I'm not *with* him. I can't believe you're doing this, Justin. I thought we were friends."

"I told you I wasn't gonna stay in your friend zone."

How did I get in the middle of this?

"Enough!" I yell, much louder than I intend. I'm clenching my fists, trying to restrain myself. "What do you want?"

"I want Kaitlin," he says.

"You can't have me."

"I know you don't mean that, baby."

"Stop calling me baby. I'm not your fuckin' baby!"

"Lemme handle this, okay?" I say to Kaitlin.

"Fine."

She backs up a couple of feet, but remains on the porch.

Then I say to Justin, "Look, I don't know what your end-game is here by harassing me, sending me those texts, but I'm taking a wild guess here—you need money. Am I right or am I right?"

I gaze past him, looking into the house. I can see an old couch, a coffee table strewn with beer cans, pizza boxes and other garbage. It's not hard to deduce what his life is like.

"Well, I have money," I say, "which means this situation is

very resolvable. How about ten thousand dollars and you stop harassing us. Deal?"

I'm willing to pay much more to make him go away. Hell, my money doesn't feel like my money anyway; it feels like a pile of chips I won in a poker game.

"I don't want your money. I want Kaitlin."

Now I know where I've heard his voice before—it was when I was dying, in the parking lot in the snow. The voice I heard—*I saw you, Steven Blitz*—was *his* voice. I received a text that *he* sent with the same message, but how did I know this happened in my other life? Was it actually *in* my other life or, at that moment, did strands of my lives merge?

"You okay?" he asks.

I realize I must have a very strange, far-off look.

"I'm fine," I say. "I…I don't think you're being reasonable."

"I told you what I want," he says. "Kaitlin has to marry me or I'm going to the cops."

"Marry you?" Kaitlin says. "Are you out of your fuckin' mind? I'm not marrying anybody, probably ever, and especially not you."

My approach clearly isn't working. And hell, even if I get him to agree to accept a payoff, how can I trust that he'll stick to his word? How do I know he'll really go away?

I lunge toward him and grab his neck. With strength I'm surprised I have, I force him back into the house, then lift him up against the wall with so much force that a mirror that was hanging nearby crashes onto the floor, scattering glass.

"Let him go!" Kaitlin screams at me. "Let him go!"

I don't let go. I lift him higher, holding him about a foot off the ground. I don't know how I'm doing any of this because he must weigh at least twenty pounds more than me. I'm pushing into his neck now, with so much force I can feel bone. I'm just trying to scare him, so he has something to think about before he makes new demands or threats. I can see his fear, his weakness, but it doesn't make me let go. It makes me squeeze harder. He's flailing, trying to grab my neck, but he can't reach it. He's scratching at my neck meekly, trying to fight back, but without much strength. It feels good to be in control for a change—to *do* something, rather than merely react.

Kaitlin is still screaming, but all I keep thinking is, *This isn't enough—I haven't scared him enough yet*. I keep squeezing, harder, until he stops gasping and his body goes limp. I'm still pushing and squeezing, feeling like I can crush his neck between my hands. Finally, I let go and his body collapses onto the floor.

"Oh my God," Kaitlin says. "You killed him. You fuckin' killed him."

Looking down at the limp body, I'm startled, like I just woke up from a nightmare. But I'm not shocked by what I did, I'm shocked by how I feel.

I just killed a man and I feel normal. I feel fine.

FOURTEEN

"You didn't have to kill him," Kaitlin says. "He wasn't going to hurt you."

"It was an accident."

"It wasn't an accident. You wanted to kill him. You could've stopped, but you didn't."

It's difficult to argue with this.

"I can't believe you did it *again*," Kaitlin says. "And you said you can take care of things? You wanted me to *trust* you? Yeah, right. You're crazy. You're *insane*."

"That isn't true," I say, mainly to myself. "I know this isn't who I am. I'm not a killer. I'm a good man. I know I'm a good man."

"Who're you talking to?" Kaitlin asks.

"I wouldn't do this," I say. "I only did it because of the situation I'm in, but it wasn't my *choice* to be in this situation, was it?"

"Wait, so now you're gonna tell me you don't remember doing it? Or what story are you gonna have this time?"

I turn to face her.

"I didn't intend to kill him," I say. "You saw what happened. I was just trying to scare him, that's all."

"Seriously? You've killed two people now and you *still* think you're not a killer?"

She has a point. I could feel blameless for killing her father because I wasn't actually there, committing the murder, at least not *this* me, but how can I rationalize killing Justin? I was *here*. I did it.

"Under ordinary circumstances I wouldn't have killed your father either."

"No, it was just like this time," she says. "I saw that look in your eyes—the same anger, the same sickness. You got caught up and you wouldn't stop. You wouldn't stop." Her eyes widen as fear grips her. She's probably realizing that being here, alone, in a secluded house, with a man whom she's witnessed kill two people, including her father, might not be the safest place to be. I notice her gaze shift briefly, back toward the front door, as if plotting a getaway.

"Don't try it," I say.

A long pause, then she bolts toward the door. I grab her before she gets there.

She screams, screeching. "Let go of me! Let go!"

I'm not concerned about anyone hearing her—the house is too secluded. Still, I need her to calm down.

"Don't kill me!" she screams. "Please. I don't wanna die!"

Murdering her, to silence her potential testimony, is what any real killer would do. If one of my psychopathic clients like, say, Jeffery Hammond killed someone and there was a witness nearby, he would undoubtedly kill the witness to save himself. He wouldn't hesitate—he'd just do it.

But I'm not like Jeffery Hammond. This version of me has made some bad decisions, but I'm still essentially the person I was in my pre-1998 trajectory. Killing isn't my nature—I don't fantasize about killing or need to kill to satisfy twisted urges. I'm not *sick*. Despite what I've done, I'm a decent, moral man. Anyone can kill, but not everyone is a killer.

"I won't kill you or hurt you," I say. "I promise."

"Why should I believe anything you say to me?"

She makes another good point—I haven't exactly been reliable lately.

"You have no choice," I say. "Your situation is the same as before you got here—it's actually worse. Now you're an accessory to two murders."

"Bullshit. I didn't do anything."

"You're the one who knows Justin, you're more connected to him than I am. If a jury was trying your case I guarantee you, you'd be convicted."

Her eyes are bloodshot and glassy—she's on the verge of losing it. "Why do you keep doing this? Why do you keep hurting me, ruining my life? Why won't you just leave me alone?"

I feel bad for making her upset. See, this proves I'm not a psychopath. A psychopath wouldn't feel anything, but I definitely do.

Resting a hand on her shoulder, I say, "I'm trying to change things, to make things better, the way things should be, but it's complicated—more complicated than you can understand."

"What does that even mean?"

"If I told you everything, you'd never believe me, but let's just say that while it seems like your father and Justin are dead, they're not actually dead, not everywhere. Somewhere else they're very much alive right now, and we're in other places too."

She looks at me like I'm a stranger.

"Wow, you really are nuts. Like seriously fucking nuts."

"Trust me, everything's going to be okay."

She swats my hand away. "Really? Stop telling me to trust you. And things are *never* gonna be okay. You killed two people, you killed my fucking *father*. The cops are already on my ass about that, and now what're we gonna do with *him*?" She gestures with her chin toward Justin. "We can't just leave him here like that?"

My mind is churning. Then I say, "This is a good thing, that

Justin's dead. I mean, I'm upset that he's dead—obviously I didn't *want* this to happen, but now that he's dead at least we don't have to worry about him blackmailing us anymore…Does he have any other friends?"

"Who?" Kaitlin asks.

"Justin. Do people come here? I mean regularly?"

"No, I told you he is…*was*…a total loser. I was one of his only friends, and I wouldn't even call us friends."

Not now, you wouldn't.

"Okay, we'll leave him here for now and come back to-morrow."

"I'm not coming back here," Kaitlin says.

"Yes, you are—yes, *we* are. D'you want to spend the rest of your life in jail? We'll bury him next to your father at Pound Ridge, but we'll need shovels. I'll buy them later or tomorrow morning. We could look around here for a shovel, but that's a bad idea, to leave more evidence than we already have at a crime scene. We're going to have to wipe everything down as it is—we can't leave any prints or hairs or anything behind."

"You seriously want to just leave him here," Kaitlin says, "like *this*?"

She makes a good point—leaving him sprawled here, in plain sight, is a dumb idea.

There's a closet nearby, in the short hallway leading to the living area. I open it and see there's room. Then I return and kneel in front of Justin and remove his cell phone from his front pocket.

"You're stealing his phone?" Kaitlin asks.

"There's a photo, at least one photo, of us on it, remember? Hopefully he didn't print any out or send them to friends."

"I told you, he doesn't have friends."

I think I hear something from outside. I part the dusty curtain and peer through the dirty window, but no one is there. It was probably just the wind.

"I hope you're right," I say.

I turn off Justin's phone and put it in my pocket.

"We'll bury it with his body tomorrow. Come on, I need your help."

"I'm not touching him."

"Don't think about it, just do it. Forget it's a body. Pretend it's a piece of wood."

She smiles knowingly.

"What is it?" I ask.

"You really don't remember? That's exactly what you said when you wanted me to help you drag my dad…into his grave. 'Forget it's a body, pretend it's a piece of wood.' "

"I did?"

"Wow," she says, "you really need help. Maybe you even belong in a mental institution."

I grab Justin by his shoulders and drag him to near the closet.

"Okay," I say, "there isn't much room so we have to stand him up. Let's go."

She helps me lift him—well, his torso.

"He's fucking heavy," she says.

"Use your legs. Come on, you can do it."

"I can't."

"Yes you can."

It's a struggle, but we're finally able to get the body upright. Then I take over and maneuver the body between some boxes and the side of the wall. I'm staring right at Justin's face—his wide-open eyes and slacking jaw exposing crooked bottom teeth. Something brown is stuck between two of the teeth— pepperoni maybe. I shut the door.

I'm breathing hard and sweating. "Okay, we can go now."

"What about fingerprints and all that stuff?" Kaitlin asks.

"We'll take care of all that when we come back tomorrow afternoon. There's no point in doing it now because we'll only contaminate the scene more when we get the body out of here. I'll bring cleaner and washcloths. Come on, let's go."

We return to the car. I put Justin's phone into the glove compartment, then drive away. It's a relief, knowing that Justin is dead, and that he can't harass me and blackmail me anymore.

Kaitlin, looking away, staring out the window, says, "I have a bad feeling about all of this. A really bad feeling. Something awful is gonna happen and my instincts are never wrong."

We drive all the way back to Katonah and I drop her at her house without saying another word.

"Let's move."

It's after dinner. Lilly's already in bed and Laura and I are in the living room, on the couch, watching the talking heads on CNN discuss the latest on the resolution of the nuclear crisis and what it means for the world. Laura glances over at me, confused.

"Move? Move where?"

"Anywhere," I say. "Let's just go somewhere. What do we have going on in Westchester anyway? We have no real roots here."

"What do you mean? We've lived here for years."

"Okay, so enough is enough. We need change, rejuvenation. Let's do it—we can afford it. California, or Europe. You always wanted to live in Paris."

"Paris? Since when did I want to live in Paris?"

We'd talked about moving to Paris during a vacation there in 2007, but that vacation probably never happened.

"I mean metaphorically," I say. "You've always had an ex-pat, adventurous side, you travelled to Guatemala and Belize."

"That was right after college," she says. "We have careers now, Lilly's in school…"

"Come on, people do it all the time, people with bigger families than ours. It's just a matter of working out the details, then we can have new lives."

"What's wrong with our lives now?"

Thinking about Justin's body, decomposing in that closet, I say, "Nothing, of course. I mean we have great lives now. I think it's important not to be complacent, though, just because things are great. I think being in a new city could be invigorating for all of us, especially Lilly. I mean, don't take this the wrong way, but you've spent practically your entire life in this house, I think it would be great for Lilly to see more of the world. In Paris, we could go on trips to England, Italy, Spain, Greece. Imagine the experiences she could have, it could affect the rest of her life."

"What about work?"

"We have enough money. We don't have to think about work for a while, maybe ever, and I'm getting a little burned out anyway."

"You are? Since when?"

"The feeling's been building—for a long time. I can consult or just take off for a while and then figure out my next move."

"And what about me? I can't just leave in the middle of the school year."

"People do it all the time. Let's just do it, take a leap."

"I have to admit, it sounds exciting," she says. "And maybe, maybe it's not so crazy. You're right, I've been in this house forever and some change would be good. It's just so sudden, and I can't believe I'm saying this, but okay, I promise I'll think about it, okay?"

I wasn't planning to suggest moving; I just blurted it out. But now that I said it I'm convinced it's the best move for all of us. I already lost Laura once, when she wanted a divorce and, the way things are going, I'm on the verge of losing her again. Getting a fresh start, far away from Westchester, and the buried bodies and my other secrets, feels like our best chance.

Later, in bed, Laura's on her laptop, researching Paris, saying, "What about the language?"

"What about it?"

"We don't speak French."

"We'll get tutors."

"Where are we going to live?"

"We'll rent first, or do Airbnb."

"What's that?"

Oops.

"I mean stay at a B and B, or hotel till we find a place. But eventually we can buy."

"Buy an apartment in Paris?"

"Why not? We don't have to rush into anything, but we'll take our time and find a big apartment with a view of the Seine. Imagine walking Wasabi along the Seine every morning. We'll make new friends, Lilly will make new friends, we'll all have new lives."

She starts searching for apartments, showing me pics, and I can tell she's getting more excited about the idea.

When I join her in bed, I already recognize a big change in her. She's ravenous, like she can't get enough of me, but it's more than that. There's a connection between us, a bond, unlike anything I've ever experienced with her. Even when we first met, it never felt like this.

Afterward, with our naked bodies intertwined, she whispers: "Okay, I'm in."

✻

I wake up invigorated, relieved, light, but I know I can't relax yet. Although I can see a finish line, I know how quickly a finish line can turn into a brick wall. I won't feel safe until Justin's body is buried and I'm on a plane to Paris.

I drive about twenty minutes to the Cross River Shopping Center, a strip mall I've been to often. There was never a hardware store there before—but there is now. I purchase two large shovels, using cash so there's no record of the transaction. While I'm aware that there is video surveillance footage of me purchasing the shovels that could be damning in a trial, I remind myself that I don't have to worry because, in all likelihood, there won't be a trial. The bodies won't be discovered and I'll be living a new, happy life in Paris.

Then, as I'm pulling out of the lot, still looking in my rearview, I see him.

Jeffery Hammond is driving the car directly behind me—a black Honda. It's definitely him and, naturally, I'm not expecting this. We're about seventy miles from Manhattan in a small Westchester town. There's no way to rationalize this, there can't be any random reason why he'd be here.

I hit the brakes and my car jolts to a stop. This must alarm Hammond because he puts his car in reverse and speeds backward away from me. Another car, pulling out of a spot, has to stop short to avoid a collision. I do a three-point turn to follow Hammond, but by the time I get my car facing in the opposite direction, Hammond is already speeding away.

I want to ignore the panic I'm experiencing, convince myself that it means nothing, but I can't. There's no logical reason why Hammond would be here, other than that he's following me. But why? Things got a little awkward at the studio yesterday, but to come all the way to Northern Westchester?

I exit the lot and head home. My hands are moistening the steering wheel, my heart is pounding so hard it's making my whole body shake. There's another possibility I have to consider—that I hallucinated. Although I'm sure I saw Hammond and no one else, after everything I've gone through, can I really trust my perception? How do I know, really *know*, that something's real, that it's *happening*, simply because I think I experience it? How do I know there was actually a car behind me, no less a car driven by Hammond? How do I know my perception wasn't skewed?

This idea, weirdly, provides comfort. Whether it happened or didn't happen, I'm going to go on with my life, telling myself that it didn't.

When I get home, I leave the shovels in the trunk for this evening, then call a few local real estate agents and set up times for them to come to the house. I text Laura to let her know and a few seconds later she calls me.

"I can't believe we're actually doing this."

"Well, believe it," I say. "Next week we'll be in Paris."

"I can't leave till May or June."

"That's fine, we can aim for June. I can go earlier to get the Paris place set up and then you and Lilly can join."

"The Paris place," she says. "I love the way that sounds."

After calling more agents, I call Terrence at my office.

"Hey," Terrence says, "I was going to check in later to see how things are going."

"Everything's great, thanks for asking," I say. "And I'm sorry for the scene I caused the other day."

"Hey, it's okay. The main thing is that you're all right. Take all the time you need."

"That's sort of what I want to talk to you about," I say.

I explain to him that I've decided I want to "phase out" of working at the firm, and "pursue other opportunities." He's surprised and asks me if I'm sure this is what I want, and when I say I'm positive he's very supportive.

"If this is what you want, I support the decision one hundred percent and I'm sure Elizabeth will as well. We'll make the transition as easy for you as possible, I promise," he says. "By the way, I want to thank you."

"Thank me for what?"

"After our talk the other day, I did some soul searching and I broke it off with Ashley. You were right, my judgment was poor. Also, I'm sorry if I was a little harsh on you, I know you've been through a lot lately, with your surgery and then the accident, and I've been feeling bad. I should've been more understanding."

"Don't feel bad," I say. "It's all my fault. I know how crazy I must've sounded, but I'm working it out, and it's all good now. I look forward to working out all the details with you and Elizabeth."

When I end the call with Terrence, I feel energized. This is really happening—soon my new life in Paris will be a reality.

I spend the rest of the day browsing Paris real estate listings. One apartment in particular grabs me—a three-bedroom flat in the 6th arrondissement, not far from Saint Germaine and Luxembourg Gardens. It has a large windowed kitchen, high ceilings, and a balcony with a view of the Seine. It's easy to imagine walking Lilly to a neighborhood school every morning where she'll play happily with her new Parisian friends, and in the evenings Laura and I could leave Lilly home with a sitter and have candlelit dinners and take long, romantic walks.

I contact the broker for the apartment, who tells me the

apartment is available immediately. I send a non-refundable deposit and the flat is ours.

On her way home from work, Laura picks up Lilly from a playdate.

"Everybody sit on the couch," I say, "I want to show you something."

With Laura and Lilly sitting on either side of me, I show them the pics on my phone of our new apartment.

"Oh my God, it's gorgeous," Laura says.

"And it's all ours," I say.

Laura looks at me. "What do you mean, *ours*?"

"I put a deposit on it," I say. "I know I should've checked with you first, but I wanted to surprise you and if you don't like it, it's no big deal, we can find another place."

"Are you kidding me?" Laura's face brightens. "I love it."

She hugs and kisses me.

"Where's Paris?" Lilly asks.

"It's in France," I say.

"I know where that is," Lilly says proudly.

"Our family's going on an adventure," Laura says. "In the summer, our whole family is moving."

"What about my friends?"

"They can visit us. But the most important thing is you'll be with Mommy and Daddy."

Lilly seems sad, then asks, "Can Wasabi come?"

"Of course Wasabi can come," Laura says.

"Okay!" Lilly smiles.

Lilly goes upstairs to play and Laura and I can't stop talking about Paris and the future.

"I have so many decorating ideas already," Laura says. "I haven't had a chance to decorate my own space from scratch for years. What do you think of these cabinets?"

She shows me the display on her laptop.

"Love them," I say.

"Me too," she says. "This is like a dream."

The doorbell rings.

"Who can that be?" Laura asks.

"No idea," I say.

Humming bars from *Que Sera Sera*, I go to the front door and look through the peephole. Two men are there.

"Can I help you?"

"John Delaney," one of them says, like this should mean something to me.

"Sorry, who?"

"It's me, John Delaney with the Bedford Hill Police Department," he says. "Can we come in please?"

FIFTEEN

John Delaney is about my age, in a button-down shirt tucked into slacks. Next to him, but hanging back a little, is a younger guy in a sport jacket.

"Hey, Steve," John says, still acting like he knows me.

He *does* seem familiar, but I have no idea why.

"Yes?" I say, sounding appropriately concerned and confused, hoping this isn't about what I think it's about. *Coincidences happen*, I tell myself.

"I'm afraid there's a situation we need to discuss."

"Situation? What situation?"

Laura has approached from behind me. "What's going on here?" Then she sees the cops. "Oh, hi, John, how are you?"

"Pretty good, Laura."

I want to know how Laura knows this cop, how *I* know this cop, but I know asking will make me sound crazy.

"This is my partner, Raymond Ortiz," John says, "I'm not sure you've met."

"We haven't," Laura says, "how are you?"

"Nice to meet you," Raymond says, but he sounds businesslike.

"What's this about?" Laura asks.

"Yeah," I say. "That's a really good question."

John and Raymond are looking at me, but it feels like they're trying to see into me.

"Can we just come in to talk?" John asks. "I think it would be better if we sat down to talk."

"Sure," Laura says. As they enter, she adds, "Is everything okay? Is your family okay?"

"My family's fine," John says.

We go into the living room area where John and Raymond sit on the couch and Laura and I sit on chairs across from them. My palms are hot and sweaty. I want to rub them on my pants legs, but I don't.

"This is about your babysitter, Kaitlin Willet," John says.

"*Ex*-babysitter," Laura says. "She quit yesterday."

"Right, she told us that," John says. "Did she tell you her father Dennis Willet is missing?"

Although I'm looking at Laura, in my peripheral vision I can see the detectives watching me.

"What?" Laura says, alarmed. "Oh my God, no. When? How long has he been gone?"

"Since last Wednesday," John says.

"How is that possible?" Laura asks.

"His office got concerned at the end of last week," John says. "She said she thought he might be travelling, but we haven't found any evidence of that."

"It's true, they had an odd relationship," Laura says. "We've been concerned about her father actually."

"Concerned how?" Raymond asks.

"She never told us any specifics, but we suspected there was trouble there."

"Did she tell you anything recently about her father?"

"No," Laura says. "I mean, not in the past few weeks."

"Why are you here?" I blurt out. "What does this have to do with us?"

These seem like appropriate questions any innocent man would ask.

John and Raymond exchange looks.

"That's a good question," Laura says. "What *does* this have to do with us?"

Then John says to me, "Maybe you should tell her."

My heart stops beating for a moment and part of me wishes it stopped permanently.

"Tell me *what*?" Laura asks, catching on that this won't be good news.

"Yeah," I say. "Tell her what?"

"Okay, if that's the way you want to do this," John says. Then, to Laura, he adds, "This isn't the way I want to do this, but we've learned that Kaitlin and Steven were—"

"It's not true," I say to Laura.

Laura looks devastated, like she just learned about a death in her family, and in a way she has.

"What?" Laura's already seething. *"What's not true?"*

It's awful seeing her this way, and I know exactly how she feels because I felt the same way when she told me about her and Beth.

"It's not true," I say. "There's nothing going on, I swear."

I feel justified, and entirely truthful, because it's true that I, the *I* who's here right now, did not have an affair with Kaitlin.

"Then what the hell's going on?" Laura says to the detectives.

I haven't seen her this enraged since…well, since *Other* Laura asked me for a divorce.

"Nothing," I say. "Really."

"We talked to a few of Kaitlin's friends who all corroborated the same story," John says. "And Kaitlin herself just confirmed it."

Is this true or are they just trying to force a confession from me? If it's true, and Kaitlin did talk to them, what else did she tell them? Did she tell them about killing her father and where the body's buried? Did she tell them about Justin?

"You son of a bitch," Laura says to me. "And the other day, you lied, you lied to my fucking face, making me feel like I was just paranoid, crazy. And what about all this Paris bullshit? Renting an apartment today? Getting us excited about a future that doesn't exist? You were trying to get us to move to Paris with you? Why? So you can have more affairs there?"

"No, Paris was about *us*," I say. "And this isn't what you think it is. I swear. There's so much you don't know."

I know my words are useless now. There's nothing I can say to fix this.

"What's this about Paris?" Raymond asks.

"He suddenly wanted us to move to Paris," Laura says.

"If you try to leave the country right now, we're gonna have a serious problem," Raymond says.

"Really?" I say. "Do you have a warrant for my arrest? Can you charge me with any crime?"

Raymond and John exchange looks, knowing they can't win this argument.

Then John says, "You're a person of interest."

"You can't prevent me from leaving the country without pressing charges, and if you could, you would've already. Face it, you have nothing on me because there *is* nothing on me. This is just attempted intimidation."

"Let's get back to last Wednesday," John says to me. "Can you tell us your whereabouts, please?"

Last Wednesday I was in an alternate reality. I can't give him an honest answer because I don't know what the honest answer is.

"Wait," Laura says, shaking her head and squeezing her eyes shut in an exaggerated way. "Let me get this straight. You're here because you think my husband has something to do... something to do with what happened to Kaitlin's father?"

"No one said anything happened to him," Raymond said.

"Your whereabouts last Wednesday," John says to me. "Can you please tell us where you were from the time you woke up till the time you went to sleep?"

The silence seems to last a minute, but it's probably only a few seconds.

"I don't know," I say.

"It was only last week," John says. "You must remember some—"

"I don't," I say. "I was in an accident, I had severe memory loss."

"You said your memory's fine." Laura's sneering at me.

"Well, it's not," I say. "I really can't remember anything from that day here because I didn't experience that day here."

"You know what I think?" Raymond says. "I think you're full of shit."

"Tell me about it," Laura says.

"Look, I'm having this conversation here out of respect," John says, "because we know each other and our daughters know each other. But if I have to take you in to the precinct I will."

"I won't be able to tell you anything there either," I say.

"Look, I know you're a lawyer," John says. "So if this is about not talking to us without a lawyer present feel free to—"

"I don't need a lawyer," I say. "Because I have no information about any of this, I can't incriminate myself. I mean, to be guilty of a crime, a person has to exist, right? Isn't that a prerequisite? I'm telling you the honest-to-God truth. I don't have memory of that day…specifically."

"Specifically?" John says. "What the hell does that mean?"

"It means I can't tell you where I was last Wednesday because I wasn't here…in this reality, in this world."

"What the fuck?" Raymond says.

"Yeah," Laura says, "what the fuck?"

"Sorry, I'm lost too," John says. "You *weren't in this world*? Then where were you? In the city? Out of state? Travelling? You had to be somewhere, so where were you?"

"I was somewhere, but I wasn't *here*. I was…well, I was living another version of my life."

"Another version of your life?" John says. "The hell's that supposed to mean?"

"It means he's been living a double life," Laura says, "lying to my fucking face."

"No," I say. "That's not what it means. It means…it means I was living another life *literally* before I got here. In another dimension, I guess."

John and Raymond exchange looks. Raymond is smiling with one corner of his mouth, shaking his head.

Then John says, "So how'd you get here? In a spaceship?"

Now Raymond actually laughs. Laura remains glaring.

"I don't expect anyone to believe it," I say. "That's why I haven't told anyone about it yet, not even my wife…" I look at Laura… "and she deserves the truth. So this is it—the absolute truth."

"Okay," John says, "let's cut the bullshit and—"

"I died last weekend," I say. "I know this sounds ridiculous, insane, and I can't prove it because I don't have access to my dead body, or *that* dead body, but please just hear me out. I wasn't in an accident, I was stabbed in a parking lot."

"Jesus Christ," Laura says, "again with that parking lot bullshit? You're going to tell me you were in a glass ball again too?"

"Glass ball?" John asks.

"Yes, I was in a glass ball," I say. "That's what it felt like anyway—like I was watching myself, through a rapidly spinning glass ball until the ball broke up into bits and vanished. Then when I woke up in the hospital on Sunday morning I discovered that the entire world had changed. The date was the same, and some events seemed to match up, for example there had been a snowstorm the night I died too, but then I discovered that there were a lot of differences too. For example, in my world Donald Trump is President of the United States."

This gets another snicker from Raymond.

"It's the fucking truth," I say. "And there, in this other world, on September eleventh, 2001, the Twin Towers were destroyed by terrorists. I can give you details—all the ones I remember anyway. Some of the hijackers' names, where they attended flight school—everything I remember that was reported in the news. I tried to report it to Senator Schumer's office, but they referred me to the FBI. If you want to take the case you could be heroes—these terrorists might be alive, planning other attacks on our country. Think of all the lives you could save. Oh, and there are other major changes too—too many to name, and I can spend the rest of my life comparing and I still won't get to the end of it. You don't have Facebook, but it's sort of like MyWorld, and Blockbuster went bankrupt and—"

"Okay," John says, "I've heard enough of this nuttiness."

"My personal life changed drastically too," I say. "For example, in my other life, believe it or not, Laura was cheating on me, and we didn't have our daughter, she didn't exist."

"*Me* cheating?" Laura said. "So this is what you do when you get caught cheating? You blame me? Talk about twisted. I always knew you were self-centered, but I never knew you were a full-blown narcissist."

"You were cheating on me with Beth," I say. "That friend you mentioned."

She looks shocked. "You seriously believe Beth and I are—"

"Not in this version of your life," I say. "But in another version, yes."

"Okay, enough." John is standing. "We're not interested in your marital problems, we're investigating a disappearance, and if you can't tell me—"

"See, I knew there was nothing I could possibly say to make you think I haven't lost my mind. Unless you experienced what I'm experiencing you'd never believe it. I still don't know why this happened to me, or how I wound up in this exact version of my life. See, because, for example what I've noticed is that all the changes in this world seemed to have started happening in early 1998. Before that point the worlds are exactly the—"

"Steven," John says. "This is the last time I'm going to—"

"I'm telling you the truth," I say. "I used to be like you—I thought death meant the end—but all of us have lives that coexist with our other lives and as long as the other lives continue, *you* continue. It has to do with our decisions. Every decision we make creates a new reality—what to eat for breakfast, to run or walk to make a bus. If you walk your life goes in one direction, if you run it goes in another, but both lives *continue*, so we all have infinite lives that coexist with the life we're experiencing, that we think is our actual life, but it's only an illusion."

"C'mon, John," Raymond says.

He tries to get by me, but I cut him off, blocking him.

"Listen to what I'm saying," I say. "The decision I made in January 1998 could've been innocuous. Maybe instead of having a piece of fruit for dessert one evening, I chose to have ice cream. This altered the course of reality for the person I purchased the ice cream from, perhaps delaying that person's day slightly, to cause the person to get into an accident later, killing that person, and thus altering the life of that person and that person's family. Don't you see? That one decision could've turned into a tsunami that altered the course of history to the extent that 9/11 didn't happen, but the Dirty Monday attacks did. See? One strand isn't necessarily better than another, it's just different. I'm wealthier in this strand and have a daughter I love, but I've made a lot of bad decisions too. I know this sounds insane, but I believe there are infinite versions of all of our lives happening simultaneously. When you have a feeling of déjà vu, it's because there are overlaps in the strands. For example, when I got to the bend in the road that night, I felt like I'd been there before, because I was having a simultaneous experience. Now, bear with me because this is where it gets really freaky—these overlaps create portals into the other strands that you enter into when you die. In my case, one of my strands got into a car accident, but another strand made a different decision and wound up getting stabbed at a gas station, so instead of dying like I should've, my life continued in the 1998 strand."

I feel manic and it must show, given the wide-eyed glares I'm getting from John, Raymond and Laura.

"I don't know what you're trying to do here," John says, "if you think this is amusing or if you're having medical issues, but you've wasted enough of our time."

"Think about the irony of it all," I say. "We all go through life feeling so powerless, but actually every decision each of us makes has the potential to change the course of the world, and maybe the universe."

Raymond follows John toward the front door.

"You'll hear from us again," John says.

"Wait, now I know!" I shout.

John and Raymond stop and turn back toward me.

"Know what?" John asks.

"How I know you."

"Our daughters went to the same day camp," Laura says.

"No, that's how we know each other in *this* strand." I say to John, "Seriously—it's all clicking now. I know why you look so familiar, it makes total sense. You were scruffier in the other strand, dressed slovenly, so I didn't make the connection right away. Where'd you get that watch?"

He's wearing a silver and gold Rolex.

"My watch?" he says. "It was my father's. What the hell does my watch—?"

"I bet he gave it to you before nineteen ninety-eight, am I right?"

His non-response tells me I am.

"See, I knew it. You were wearing that watch the other night."

"What other night?" He sounds fed up, near his breaking point.

"The night you killed me," I say. "It was you—in the parking lot with Kaitlin, the old version of Kaitlin. In the other strand you weren't a cop. You were a drunk fuckup in an abusive relationship with my babysitter, who wasn't my babysitter in that strand because I didn't have a child, but it makes sense because she's attracted to older guys and that might not be affected by the strands. Lemme guess—you made the decision to be a cop after nineteen ninety-eight." Again, I can tell I'm right. "See? That was the other strand. See the power of our decisions? In the other strand you probably decided not to be a cop, but you had the same personality. I bet you were a bully in school, got into a lot of fights. The version of you who stabbed me in the gut was a real asshole, so you must have some asshole and psycho in you, even if you do a good job of hiding it."

Shaking their heads, Raymond and John exit.

Holding the door open, I shout at their backs as they march away, "I have power now too. I can't predict the future exactly— I don't know tomorrow's lottery numbers, and there's free will and luck—but I know about the *nature* of people. Not only of you, detective, but of other potentially violent people. I know things other people don't!"

They get in their car and I watch them drive away.

When I return inside, Laura has left the living room. I hear her sobbing in the kitchen. I'm about to go in there, then reconsider. I'm not sure what I can say to her right now; it's better to give her some space.

I go upstairs to my office and, on my laptop, I check mail. The broker in Paris wrote me, letting me know that the apartment rental has been confirmed.

A moment later, Laura enters, glares at me with pure hatred, then says, "I want a divorce."

"Oh my God, this is wild," I say. "This is exactly how it happened the other time."

"What?" She sounds more angry than confused.

"In our other life," I say. "I was working on my laptop, and you came in, just the way you did now, and asked for a divorce. Except it was different then because you weren't taking your meds for your manic depression, the way you do now. But your tone—your tone is the same."

Not listening to me, she says, "You humiliated me and lied to my face, and that's it, I've had enough. I want you to move out tonight. Go stay with your brother."

"You said that the other time too! See? I *am* right about all of this."

"I'll say it once again," Laura says with her eyes closed. "I… want…you…to…move…out."

"This is ridiculous," I say. "I didn't actually do anything to hurt you, Laura, nothing I can control anyway. You have to believe me—I know what it's like to have our marriage end and I don't want to go through that again."

"Go, Steven. Now!"

"The last time I listened to you and left it didn't exactly go so well, and isn't the definition of insanity making the same mistake again and again and expecting a different result? Well, to prove to you that I'm *not* insane I'm not going anywhere."

"Fine," she says, "if you won't leave, I will."

She heads upstairs.

Following her, I say, "Where are you going? Wait, let me guess. To Beth's?"

"It's none of your business where I go."

"I think it is my business where my wife goes."

"Stay the fuck away from me."

She enters Lilly's room.

"Wait, what're you doing? You're not taking Lilly. Come on, Laura, let's just sit down and discuss this."

Laura wakes Lilly and tells her to pack a suitcase with her "favorite things" because they're leaving. Naturally Lilly's hysterical and Wasabi's barking like crazy. I'm mostly trying to calm Lilly down, assuring her that "all parents fight" and that everything is going to be okay. Then, while Laura is packing in the bedroom, I enter and lock the door so we can talk in private.

"What're you doing?" Laura says.

"Please, just hear me out," I say. "If you've ever loved me at all, hear me out."

"Unlock that door right now."

"Remember your promise to me."

"*My* promise?"

"That you'd always give me the benefit of the doubt, no matter what."

"Well, I lied," she says. "Like how that feels?"

"Didn't you hear anything I was saying down there?"

"About how you died?" Laura says. "About your *strands*?"

"It's all true."

"I can't believe you went to this extent, getting me so excited about Paris, believing we actually had a future."

"If you could just—"

"I can't believe what you've turned into," she says. "I was hoping after the accident you'd really changed—sometimes a near-death experience can do that to a person. But this is who you truly were all along—you're the sickest, most twisted man I've ever met, and I won't let you hurt me anymore."

"I'm not who you think I am, Laura. I'm not a cheater. I love you and I'll always love you if you love me!"

"Stop it! Stop hurting me!"

Lilly, thinking I'm actually hurting her mother, is banging on the door, yelling, "Don't hurt Mommy! Don't hurt Mommy!"

I let Lilly in, telling her, "I'm not hurting Mommy, see? Mommy's fine. I love Mommy."

"The fucking hell you do," Laura says.

I grab onto her arms with her facing me. I'm not squeezing her hard, but firmly enough to make the point that I don't want to let her go.

"*Please*. All I'm asking is that you give me a chance to prove to you that there is more going on here than you realize. If you've ever loved me at all, you know I'm a good person, that there's more to me than the sum of a few bad decisions I've made. In Paris, you'll see the real Steven Blitz. I know how crazy this all sounds, but please, just give me a chance to prove it to you. I'm begging you for a chance. That's all I want—a chance."

"Were you fucking our babysitter or not?"

"No," I say. "*I* wasn't. I mean, how can I be responsible for something I did when I wasn't actually here?"

She seems too exasperated to yell anymore. "Please let go of me," she says.

I know there's nothing I can say to make her believe me or understand. If I were her, I wouldn't either.

I let her finish packing. When she and Lilly are leaving with their suitcases, I'm waiting downstairs near the front door. I squat in front of Lilly to talk to her at eye level.

"Daddy loves you and Daddy will always love you, so don't be afraid, okay? Everything will be fine, I promise."

Looking down, avoiding my eye contact, she nods.

"Let's go, Lilly."

I kiss Lilly on top of her head, then I watch them leave.

I hear Laura's car start up, then drive off.

I've never felt so alone. The idea of killing myself seems very appealing. I might never see my family again and who would miss me? I've cheated, killed, and seem to have made a negative impact on most people I've encountered. Besides, if I kill myself, maybe I won't die, I'll just continue living another strand of my life, a strand that's better than this one. Suicide might be my best option.

I'm ready to drive my car inside my garage and kill myself with carbon monoxide poisoning, which seems like an appealing, painless way of doing the deed. Then I hesitate—how do I know for sure my life will continue with another strand? Maybe what happened to me was a one-time thing, and the next time I die it will be permanent. Besides, if I do wind up in another strand, how do I know it will be better than this one? Maybe it'll be worse. While there are a lot of negatives in my current life, there are a lot of positives. I have a daughter I love, I'm wealthy, and until less than an hour ago, I had a wife who loved me.

I know I can still fix this, but not if Kaitlin talks to the cops again. She already told the cops about our affair, but how long will it be until she tells them about the murders? Paying her off won't be enough; if I give her money, why couldn't she just ask for more? And if she did ask for more, how would I be able to say no? I'd never be able to relax in Paris or anywhere else, knowing Kaitlin could potentially show up at any time.

I'm aware that I'm not thinking like myself, that I'm thinking like a psychopath, but I also know that this doesn't mean I *am* a psychopath. I'm being pragmatic, not psychopathic—there's a huge difference. I need to use logic to prevent more damage and to—if not rectify what I've done—at least salvage the rest of my life and not hurt the people I love more than I already have.

I go up to my bedroom and change into jeans, a sweatshirt, and work boots that I find in the back of my closet.

I text Kaitlin: *Be there in 20*

She responds: *K*

I'll have to be careful—make sure the police aren't following us and that Kaitlin's not wearing a wire. After we transport Justin's body and dig the hole, I'll strangle her, the way I strangled Justin, and then I'll bury her with Justin. I won't feel any guilt or remorse for killing her because her life is miserable right now and when she dies, her life will probably continue in another strand, and she'll very likely wind up in a much happier version of her life. In a way, by murdering her, I'll be doing her a big favor.

Meanwhile, in *my* reality, when all the bodies are buried, I can focus on fixing my marriage and living a happy life in Paris.

At two P.M., I leave my house. I should have enough time to

pick up Kaitlin, transport Justin's body, dig the hole, kill Kaitlin, and bury Justin and Kaitlin before it gets dark. I have Justin's phone with me to bury in the hole too.

As I'm getting into my car in my driveway, I hear a noise—someone rushing up from behind me. When I try to turn, it's too late.

SIXTEEN

The pain is worse than anything I've ever experienced. Mainly my head kills, but my neck and shoulders are throbbing too. It seems like it takes all my energy to lift my eyelids, and not even halfway. My vision is very blurred and I feel unsteady, like I'm on a ship in rough water. I'm in an upright position, sitting, but I can't move at all. I might be groaning or wailing, but I'm not really aware of anything except my tremendous pain.

Then I see that I'm facing a figure—a man—standing in front of me. For several moments, he's just a blur, then I'm able to make him out. I know who it is, but it takes several seconds until I can attach a name to his face.

Hammond.

He's several feet away, watching me. My eyes dart around as I realize I'm in his studio in Astoria. I can't move because I'm tied to a chair. There's light coming from directly above me, from a single bulb, but the rest of the space, including the area where he's standing, is in shadow.

"You're alive," he says like he's somewhat surprised. "For a while there, I thought you wouldn't make it. That would've been good for you, not so good for me."

I'm in so much agony it's hard to think clearly. I remember my last conscious moments—leaving my house, someone rushing up behind me. Hammond was probably following me all day and then he hit me over the head with something. The sequence of events is logical which seems to mean I'm still alive—living the version of my life I've been living. I don't know why he hasn't killed me yet, but I know he's going to—it's a matter of when, not if.

"So…" I pause to get a full breath, then say, "… is this how you treat all your prospective buyers?"

I know he gets off on frightening his victims, so I'm trying to make him uneasy. The strategy seems to work—for a couple of seconds. Then he leans toward me and slaps my face so hard my neck strains from the whiplash. I flash back to when Laura slapped me the night she asked for a divorce. The pain is similar.

Then Hammond says, "I think, given the circumstances, I should be the one asking the questions, don't you?"

My cheek is stinging, but it makes it easier to focus somehow.

"Ask away," I say.

"Why did you come here the other day? And don't give me that bullshit about wanting to buy a painting."

I notice that he's holding something in his left hand—a chainsaw. This doesn't surprise me. He's told me in great detail, with no emotion, about how, while he sawed his victims to pieces, he loved watching the blood splatter around him. *Killing makes me feel I'm Jackson Pollock*, he told me. *Like I'm creating a masterpiece.*

"I bet you love this," I say, "don't you?"

"What did I tell you about asking questions?"

"I'm here, tied up, defenseless, which makes you feel in control, like you can do anything you want to me. That's what it's all about, isn't it? Control. Like when you're painting. You control everything on the canvas."

"Shut up."

"Come on, what're you waiting for? It'll be like creating art. Don't you want to feel like Jackson Pollock? Like you're creating a masterpiece?"

He's craning over me, like he's about to slap me again, then he stops and stares at me, then says, "Why did you just say that?"

"Say what?" I ask.

"About Pollock. I've said that before, to other people I've... but I've never told anyone who's still alive."

"So you *have* killed," I say. "Did you kill Mark Miranda and Eduardo Ortiz? Are there others? You're going to kill me anyway, so you might as well confess."

He moves in closer to me, but he doesn't slap me. He just stares at me, like I'm a problem he can't solve.

"I'll ask you one more time. Why did you say that about Pollock?"

"Maybe it was just a coincidence," I say. "If you believe in coincidences, and you aren't a fate guy. I don't believe in co-incidences—not anymore. I think all coincidences can be explained."

"You didn't come here to buy a painting. I know when some-body doesn't give a shit about my art and as soon as I looked you in the eye, my shit detector went off full blast. Also, you lied about how we met. Telling me that bullshit that we met at that gallery opening when there were about ten people at that opening and I knew all of them. You came for a *reason*. You seemed to know things about me, things that no one else could know."

"I told you, I like to research before I invest."

"I know you're not a cop because I checked you out. You really are a lawyer. Did somebody hire you? Do you do P.I. work on the side?"

"No, but you're right, I do know everything about you. I know what you are, I know *what* you are."

"Yeah? What am I?"

Looking right at him, with no fear, I say, "You're a psychopath."

"Interesting." With a sly smile, he rests the chainsaw on my right shoulder. "Guess it takes one to know one, huh?"

"I'm not like you, Jeffery. I feel remorse, I have a conscience."

"Yeah? It didn't seem that way yesterday."

I know what he's alluding to. Is it possible he knows? But how could he know unless he was there?

"I don't know what you're talking about."

"I think you know exactly what I'm talking about."

I recall hearing a noise from outside Justin's house. Is it possible Hammond was there or is he just bluffing?

"No, actually I don't," I say.

Now the tip of the cold chainsaw is against my neck.

"I watched you kill that guy, at that old house in Westchester. And you're seriously telling me you're not like me? You're *exactly* like me."

"So you were following me yesterday too, huh?"

"Yeah, I was. I thought I'd just find out who you are, what you know, but I didn't expect to see what I saw. Why'd you kill that guy? Just for the hell of it?"

"No, because I'm not a psychopath."

"Keep telling yourself that. You looked pretty damn psychotic when you were choking that guy to death. You looked like you were enjoying it, too—I know what *that's* like. Come on, you can tell me. Killing's the best rush ever, isn't it? And it's addicting too. Do it once and you can't get enough."

"I know that's how it makes you feel, Jeffery, because you don't even need a reason to kill somebody. You kill because you can't control yourself. You do it because you have urges and you need to indulge those urges. For you, it's never enough."

Pushing the saw against my neck, maybe piercing my skin, he says, "I'm losing patience. Why the fuck did you come here the other day? How do you know things about me? Who did you talk to?"

"I'm your lawyer," I say.

Maintaining the pressure with the saw, he says, "My lawyer? I don't have a lawyer."

"In a different version of your life you do. In a different version of your life you were on trial for killing three men—three men you've probably never met in this reality."

"In *this* reality?" He smiles. "See? You *are* as crazy as I am, maybe crazier. At least I know I'm not normal. The people who think they're sane but clearly aren't are the real lunatics."

"Turn yourself in," I say. "You'll never get away with any of this, so just go to the cops right now. Confess. You'll save lives, the lives of the people you haven't killed yet. You can get some redemption."

I know I'm wasting my breath. He'll never stop killing until he makes a mistake and gets caught. Living on the edge, always trying to get that next rush, is what drives him.

He raises the chainsaw over his head and turns it on.

Over the din of the churning saw, he raises his voice: "Maybe I'll start off with your right arm. What do you say?"

"Do whatever you want!" I shout back.

He seems perplexed, like he doesn't know what to make of me. I recall Hammond, during one of our interviews, telling me that when victims beg for their lives it makes him feel more powerful. He's used to seeing fear in his victims, and I'm showing none because I have no fear. It's easy to take death lightly when you've already died.

The chainsaw slices off my arm. I wail because I have to wail, but I'm still not afraid.

Then he severs my other arm. I see my arms on the floor and my blood spurting all over Hammond who doesn't seem to care or even notice. I'm still wailing, but the pain is starting to fade, and so is everything else. I think he's sawing off one of my legs now; I'm not sure. I'm watching my bloody body spin in a glass ball. All my pain is gone. I hear a man's voice—*I got you, Steven Blitz*—and I want to stay here, painless like this, forever.

SEVENTEEN

Blurry, serious faces gaze down at me.

"His eyes're open, his eyes're open."

"Guess that's good news."

A siren is blaring. My eyes try to dart around. The bed or whatever I'm on is bouncing. I feel pressure on my chest and pain in my head.

Bright, fluorescent light seems familiar.

I feel pain all over, but mainly in my head, back and arms—I *have* arms. Does this mean I'm in another strand?

I turn my head to the right, toward a window, which also appears familiar, though I'm not sure why. I see the leafless branches of a tree swaying in the wind. Around me I notice the medical equipment.

Hospital. I'm in a hospital.

Except for my head, I'm not in any pain, but maybe I'm on painkillers. I can wriggle my toes so at least I know I'm not paralyzed. I'm not connected to any feeding tubes or oxygen devices. I'm thinking clearly.

I flash back to Queens—Hammond chopping me up with the chainsaw.

Glancing around again, I realize why this looks so familiar.

Because I've been here before.

I'm at Four Winds Hospital in Katonah, the same hospital I was brought to after John Delaney stabbed me in the parking lot.

Why am I here? How come I'm not in a hospital in Queens?

"Hello." I try to project my voice, but my throat is too dry. After a few more tries I let out a louder but still gravelly, "Hello."

Marie, the nurse who treated me last week, enters. She looks pretty much the same except she's gotten a haircut. She had dark shoulder-length hair; now it's a short bob, framing her face.

"Marie, it's really you."

She's checking my blood pressure.

"How're you feeling?" She's not smiling, and doesn't seem nearly as friendly as the last time we met. Maybe it's been a long day at work?

"I'm okay," I say. "When did I get here?"

"Last night," she says. "Pressure looks okay."

"But how?" I ask.

"How?" She's looking at the monitor, maybe checking my other vitals.

"Yeah," I say. "How did I get here? I mean all the way from Queens."

Still avoiding eye contact, acting cold, she says, "I don't know anything." Now she looks at me. "But I am curious, how do you know my name?" As if answering her own question, she glances at the name tag she's wearing. "Oh, that makes sense, I always forget I have that on."

"You don't remember me, do you?" I ask.

"Remember you from when?"

"I thought you seemed confused. I was here last weekend. I have a wife, Laura, a daughter Lilly. A brother, Brian."

It's not registering.

"You really don't remember me?" I say.

"I don't believe we've ever met before, Mr. Blitz."

She must've just forgotten.

"Of course we did," I say. "Remember, I'm the lawyer. The doctors wanted to keep me here another day because of my past neurological issues, but I insisted on leaving. Remember, I had memory issues…"

Looking at my chart, she says, "What past neurological issues?"

"My brain tumor," I say.

"Oh, so you're aware of that," Marie says. "An issue was discovered when you arrived, but we weren't sure if you knew about it."

"I had surgery to remove it," I say. "I'm cured."

"Not according to what we saw. We discovered it in an MRI, so you're going to have to discuss this with Dr. Phillips, okay?"

"I don't know who Phillips is, but Dr. Assadi knows all about my history."

"Who?"

"Dr. Assadi. The neurologist who treated me the last time I was here."

"There's no Dr. Assadi on our staff."

"What about Dr. Chu?"

"Are you sure you were at Four Winds Hospital?"

"Yes, I'm absolutely…" Inadvertently I touch my head, feeling that I have much more hair than I did in Queens. "How'd *this* happen?"

"What?" Marie's even more confused.

"I have hair," I say. "So much hair. This is impossible."

Now she's giving me a look like she thinking I'm crazy which, yeah, gives me a strong feeling of déjà vu.

"Oh my God," I say. "This can't be happening again, can it?… What…what day is it?"

"Today is Friday," Marie says cautiously.

This makes sense. Hammond kidnapped me on Thursday.

"Well, all your vital signs look good," Marie says. "I'll have Dr. Phillips—"

"Who's President of the United States?" I ask.

"Excuse me?"

"Is Al Gore President of the United States or not?"

Now Marie's looking at me like…well, like I've officially lost my mind.

"Um…not," she says.

"Fuck," I say. "Then who's President?"

"You don't know who the President is?"

"No, that's why I'm asking you."

"Donald Trump," she says.

"Oh my God." I sit up. "I'm back? I'm really *back*? It's winter 2020?"

"Lie down, please, Mr. Blitz."

"Is it 2020 or not? *February* 2020?"

"Yes."

She's trying to push me back by my shoulders, but I resist.

"Wow." For a few moments I'm elated. This means I didn't kill Kaitlin's father or Justin or *anyone*. It also means that Jeffery Hammond didn't dismember me, or kill me, and that he's in Rikers, locked up where he belongs.

Then I think of the *other* connotations.

If I'm really back, doesn't this mean Laura is leaving me to be with Beth? That 9/11 happened? That my daughter doesn't exist?

"What about Lilly? Is Lilly here?"

"Calm down, Mr. Blitz."

I'm trying to sit up. "Is she here? Is my daughter alive or not?"

I feel out of control and know I'm rambling. Marie manages to push me back to a lying position.

"Mr. Blitz, you're going to have to relax now. Just focus on your breathing. I'll report your symptoms to Dr. Phillips and I'm sure he'll be here to see you soon."

"They're not symptoms," I say, "and I'm not crazy." I look around. "My phone. Where's my phone?"

"I'll have to ask the police if you can have access to it," she says.

"The police?" I say. "The police are here?"

"Yes, there's an officer right outside the door and a detective waiting to talk to you too."

I'm still trying to process this. If I'm back in my original life and haven't committed any murders, and am not a suspect in any murders, then why are the police here?

"Why is there an officer out there?" I ask. "What's going on?"

"You're just going to have to calm down now or I'll have the officer come in here," Marie says. "Please just calm down, okay?"

Marie leaves. I have so many questions that I have no answers, or even guesses, for. But mostly I'm thinking about Lilly. I'm as devastated as if I just found out that she died. Although I only knew her for a few days, I'm attached to her, and the idea that I might never see her again, that she might not even exist, feels horrific and devastating.

A slim female doctor with short blond hair enters. Like Marie, she has a serious, somewhat cold demeanor, as if she's seeing me because she has to see me, not because she wants to. I'm beginning to suspect that it has to do with the cop who's guarding the room and the detective who's waiting to see me. I'm getting a vibe that everyone is treating me like I'm a criminal.

"Hi, Mr. Blitz, I'm Doctor Phillips."

She's looking at my chart, not smiling or making eye contact. I notice that she's holding an iPhone with a familiar case.

"My phone," I say. "Is that really my phone?"

"It's the one you had when you were admitted here," she says.

As she hands me the phone, I see that it's in fact my phone; I last saw it the night I got stabbed in the snow at the gas station.

"It's my phone," I say, as I caress it with my fingertips. "It's really here."

I realize that Dr. Phillips is observing me with a serious, clinical expression. "Happy to have your phone back, huh?"

"I don't know if happy's the right word. More like amazed."

"I understand you're having some memory issues," she says. "Do you remember what happened to you?"

I'm going through my apps—they're all there. Then I check my texts; I have threads from familiar contacts like Terrence and Brian, but I don't recognize the recent messages.

"What the hell?" I mutter to myself.

Dr. Phillips repeats her question, maybe for the third time.

"Oh…when?" I ask.

"Before you lost consciousness," she says.

"You mean as far as I know?" I ask.

"What else could I mean?" She's losing patience.

"I thought I was murdered by an artist named Jeffery Hammond," I say. "Yes, *that* Jeffery Hammond—the one you've heard about in the news. I'm his attorney actually. I have no idea how I wound up in Westchester, but I'm guessing you're going to tell me that I wasn't taken from Queens. Is that correct?"

"That's correct," she says.

"That means that Jeffery Hammond is actually on trial for murder and I'm representing him."

"I understand that's correct too," she says. "So are you having memory issues or aren't you, Mr. Blitz?"

I'm looking through the text thread with Laura. I've apparently sent many texts over the past several days. I scan them:

I have to see you
I know you love me, I know you don't love her!
What the fucks wrong with you? How can you do this to us???
Answer me!!!

I have no recollection of sending the texts; it's like I'm seeing them all for the first time. I texted Brian with recent messages:

I have no idea where she is
Haven't heard from her at all.

In a text exchange with Terrence, we seem to be discussing the *ongoing* Jeffery Hammond murder trial.

"Jesus," I say. "This is insane."

"What is?" Dr. Phillips asks.

"What do the detectives want from me?" I ask. "I don't know anything about that either."

There are so many things I want to check out online. Into the browser I type in Google and I'm delighted to see it exists.

"I can't discuss any of that," Dr. Phillips says. "But do you remember anything about the car chase?"

"Car chase?" I ask, confused.

"Okay, well, you had a concussion and some minor bleeding so memory issues aren't entirely unexpected. We'll run more tests."

"But I don't have a head injury," I say. "I was stabbed. See?"

I pull up my shirt, but there's no wound there. I do notice I'm back to my heavier self, though.

"The memory issues could be related to your other issue as well," Dr. Phillips says. "I understand you are aware of the brain tumor we discovered?"

"Yes," I say, "and I guess it makes sense it hasn't been removed if I'm back to my old life."

"Excuse me?" she asks.

"Yes, I know about it, and I know it's cancerous, but I also know the surgery will go well and I'll be okay. I'll schedule surgery at Sloan Kettering when I get out of here, okay?"

Appearing confused, Dr. Phillips says, "Okay, well, we'll discuss how to coordinate all of that with the police at an appropriate time."

"The police? What do the police have to do with me setting a time for my surgery? Why won't you tell me why the police are here?"

Dr. Phillips is already leaving.

With her back to me she says, "I'll update the detective on your condition and he'll be in here shortly."

I read through more of my texts with Terrence at the Hammond murder trial. It definitely seems to be going on, as some of the texts have to do with testimony from Alex Brisco, the arresting officer, and our cross examination of Brisco. Of course, I have no memories of any of this because on the days of these texts I was in the other version of my life. The last text I sent to Laura, last Sunday evening was "Can we talk?" On that night, in my other life, I was home with Laura and Lilly.

I Google the Hammond trial and skim several articles about it, including a quote from me: "My client maintains his innocence."

All of this feels beyond surreal, of course. Am I really back in the old version of my life, or is this a different version?

I do a series of searches and see that terrorists attacked the United States on September 11, 2001, Obama was president for eight years, the Dirty Monday terrorist attack in Rome didn't happen, *The Sopranos* and *Game of Thrones* TV shows exist, Netflix slaughtered Blockbuster, Bill Cosby is in prison, the #MeToo movement exists, Bernie Sanders won the Nevada

Caucus, and a novel coronavirus has been spreading rapidly around the world. I log into my bank account and see I'm not rich; I have just about the same in the bank as I had before John Delaney stabbed me in the snow.

I'll have to do my research at some point, but it certainly seems like I'm back in the original version of my life. The only "missing time" seems to be the past week, when I was living my other life.

"So you woke up," a man says. "I'd be lying if I said I wasn't disappointed."

I see that Detective Raymond Ortiz, the partner of Detective John Delaney, has entered the room. He looks like the other version of Ortiz who visited me at my house yesterday—well, in the *other* yesterday—but there are differences, which makes sense. Now he's in a nicer dark suit and has a neater slicked-back hairdo.

"Yeah, it's me, you cocksucker," he says. "I heard you have a brain tumor too. Good, I hope you die in pain in prison, you piece of shit."

"Excuse me?" I have no idea why he's so belligerent.

"You heard me," he says. "You thought you'd get away, huh? Meanwhile you could've gotten me and my guys killed."

"I…I have no idea what you're talking about."

"Yeah, I thought you might try to pull the amnesia card. Save it for the courtroom, though you're not gonna have much luck there, fuckin' prick."

"Whoa, whoa, let's slow down," I say. "Honestly I have no idea what's going on here, but I think I can explain."

"Explain? Yeah, you're going to have a lot of explaining to do."

"Where's your partner?"

"Partner?" Raymond says. "I don't have a partner."

"*Here* you don't," I say. "That makes sense. Because here the man who would've been your partner, John Delaney, is a scumbag loser who tried to kill me. I mean, *if* he tried to kill me. I might not have actually met him. In this version of my life, I might've made a different decision and maybe my life veered in a different direction."

"I have no idea what you're rambling about, but I told you to save your breath," Raymond says. "That is, unless you're ready to confess."

"Confess?" I have no idea what he's talking about—I haven't committed any crimes in this strand. "Confess to what?"

He moves closer to me, his forehead veins bulging and his face red, and says, "I told you, I'm not fucking around anymore. We have your blood on the scene, in the trunk of your car, you're not getting away with this shit. You think you can play us because you defend killers, but I can see through that bullshit. I know who you are."

"Look," I say, "I'm not trying to confuse you. If you tell me what you think I did, maybe I can tell you if I did it."

"This isn't a *theory*," Raymond says. "This is fact—I got you, Steven Blitz."

"*That* I remember," I say. "I heard you saying that after I got killed in Queens. I had déjà vu. See? This proves it."

Raymond backs away a little, but still stares me down.

"So this is your new act, huh?" he says. "New strategy? You're gonna play the crazy card?"

"I'm not crazy. I just *know* things. Maybe it's things I'm not supposed to know, that no one's supposed to know."

"Okay, fine," Raymond says. "That's the way you want do it, it's up to you. I told you—it's game over, you're going down. I thought maybe you'd just want to get it off your chest, make your life a little easier."

"And I'm telling you I have no idea what you're talking about," I say. "I don't even know what bodies you're talking about and what blood."

"The bodies of your wife and her girlfriend," Raymond says. "Does that ring a bell?"

"What?" This can't be true. "What're you talking about?"

"You heard me?"

"*Bodies*? You don't mean....No. Please...please tell me that didn't happen."

"Gimme me a fuckin' break."

"I wouldn't hurt Laura. And I never even met Beth."

"But you know who Beth is."

"Laura mentioned her to me, in both versions of my life."

"Both versions of your life," he says with mock amusement.

"That's right," I say.

"So I guess you're not gonna confess, huh?"

"Confess to what?"

"Murdering your wife and her girlfriend."

This must be a play, a set-up.

"I'm not a killer," I say.

"Bullshit!" Raymond screams in my face. "You killed them and you're going down for it."

"Okay, so go ahead then," I say. "Tell me what you think I did."

"Think?" he says. "I *know* what you did. You confronted your wife and Beth Chang outside of Chang's house in South Salem on Wednesday evening. First you killed your wife with a butcher knife you brought with you, then you chased Beth down and killed her. You tried to cover it up by taking the bodies over to Pound Ridge Reservation and burying them. A hiker found the bodies this morning."

Pound Ridge Reservation is where Kaitlin and I buried her

father—her father who's probably still alive—and where I planned to bury Justin and Kaitlin.

"That makes sense," I say.

"How does it make sense?"

"It feels like déjà vu because it happened in a different life."

"A different life?"

"Yes," I say. "I'm living other lives right at this moment, so even if a version of me did what you claim I did, *I* didn't kill anybody. I know you might not believe that with the physical evidence you have, but I'm asking you to go beyond the physical, okay? I want you to open your mind—think harder."

He glares, then says, "So now you're playing the amnesia card *and* the crazy card, huh? You have no chance with an insanity defense. This is first degree, premeditated homicide. *Double* homicide."

"But how can I be responsible for anything I do in a life I'm not living?"

"What the hell's that supposed to mean?"

"In *this* life, I didn't do anything bad, I didn't cheat on my wife and I didn't commit any crimes. The last thing I remember is getting stabbed to death in a parking lot a week ago."

"Lemme get this straight," he says. "We have your blood at the scene, in your car, and your DNA on the bodies, but you're gonna tell the jury you died for a week and then came back to life? I'm sure that'll work out great for you."

He's not rolling his eyes, but he might as well be.

"I understand you have evidence, but that doesn't mean that I committed these crimes. Somebody could've set me up."

"Like hell someone set you up," he shouts. "You're a fucking killer!"

"But I'm not," I insist. "I know who I am...and I know I'm not a killer."

As I say this, I think, *Is this true?* Do I really *know* that I didn't kill Laura and Beth? I know that killing is not my nature, I'm no Jeffery Hammond, but does that mean I'm innocent? Of course non-psychopaths can kill; I've defended many clients who committed "crimes of passion," and I'm sure in some of the infinite coexisting versions of my life I've made bad decisions and acted impulsively.

I recall how hurt I was when Laura told me she was leaving me. Driving in the snow, I was feeling tense and decided to pull over to buy a pack of cigarettes. That decision led me to getting stabbed, but what if I didn't make that decision, and continued living *this* version of my life? It's true that, before I pulled over at the gas station, I considered going back to the house and following Laura and confronting her and Beth, so if that strand continued, is it really far-fetched that over the past few days, I could've gotten obsessed with getting Laura back, lost control of my anger, and while I was defending Jeffery Hammond for multiple homicides, committed a horrendous crime myself?

"Fine, if you won't confess, we'll play the long game," Raymond says. "It doesn't matter. You're going down no matter what."

"I want a lawyer," I say.

Terrence will defend me. This version of Terrence is a moral, reliable guy, and a great attorney—if anybody can get me out of this, it's him. But what will my defense be? Can we convince a jury that I didn't commit these murders because I was simultaneously living another life? Can living in another existence be an alibi?

"Oh you're gonna need a lawyer," Raymond says, "you're gonna need a whole team of lawyers, but it still won't help you, you fucking psycho. Steven Blitz, you're under arrest for the murders of Laura Blitz and Beth Chang. You have the right to remain silent. Anything you say…"

As he continues, I remind myself that this isn't happening,

not the way it seems to be happening anyway. Although Laura and Beth seem to be dead, they aren't *really* dead, the same way I know that Lilly is actually alive—in a place I can't access right now, but that doesn't mean she isn't there. Even if I can't see certain people, or experience them, that doesn't mean they don't exist. And if they're somewhere else, that means I can be somewhere else too. This version of me is under arrest, but millions or maybe billions of other versions of me, who've made different, better decisions than this version of me made, are living happy lives right now.

I must be smiling because after Raymond finishes reading me my rights and explains that I'll be taken into custody later today, he says, "You kill your wife and her girlfriend and you think it's funny? You know what I think? I think you're as crazy as the scum you defend."

At this moment, in another existence, I'm with Laura and Lilly, having a steak dinner, while Wasabi sits nearby. It feels so great to have a family whom I love, and who loves me, and it's comforting to know that the next time I die I'll have a chance to love them again, make better decisions, and make everything right.

There are always chances to fix things. Nothing is ever permanent.

"Hope you enjoy rotting in hell, you piece of shit," Raymond says as he heads out.

I want to stop him, tell him again that he's got it all wrong, that I'm not actually a killer, or at least not *always* a killer, that he doesn't understand the truth about me, or anything really, but I let him go, feeling sorry for the poor guy.

He has no idea what he's missing.